I'll Take The Chance

Re Venge

Published by Re Venge, 2024.

I'll Take The Chance

A Work of Fiction

This is a work of fiction. Names, characters, places, and incidents either are the product of the author's imagination or are used fictitiously. Any resemblance to actual persons, living or dead, events, or locales is entirely coincidental.

Published by:

Re Venge

Basud, Camarines Norte, Philippines 4608

Email:

rvenge594@gmail.com

Book design by: Re Venge

Author: Re Venge

Chapter 1

The night was dark and stormy, with thunder and lightning clashing in the night sky. Heavy rain pelted the streets, giving the night a surreal and menacing atmosphere. All the hustle and bustle of the nightlife had died away as people returned to their homes seeking safety. The wind was strong, howling through the streets as it picked up speed. It seemed everywhere at once, shaking buildings and making trees sway. Every so often, a gust of wind would come, almost as if it was trying to shatter the windows of the buildings.

The thunder and lightning made it feel like the sky was splitting in half, with flashes of light competing with the darkness of the night. The rain was relentless, pounding down on the streets, flooding them and making them unrecognizable. It seemed strange, eerie stillness, forcing the city to stay in its homes.

Despite that scenario, in one of the pubs in Vienna, Austria, a man sits alone at the bar counter. All of the people who went to the pub returned home. But the pub owner can't send this customer out of the pub even though he wants to close his pub because of the bad weather. The pub owner had just decided to close the pub when that man, who was their last customer, left the pub.

On a bar counter, the bartender served him glasses of brandy. The man was still drinking. He had taken a deep breath and drank a glass of brandy. After emptying the brandy glasses on the counter, he ordered several more.

The female bartender approached him with a warm smile. "Another glass of brandy, sir?" she asked.

The man looked up, his eyes meeting hers. "Yeah," he replied, with a frown on his face, ignoring her warm smile. He didn't smile back.

As she poured the amber liquid into a glass, the bartender took a moment to study the man. She noticed the lines etched on his face, evidence of the burdens he carried. With a gentle touch, she placed the glass in front of him.

He took a deep breath, his fingers tracing the rim of the glass. "Why did those things happen to me?" the man muttered to himself, his voice filled with despair and frustration.

As the man took a sip, the bartender decided to break the silence. She leaned against the counter, her voice soft and comforting. "If you ever need someone to talk to, I'm here," she offered, her words sincere.

He glanced at her, surprise flickering across his face. "You'd listen?" he asked, a glimmer of doubt in his eyes.

The woman nodded, her empathy evident. "Of course. Sometimes, it helps to share our burdens with a stranger."

The man took another sip, weighing her words. After a moment, he responded, "Never mind. It's too personal, and I can't tell anyone." He dismissed their conversation.

"Alright." She smiled to hide her embarrassment as he dismissed her.

He is Dren Wolf. He is an angel investor who invests his own money in different holding companies. He is also the owner and CEO of DW Manufacturing & Distributing Company. It is a large manufacturing and distributing company of milk that is located in Vienna, Austria.

As described by many, he is a billionaire with a devil-like attitude and an angel-like appearance. He is known to be moody and create fear in the hearts of those who work for him because he is a little bit unwell.

Dren has a psychological condition. His dark secret which is unknown to the society to which he belongs. When he was 14 years old, he was diagnosed with a personality disorder. A split personality disorder. Only the doctor and his Uncle Ivano knew about it. His Uncle Ivano made it a secret to everyone.

Dren is feeling shattered because today is his birthday but also the anniversary of his parents' death. Until now, he still can't accept that his parents' were gone. He lost everything when they were gone. But he is thankful that his Uncle Ivano , his father's best friend, saved him and took care of him until he became what he is today.

Dren was awake in deep thoughts when the bartender gave me his order. He drank all three glasses of beer that he ordered. He dropped by a pub again, just to drink so that he could forget how his parents were lost...

That was 18 years ago, but the memories are still there in his heart and mind. The year is 2003, and the location is somewhere in Asia.

It was his 10th birthday. They are on a luxurious passenger cruise ship owned by his parents. He was eating dinner together with his parents and Ivano. Ivano is his father's best friend. They decided to treat Dren to a sumptuous meal in one of the finest restaurants on board that large cruise ship.

But Dren felt afraid when he heard a loud explosion nearby. Suddenly, all the lights turned off. Dren couldn't see anything for a few minutes until there were flashes of light coming from emergency lights and flashlights. Then he heard commotion. Inside the cruise ship, passengers are in a state of panic.

Dren heard some passengers say there was faulty electrical wiring on the ship that caused that loud explosion. It caused huge damage to the ship and caused a total loss of electricity. The ship was stranded in the middle of the ocean. He heard that the ship was about to sink.

The passengers grew more anxious. The crew on the ship called for a rescue. The rescue team immediately arrived and started saving the passengers from the sinking ship.

Some of the crew approach them so that they can transfer on the other ship safely. They want to protect Dren's family in any danger because they are the owners of the cruise ship.

But the next incident was not expected. Then there was a series of loud explosions that happened again. It caused a big hole on the side of the ship. Then big waves splash on the ship, and the seawater starts to enter the ship's hole.

Dren's father was holding his mother who didn't know how to swim. While Dren clung to Ivano's arms tightly because of fear. Half of the ship was set on fire while the other half was filled with water and slowly sinking. There was no choice but to jump into the water just to reach the lifeboat down there.

The crew helped their parents jump into the water first to reach the boat where the other passengers climbed to transfer to another ship that would rescue them. But before the ship crew and Dren's parents reached the lifeboat, a big wave was splashing that made the ship crew lose their grip on

Dren's parents. They tried to save Dren's parents but the big waves carried his parents away from them.

Dren heard Ivano's voice, full of fear, calling the name of their parents while holding Dren's tightly. They are still standing on the sinking ship and the fire behind them slowly creeping towards them.

Ivano was full of fear while shouting;

" Alexander! Olivia!"

Alexander was drowning but he still managed to shout back;

" Ivano! If anything happens to me, please take care of my son."

Ivano shouted back;

"I will, Alexander! I swear."

Dren felt suffocated because of the smoke coming from the part of the ship which is burning . He almost fainted. Then he never heard his father's answer again. He felt like he couldn't breathe. Knowing that there was a possibility that he wouldn't see his parents again. Ivano jumped on the water holding Dren tightly when he felt the hot temperature of the fire behind them got intense. It is either to jump into the dark water below or be burned by the fire burning behind them. Ivano tried to reach the lifeboat.He tried all his might to save Dren when the big waves splashed on them.He held Dren tight, but Dren felt suffocated in the water. He can breathe no more. Then everything went black for him.

When Dren opens his eyes again he is in the hospital. He wakes up from a coma. He saw Ivano crying beside his bed so he asked him;

" Why are you crying Uncle Ivano? "

" Dren! I'm glad you're already awake. "

Dren was confused. He asked Ivano again;

" Where are my parents?"

" I'm sorry Dren, but your parents were dead. And they were already cremated. One month had already passed since the ship sank and I brought you here to the hospital. I'm thankful that you are awake now.

Dren kept silent. He was not able to speak when he heard what Ivano said to him. That bad news feels like a bomb that exploded in his ears when he heard it. His parents were gone. It means he is now an orphan.

Dren cried silently. He couldn't accept the fact that his parents were gone. He wanted to cry a lot.

" Cry out loud if you want Dren. It will help you ease the emotional pain that you have." Ivano said to him.

Dren suddenly shouted because he couldn't bear the heartache that he felt upon his parents death;

"Noooo!!! How can my father leave me? "

"Your parents don't want to leave you, Dren, for sure, but they just didn't survive." Ivano said in a sad voice. It is also painful to him that his best friend Alexander was gone. And he wouldn't see him again.

Dren didn't answer. He just cried and cried a lot. He taught that he can't go on with his life without his parents.

"Don't worry, I'm here to take care of you. I will bring you to my own country. There, in Austria, you can start a new life. I will just settle all the things that your father left her in Albania. Then my wife and I will go home to Austria. We will bring you there."

" Thank you, Uncle Ivano." Dren said while he sobbed.

Chapter 2

When Dren was back in reality he drank the last glass of beer that he ordered. He decided to go home. He still has a job for tomorrow. He needs to go home right now.

Drenwent outside the pub. He is feeling dizzy. It sucks! He needs to lean on the car before he can get inside. He feels too dizzy. He feels sleepy right now. He can't stand up properly.

He slowly sat down on the roadside. He is talking to himself while lowering his head;

"Shit! I can't handle myself. Is this the effect of the beer that I drank?"

He needs to force himself to stand up and get inside his car to drive home. Dren stands up but he feels he will fall down. He still feels dizzy.

Dren feels like he is not falling on the roadside but in somebody's arms. He fell on a woman's arm, then everything went black. He doesn't know what will happen next but he is thankful because someone helped him.

A woman who happens to pass by helped Dren. She helps him to get inside his car. She is not a citizen of Dren's country. She came here to Vienna to continue her studies in college. She comes from the city of Tirana, Albania. She just got a chance to get a half scholarship at one of the universities here in Vienna, so she moved to this country.

She is an orphan and has no parents or siblings that he left in his own country. She didn't hesitate to leave her own country because all her cousins were cruel to her.

When she moved to Austria, she was able to find a job before the school year started. She works as a cashier at one of the late-night restaurants in the city. She goes to work at night and attends classes in the morning. Her shift at work started at 7:00 pm and ended at 3am. Then she will attend classes from 7:00 a.m. to 9:00 a.m. Since she has free time from 9am. to 6 p.m. she wants to look for a part-time job because her salary is not enough for her expenses and to pay half of her tuition fee.

Going back to Dren. He feels too sleepy right now. He leaned his head on the driver's seat. He closed his eyes while talking to the woman who helped him to get inside the car. The woman is standing beside. Her arms are

6

resting on the open window of the car. She is peering to the car's window to answer Dren's question

"Why do you help me?"

"I was walking down the street from work when I saw you on the roadside beside your expensive car, trying to compose yourself, but you can't handle yourself anymore because you are too drunk."

Dren's eyebrow raises , then he speaks to her again;

"Yeah that's why I sat on the roadside for a while, but forced myself to stand up to get inside my car. But I felt too dizzy. "

"That's why you were about to fall on the roadside?"

"Yeah but you managed to get near me immediately and you were able to catch me."

"I bet you can't drive home safely. You definitely meet an accident on the road. I can drive you home if you want."

Dren feels too sleepy. That's why he accepted her offer to drive him home.

"Thanks for volunteering."

"So where do you live?"

Dren pointed to a photo placed on the car dashboard and said;

"There!"

The woman picked up the photo and looked at it to get a clue. Then she speaks to Dren;

"I would accompany you. I know where this place is located. It is just about 250 kilometers away from here."

Dren makes no response. He closes his eyes because he feels sleepy. When the woman sees Dren's behavior she speak to him again;

"Are you sleeping now? Honestly, I felt hesitant to drive you home, but I don't know why I felt concerned for you. I can not just leave you in this situation. So I will just drive you home."

Dren moves to the passenger seat before he answers her;

"Seriously?! Whatever your reason is, I'm thankful."

The woman gets inside the car and sits down into the driver's seat then starts to drive away. While driving she speaks to Dren again;

"I drove you to the place where your mansion house is located. After 20 minutes of driving we will reach that place."

"Okay. Thank you for your kindness."
"No worries."

After 20 minutes of driving they are now in front of Dren's mansion house.

The woman parked the car in front of the mansion house. Then she stepped outside of the car and blew the horn twice. When she saw that the guards were coming she talks to Dren;

"I will leave you here. I will go home now."

Dren opens his eyes though he still feels dizzy when he hears the woman speak to him. He answers her;

"Thank you. Take care."

The woman answers him then she walks away from him;

"I will."

Dren felt dizzy. He can't manage to stand up. He can't get outside his car. He saw the guards coming together with his Uncle Ivano outside the mansion gate. His Uncle is giving the guards instructions to carry Dren inside the mansion. The guards carry him inside. Then his Uncle Ivano gets inside the mansion too.

Dren woke up to the smell of coffee aroma. He wondered where he was. He realized that he is in his own room now because the bed felt too soft and smelled fragrant.Unlike in the pub, which smells of alcohol and cigarettes is in the air. He got up from bed. He saw his Uncle Ivano sitting on a single sofa, drinking coffee. He is looking at him. But he is sitting at a distance, so Dren can hardly recognize his face because of his poor eyesight.

Dren feels annoyed when he remembers his contact lenses were lost in the pub last night.

"Bullshit! My contact lenses were lost in the pub last night."

Chapter 3

When Ivano saw that Dren got up from bed and sat down. He walks towards him. He brings him a cup of coffee and puts it on the bedside table. Then he talked to him while holding a cup of coffee;

"How are you? The guards saw your car parked outside the mansion. They discovered you in your car, unable to drive due to intoxication.I ordered them to bring you here to your room."

"Yeah. I remember." Dren answered while picking up the cup of coffee that Ivano brought for him.

"Who drove you home?" Ivano asked, curious.

Dren smiled before he answered Ivano's questions;

"I don't know who she is. I thought I saw an angel last night, and she drove me home."

"Dren? Are you out of your mind again? You're talking nonsense again." Ivano asked Dren, suspecting that Dren's psychological disorder is manifesting. He knew that it was Dren's parents' death anniversary yesterday so he knew it affects Dren's emotions and thinking a lot.

Dren laughed out softly before he answered Ivano;

"Of course not. The last thing I remember before I fell asleep last night was the woman who helped me go home." Dren said, recalling the woman that drove him home last night.

"But I didn't see any women around last night. You are just alone in your car. You drank too much last night. Maybe it's just your imagination. The truth is you drove alone last night, and before you could get inside the mansion, you fell asleep in your car. You better see your doctor again, Dren." Ivano said to Dren, feeling confused because he didn't see a woman last night that accompanied Dren.

Dren shook his head then spoke to his uncle;

"Uncle Ivano, I'm fine. I don't need a psychiatrist. That is true. A woman drove me home last night." Dren insists to Ivano that he is telling the truth.

Ivano takes a deep breath;

"Alright, You better empty your coffee cup before the coffee gets cold. "

Dren smiled and said;

"Thank you, Uncle. Don't worry, I'm fine."

Ivano was convinced;

"All right,Fix yourself. Remember, you have a business meeting today. I'll go ahead.

Dren answered;

"Alright. "

When Ivano left Dren's room, Dren emptied his cup of coffee. Then, after a few minutes, he decided to take a bath and prepared to go to work.

Twenty five minutes later he is about to go to work. He left his room to go to the basement parking area of the mansion. He selects which car to use from his collection in the basement.

He has a collection of cars and motorcycles in the basement parking area. He uses different cars every week. But today he just picked the car that he used last night.

Dren gets inside his car and drives outside the mansion. After 20 minutes of driving, he reached his company. He has two hours to prepare for the business meeting. It will be held in the adjacent building of his company.

When he enters at the main building of his

company he went to his office on the 10th floor. From the elevator he saw that some of the participants were here in his company. He is able to see them because the elevator of his company is transparent. They are visiting the showroom of the different milk products that his company manufactures and distributes to the market here and abroad. They are all angel investors and billionaires like him. They invest their own money in different companies.

Dren walked outside the elevator and went to his private office. He was lost in deep thoughts.

Dren is thinking about his co investors. They are all married. They are too sweet and thoughtful with their wife and kids. Dren feels envious. All of them have their own families. They found the right woman, who they will share the rest of their lives with. Unlike him, he is struggling to have a stable and long lasting relationship because of his mental condition. All of his relationships end in breakups. It only lasts for a month and does not even last for a year.

Dren is proud but feels lonely at the same time. Yes, women will be easily attracted to him but because they don't understand his attitude and behavior, they will easily get tired of him and the end result will be that they will leave. Dren is wondering if there will be a woman someday who will stay forever by my side.

While he is sitting in his private office he recalls the face of that woman who drove him home last night.

Dren still remembers her face and appearance. He thinks he is attracted to her but his problem is he doesn't know where to find her. He was not able to ask her last night where she was residing. And he forgot to ask even just her name.

While he is in deep thought, he starts preparing all the documents that he needs for the presentation for the meeting.

Dren still has one hour remaining before the business meeting starts so he decides to scroll his phone while waiting for the time. He checks the social media page of his company. He will check out the latest posts that have been posted by the marketing department of his company.

He is scrolling through some posts regarding a part-time job that his company is offering to working students. He offers such opportunities instead of offering scholarships or internships. In his own opinion, it will be a huge help to any student who has a part-time job.

While reading the post he saw a comment on the post of one of the applicants asking how to apply for this part time job offer.

"How to apply for this part time job offer?" The applicant's comments.

Dren decides to answer the applicant's comments via direct message because the applicant looks like the woman who helped him and drove him home last night.

"Just email your application to the company. It's not my job to answer applicants' inquiries, but I think it is also my responsibility since I'm working with this company."

The applicant replied;

"Wow! Thank you for the info. I really need a part time job."

Dren really didn't want to reply because he also had a doubt that the applicant is not really the woman who accompanied him last night, but he lost his grip on his phone. Because he is trying to catch it so that it will not fall on the floor and get damaged, he accidentally presses a word that pops up from keyboard suggestions. What he accidentally typed was sent when his fingers accidentally hit the sending button unintentionally while preventing his phone from falling down on the floor.

"Why" The message that accidentally sends.

"Shit! It was sent." Dren uttered in an irritated voice.

After a minute, he got a reply from the applicant. He reads her message.

"I need money for my tuition fee." The applicant replied.

Dren sent a reply; " Oh, okay. "

The applicant replied;

"You're the company CEO or a department head? "

Dren replied;

"An employee,"

Dren just said that he is an employee because he doesn't want to reveal his true identity, that he is the owner of the company. Their chat went on and on. He got another message from her. All he can tell her are lies. He saw that it was already time for him to go to the business meeting so he sent another message to end their conversation.

Dren's message;

"I really have to go. I am really busy right now."

Applicant's replied;

"Alright, sorry to disturb you."

Dren's replied;

"You don't disturb me that much. You can chat with me, but I will reply after work. "

Applicant's replied;

"Okay. "

After Dren read her reply, he picked up his laptop and folder. He walked out of his office in a hurry to ride on the elevator going down to the ground floor. The elevator reached the ground floor. He stepped outside and ran to the adjacent building like a fool. His employees saw him running, but none of them had the courage to laugh at him. They are all afraid of him. Of course, they don't want to get terminated. Especially those who badly need a high salary. He is giving them a salary that is above the minimum compared to other companies.

Dren is talking to himself while running towards the venue of the business meeting;

"Wait a minute! I will be late to the meeting."

He reached the building where the venue of the business meeting was located. He was still catching his breath because he felt tired from running. He saw that all the participants were inside the meeting room. He is the only one left outside. He composed himself before he entered the meeting room. When He entered the room, he looked dignified; a very dignified and charming man. He greeted them in a serious tone.

"Good Morning. Sorry I'm a bit late. Let's start the meeting."

Participants talk in chorus; "Goodmorning.*

Dren started the business presentation in a few minutes. He makes an audio visual presentation. It is about the new business that he wants to open. A manufacturing company that will produce biscuits and bread

When he finished discussing the whole project proposal, he answered all the questions from the investors. They threw him with too many questions, because they were all interested in the new project. The new project was approved by the investors because they were convinced by Dren's presentation.

When all the people leave the meeting room, he immediately pulls his phone from his pocket. He doesn't know the reason but he is expecting a new message from the applicant that he chatted with before the meeting.

He is disappointed when he gets no message from the applicant. He just turned on the music player on his phone and put on a headset to listen to the music. Then he walks toward the entrance and leaves the meeting room. He goes back to his office.

While he is in his private office Dren tries to concentrate on the documents that he is reading, but he can't so he decides to go out again from his office to take his lunch break since he can't concentrate on his work because he is checking his phone from time to time hoping the applicant message him again.

Dren was lost in deep thought while walking to the elevator to go down to the basement parking area;

Dren can't imagine himself in this kind of situation feeling attracted to someone else whom he doesn't even know the name of and he just once saw . He felt attracted to the woman and hoped that woman is also the applicant whom he chatted with before the business meeting started this morning. He decides to check the woman's post on her timeline. As far as he remembers the woman has resemblance to this applicant.

Going back to reality. He is now on the busy street of Vienna, Austria. He was driving too fast and his car almost hit a woman walking down the street when his car passed her by.

Dren blows horn;

"Peep! Peep P!

The woman shouts at him;

"You're reckless.You drive too fast, just like you are chasing the road."

Dren stopped the car beside the woman and talked to her;

"I'm sorry, Miss. "

The woman was surprised when she saw Dren's face;

"You are the drunk man that I helped last night to go home. I am curious about what kind of man you are. A drunkard and a reckless driver."

Dren smirked when he heard what the woman said. Then he teases her;

"But in fairness, I'm handsome, right? Are you sure I am that man?"

"Of course. I remember how you looked last night." The woman said.

She thinks she is not mistaken. She can still recall the appearance of the man she helped to go home last night. He's tall. Maybe he is six feet and four inches. He has a wide shoulder and a muscular build.He has an angel-like appearance.He has long, dark hair that he keeps in a man bun with some strands falling prettily on his face. His eyes are green, as green lights shine in the dark evening. He looks exactly like him.

While the woman is looking at Dren , she sees Dren smirks again before he speaks;

"Sorry, Yeah I remember your face. Anyway, Thank you for helping me last night." Dren said in a glad voice when he recognized the woman. And now he is one hundred percent sure. This woman is also the applicant whom he messaged this morning.

The woman's eyebrow raised at Dren.

"It's okay. By the way, I have to go. Nice meeting you."

"Ditto. See you around." Dren said without bothering to ask the name of the woman because he knew sooner or later he would know all the information he wanted to know about her if she were hired by his company.

Dren continued to drive to an expensive restaurant nearby when the woman started walking away from him.

While he is sitting down at the restaurant, He get his phone and sends a message to her.

"Hello.It's just my break time, so I can chat. " Dren's message.

She replied to him;

"I made my resume, I emailed it to the company. I want to chat with you again, but I am hesitant because you said you are busy."

Dren replied to her message while feeling happy;

"Glad to hear that. So what is the result? Do they reply to you? "

She replied;

"I got an email from DW Manufacturing & Distributing Company. It said that they were expecting me to come for an interview this afternoon at 2:00 pm.

Dren replied;

"I felt too glad. So hurriedly eat your lunch and prepare to go to the company for the interview. Anyway, where do you live?

She sent a reply;

"It is just several meters away from the company. According to the address they gave me, I will walk only to save money on fares."

Dren feels pity on her while sending his reply. Message sent;

"If you will be accepted into that job, it will be more beneficial to you. You will have another source of income and you can save money on bus fare because it is walking distance from your home. "

She replied;

"Yes. Really."

Dren replied;

"Alright. My breaktime is over. I have to go. Have a nice day."
She sent a message;
"Thank you once again."
Dren's replied;
"No worries. Chat me after your interview. "
She answers his message;
" Alright. I will. "

Chapter 4

After office hours Dren goes to the shopping mall to buy some stuff when his phone vibrates in his pocket. He got a message from her.

Her message;

"The job interview finished late in the afternoon because there were a lot of applicants, and I was last on the list. It's already 5:00 p.m. And my shift at the restaurant is getting closer. So I just decided to walk to the restaurant while waiting for 7:00 a.m. I know it's a long walk, but I decided not to ride on a bus to save money on fare.

Dren replied;

"So are you hired?"

She sent a message;

"I'm thankful that I passed the job interview. The HR department said that I am hired and can start work tomorrow."

Dren can't stop himself from smiling while typing his reply for her. His message was sent;

"What position is your job in the company? And what time is your working schedule?"

She replied;

"I was hired as a machine operator. I will work in the production area. My shift will start at 10:00 a.m. and end at 6:00 p.m. So after my classes tomorrow, I will proceed to work at DW Manufacturing & Distributing Company."

Dren replied;

"Alright. Do you have other part-time jobs aside from that?"

She sent a message;

"After the end of the shift at the company, I will proceed to work at the late-night restaurant where I am working at present. I have a hectic schedule. I only get 3 hours of sleep each night, but I can rest on Sunday because it's my day off.

Dren replied;

"Alright. So where are you now?"

He got a reply from her after a few minutes.

"Because I was starving, I decided to eat first at the fast food restaurant I will pass by on my way."

Dren replied;

"Okay. "

After sending his replies to her he walks outside the shopping mall near the fast food chain. While he was coming out of a shopping center walking down the street a woman bumped into him. She is heading to the fast food chain. She lost her balance and stumbled down the street. She can't move for a few seconds.

She feels pain and that makes her mumble; "Ah! My knees are aching. I can't stand up."

Dren's cell phone dropped in front of her. So he sat in a squat position and picked up his phone. Then he checked on what happened to the woman and speak to her;

"I'm sorry. Are you okay?"

The woman didn't answer him. She is now sitting on the pavement and looking at her knees, which have a small wound. The blood came out of her wound, so Dren decided to tie it up with his handkerchief. She got so angry at Dren. She was ready to throw harsh words at him, but when she looked at him, she was surprised.

"You look so familiar. Is it you again? The drunkard and reckless driver I encountered on the street yesterday and today."

"Oh it's you? I repeat my question. Are you okay? Let me help you stand up." Dren said, while feeling sorry when he recognized who the woman in front of her was.

"No need. I can manage."

The woman said but Dren still offered his hand to help her stand up because she was still sitting on the pavement but she just ignored his help and stood up immediately when she was able to compose herself. Then she stepped back away from him. He just shrugged his shoulders, put his hand in his pocket and smiled, even though he was a little bit embarrassed by her action.Then he decided to apologize again and he introduce himself to her this time;

"I am sorry, Miss. I know it was my fault for using my cellphone while walking, but I didn't mean what happened. My name is Dren. I'm the owner of DW Manufacturing & Distributing Company.

Her eyes widened when she heard what Dren said. She can't believe that he is the owner of DW Manufacturing & Distributing Company.

"You're going to be my boss?" She asked while looking at Dren.

"Yes. You applied to my company, right? Will you accept my apology? I'm really sorry." Dren said, smiling at her.

"Alright, Sir. I have to go. I will go to that fast food on the other side of the street." She said while starting to walk away from him again.

Dren: follow her while speaking to her;

"I wanted to talk to you. Don't walk too fast. You almost left me behind."

"Oh sorry, I wanted to talk to you also Sir Dren, but I feel ashamed because you're my boss. All I want to do right now is run away."

"What? Rovena, Wait!!!

Dren said. He is determined to talk to her right now. He wanted to know her further so he followed her walk down the street, going to the fast food restaurant.

But she went inside the fast food restaurant so fast without saying a word and never looked back at me. Dren was left outside the fast food restaurant. He decided to follow her inside.

Dren shook his head while smiling and mumbling. "Why does she want to avoid me? Is she angry with me? Or is she scared?

When Dren got near her again inside the fast food restaurant he asked her;

"Do I look like a scarecrow?"

"No, Sir. You know you're not. Why are you still following me?" She said to him in a curious voice.

"Because your looks and behavior caught my attention. I got interested in you. I want to know you furthermore." Dren said to her, smiling.

She won't admit and she will never admit that every time he smiles she feels mesmerized because his beautiful white teeth show up. His face lit up and his green eyes looked so innocent. He looks like an angel without wings.

She started to move away from him again. Dren smirks when he sees she is going to ignore him again. He talks to her;

"I can't just accept that I was ignored like that by a woman. You are the only woman who has the nerve to ignore me."

"I'm sorry about that. You have never been ignored by any woman? So most of the women you met were interested in talking to you and knew you further? Maybe because of your looks, charm, and status in life.

"You are different, so I was challenged by your behavior. In addition, you are pretty cute." Dren said in a serious manner while getting close to her again.

"No. I'm just tall and slim. Not pretty." she said while continuing walking away from him. But he is still following and talking to her;

"I'm not kidding. Your face looks beautiful even though you are not wearing any makeup. I can't forget your bright brown eyes with long eyelashes when I saw you last night.

"Hah! Seriously?! she said, while she turned around to look at him.

"Yeah. I wanted to know who you are because there is something that I can't explain. I got this feeling when I met you. I wanted to know if what I felt was real or if it was just an illusion." Dren said, looking straight in her eyes.

"So bad. That's weird. Please excuse me, Sir. I will just order some food. I'm so hungry.

Dren shrugged his shoulders and said;

"Alright."

Chapter 5

When she ordered food and dine, Immediately Dren ordered some food too. Then he walked over to her table and asked if he could share it with her at the table.

"Excuse me. Can I sit on this chair opposite in front of you?"

Dren said but he didn't wait for her to answer. He just put his food on the table and sat down on the opposite chair in front of her.

She was surprised;

"What do you want?"

"I just want to sit here and know your name."

She stopped eating for a while and asked;

"Why?"

Dren smiled before he answers her question;

"I just want to know. "

She takes a deep breath before she speak;

"You already know that my name is Rovena, right?"

Dren answers her;

"I just want to confirm. Nice meeting you, Rovena."

She just continued eating. She didn't respond.

Dren asked her again;

"Where do you live?"

"Just several meters away from here. " She answered before she put food mouth.

Dren laughed softly and said, "Tell me the exact address."

She feels slightly annoyed. She can't believe that he is too demanding.

Dren smirked when he didn't receive any answer from her then he spoke to her again.

"I just want to know. Is there something wrong with that?"

She gets something from her bag before she answers him;

"Here is my ID. You can read my address here."

Dren picks up her ID and reads:

"Oh it's just nearby. So you are Rovena Binder. The applicant whom I'm chatting with."

She was surprised when she heard what Dren said;

"What?! Are you also that guy who answers my inquiry?"

Dren answers her in a serious manner;

"Yes. I am."

"You never told me that you are the owner of the company when I asked you, Sir." Rovena said, curious.

"Because I think it was not necessary. Now you know." Dren answered, smiling at her.

She answers before she puts food in her mouth; "Alright."

Dren finished eating his food when he noticed that Rovena was about to finish eating her food too. She stands up immediately after she finishes eating her food and walks out of the fast food restaurant going to a busy street.

She felt relieved when Dren didn't follow her when she walked outside the fast food joint. After leaving the fast food restaurant, she began walking down the street toward the restaurant where she works. But she was shocked when she saw Dren's car suddenly parked in front of her. He immediately opened the window of his car in front of her and said;

"Rovena!. I'll drive you to where you are going. "

"What?!I.. I couldn't believe that you are still following me. I thought that you are not interested anymore in following me, but to my surprise, you are here again in front of me."

Dren smiled and insist;

"As I was saying, I will drive you to where you are going."

"No need, I can manage. I can manage to go to work alone. Will you please stop following me, Sir?" Rovena said to him, smiling.

"Come on. Hop in. It's getting cold here. Look, the snow started to fall." Dren said, insisting what he wanted.

"No, thanks." Rovena said, determined n to ride in his car.

Dren frowned and said;

"So you are determined not to allow me to know where you are working? Are you afraid I will always go to the place if I know where you are working?"

"I just don't want to get inside your car..." Rovena answered politely.

"But I insisted. It seems to some passersby that you and I are arguing, so they are looking at us now. To avoid creating a scene, You had no choice but to ride in my car and let me drive you to the restaurant where you are working."

Rovena feels slightly annoyed because some passersby look at them.

"Okay, Sir." She said, then she got in his car immediately.

The next day at DW Manufacturing & Distributing Company.

At exactly 10:00 a.m. Dren gets inside the production area. He is looking for Rovena. He asked the supervisor about her working station. After a few minutes he saw her operating the machine in her working station.

"Miss Rovena Binder?" He greets her when he gets near her.

"Sir?" Rovena said, looking at him.

"Sorry I have poor eyesight. I didn't recognize you easily." Dren said and got his eyeglass then wore it.

"Yes I bet you have poor eyesight when you don't recognize me easily."

"Now that I wear my eyeglasses, I'm sure you are Rovena. I'm glad to see you here. " Dren said, smiling at her.

"Thank you, Sir. " Rovena said.

Dren smiled back and said; " No worries."

"I can see that all your employees are afraid of you. I'm sure you are strict in implementing the rules in the company. When the employees saw you in the production area they seemed afraid of you." Rovena said, obviously feeling nervous. It was noticed by Dren.

"Yeah. That's true. But you don't have to be nervous like that. By the way, I hope you don't find it hard to operate this machine." Dren said in a serious manner.

"It's fine, Sir." Rovena answers, focusing her attention to the machine she is operating.

"Alright. Anyway I have to go. I just dropped by to see you." Dren said, started walking away from Rovena.

Rovena watched him walking away until he was lost in her sight because he walked out the production area. She can't stop herself from admiring him but of course she doesn't show it to him. She is afraid that he will misinterpret her if he learns her feelings towards him.

Time passed by so fast. It's already the end of Rovena's shift. She immediately went outside the production area because she only had one hour left and the shift on her other work will start. She almost ran out of the company building so that she could reach the late-night restaurant that she is working at without delay. Its location is more than a few meters away from here. She doesn't want to be late because the owner will get angry if she arrives late. She was walking fast down the street when Dren stopped her car in front of her. He opened the window of his car and talked to her.

"Come on, Rovena. Hop in. I will eat dinner at the restaurant that you are working at. "

"Thank you, Sir. But I can manage to go there alone." Rovena said, trying to avoid Dren because of the rumor that arises from the production area when Dren intentionally dropped by there in the morning to look for her and talk to her.

"I insisted. Get inside the car before I step outside this car and lift you inside." Dren said, giving her a warning.

"Why are you bothering me?" Rovena said, her voice slightly raised at him. She didn' t mean to ask that question that way but she just got carried away by her thoughts about the rumor she heard among her co-workers.

"I just want to. Is there a problem with that?" Dren said and smirked.

"Are you crazy, Sir?" Rovena asked in a voice slightly annoyed at Dren.

Dren laughed softly and said; "Nope."

Rovena left him, but still, he is determined to follow her. He stepped out of his car. Then he walked towards her and held her hands. He pulled her into his car. When they get near the car, he opens the door on the passenger seat and asks her to ride. Because passersby look at him and her , she just gets into his car to avoid getting attention. She shook her head while looking at him. He just shrugged his shoulders when he looked back at her. Then he goes back to the driver's seat and drives to the restaurant where Rovena is working. After more than several minutes of driving, he reached the restaurant.

"Thank you for driving me here, Sir." Rovena said in a serious tone.

"No worries." Dren said, then smiled at her.

Then Rovena stepped out of the car in a hurry. She goes to her workplace as the restaurant's cashier.

Chapter 6

As Dren had said he will eat dinner in the restaurant where Rovena is working so he steps outside his car and proceeds inside the restaurant.

When he was inside the restaurant he chose a table at the corner good for one person. Then he calls the waiter and makes an order.

While waiting for his order he is scrolling through his phone but she is glancing at Rovena from time to time who is now busy doing her work as a cashier.

After several minutes the waiter serves his order. He starts eating his food but his eyes and mind are not in his food but it is fixed at Rovena.

After an hour, Dren finished eating his dinner. He decided to go home. It was 9:00 pm when he reached home. When he reached home, he decided to look for Ivano. He wanted to talk to him about how he felt about Rovena

He found him in the garden while drinking coffee. When Ivano saw Dren, he immediately talked about the result of the conference meeting yesterday. Ivano is glad about the result of the meeting.

"Good evening, Uncle."

"Good evening. I'm very proud of you, Dren. "

"Oh, why?"

"Because you meet the expectations of the investors and board members.That's why the new business will be approved when you present it to the meeting.

"Thank you. Uncle. "

"You're welcome. By the way, what brought you here? "

Dren smiled before he talked to Ivano. He felt a little bit nervous about the topic he would be opening up to him.

"I just want to tell you something."

"What is it all about?"

"About a woman."

"A woman?"

"Are you falling in love?"

"Not at all.I mean, it's too early for me to say that I love that woman. I just met her. And now she works at my company."

27

"Oh, so what do you want to tell me about her?"

"I'm just confused about why I have this feeling that I'm so attracted to her . I just met her yesterday. "

"Maybe she is the one who is meant for you. That's why you feel that way about her. "

"Meant for me? If she is, why does she keep on avoiding me? "

"There are too many reasons why Dren."

"What reasons? She senses that sometimes I'm insane."

Ivano laughed when he heard Dren say those words.

"That's not what I mean, Dren. Maybe she just felt shy because you are her boss. The differences in the status of life that you and she may have may be the main reason."

"Maybe you are right. But it doesn't matter where she belongs. "

"For you, it's not a big deal, but for her, maybe it is. Maybe she feels shy whenever you're around her. So she is trying to avoid you. Or maybe she is attracted to you, but she chooses to avoid you to hide her feelings. "

"So what will I do then? She doesn't need to hide it from me because I feel the same way about her. "

"Why don't you just tell her? "

"I tried to tell her but she just ignored me ."

"Don't give up easily.You need to tell her over and over until she believes in you. Be like me, Dren. I have the courage to tell the woman I want that I have feelings for her. That's why I'm happily married. Because I'll take the chance to tell the woman I love my feelings."

"I will also do that, Uncle"

"So all I can say is you need to take the chance you have to let her know how you feel about her. Don't wait for the time when you will see her walking down the aisle of the church marrying another man. "

"All right."

"All right, good night."

"Goodnight, Uncle."

Then Ivano and Dren get inside the mansion and go to their own room. Dren can say that Ivano is really happy in his marriage life even though he has no child because his wife has no capability to bear a child. Even so, he loves her wife so much. And because Ivano has no child he treats Dren like his own son. He acts like a real father of Dren. He raised Dren very well until Dren became what he is at present.

When Dren reached his room, he lay down on his bed, then he got his phone and started sending messages to Rovena;

"Goodnight and take care. See you at the company tomorrow."

He is waiting for her reply while listening to music from his phone and reading a fashion magazine. But almost half an hour had passed and he got no reply from her. He feels disappointed. He just comforts himself by thinking that maybe cellphones are not allowed in her work so she can't reply to his message.

Dren decided to go to sleep instead of waiting for Rovena's reply. He will just talk to her tomorrow at the company.

But before he can close his eyes he received a message from her;

"Goodnight, Sir."

Dren replied;

"Please refrain from calling me "Sir" if we are not in the company."

Rovena replied;

"But why?"

"I think it's not really needed to call me that way if we are not in the company."

Rovena replied;

"Alright, Dren. I have to go back to work.It's just my coffee break that's why I was able to reply to your message. "

Dren replied;

"Alright."

After their conversation, Dren fell asleep while on the other hand Rovena is thinking of Dren while doing her work. She can't deny that she feels attracted to Dren and she can say that he feels the same way towards her. But Rovena is just hiding her feelings because she knows it's not right to fall in love with Dren.

She knows status in life matters. Based on the reactions of other employees in Dren's company when they saw Dren talk to her.

She heard an unpleasant judgment from them. And she can't bear hearing their accusation towards her so she needs to avoid Dren. Thinking of that situation makes her feel sad.

Chapter 7

One week Later.

It's 3:00 a.m.Sunday.

It is the end of Rovena's shift at the late night restaurant. She walked down the street to go home. Even the snowflakes are falling down.

Rovena noticed that the street was full of snow. The weather is bad. Many of the cars were stranded on the street because of the heavy snowfall. She walked as fast as she could. After almost 30 minutes of walking, she reached her boarding house. She immediately got inside and changed her clothes, soaked in the falling snowflakes.

Since It's her day off, she plans to rest all day today. She plans to sleep the whole day. After changing her clothes, she brushes her long beautiful shiny hair. After brushing her hair, she laid down on her bed to sleep. But when she was about to close her eyes, she heard a knock on the door. She wonders who the hell is knocking on the door at this hour. It's only 4:00 a.m. in the morning. She gets up from her bed to open the door to see who is outside. When she opens the door she sees Dren standing on the doorway.

"Good morning, Rovena." He greeted her with a wide smile on his face.

"What are you doing here, Sir?" Rovena asked, confused.

"Would you mind if I came in?" He said instead of answering Rovena's question.

"Okay. Get inside and take your seat, Sir. " Rovena said.

When he got inside her room, he sat down immediately on the single sofa that he saw because he could not stand up any longer. He feels dizzy now because of the effect of the alcohol that he drank. He is drunk. He went to the pub late at night, and he drank until the pub closed.

Because of the bad weather, the street was covered with snow and the road was slippery. He is afraid that he will have an accident if he forces himself to drive home.

Why is he drinking again? Because he misses his parents again. He still feels bitter that he can no longer see his parents again. Even though it's been a long time ago since his parents passed away he still misses him and still can't accept that they are gone.

Because he cannot drive until he reaches his home, he decided to look for Rovena's apartment. He knows it's near the pub because Rovena once told him her address when he asked her. And he is not mistaken. After a few minutes of looking for her apartment he saw it. But when he saw the time on his wristwatch that Rovena was still at work so he stopped first on the opposite road of her apartment to wait for her.

When he saw that she had arrived from work, he decided to go to her apartment to ask a favor from her so that he can sleep over in her apartment just for a while because he can't drive any more.

"Would you mind if I slept here for a while?" He asked Rovena, who was still standing near the door.

"It's okay. No worries. Are you drunk, sir?" Rovena said, a little bit curious.

"Yes, sorry to disturb you, but I can't drive home anymore." Dren said to her,

"All right, I will just make a cup of coffee for you, Sir. "

"Yes, Please, Rovena." Dren said while massaging his forehead because of a headache.

Dren is not aware that he is staring at Rovena because he is confused about what he feels. He can say that his feelings for Rovena grew much stronger. He hopes that he can tell his feelings for her one of these days. He is hoping that Rovena will give him a chance to become her fiancé.

He is back to his senses when he hears Rovena talk and asks her. He nearly falls off the chair where he is sitting. He feels a little bit embarrassed because of that.

"Why are you staring at me, Sir?" Rovena asks, feeling a little bit afraid of Dren.

Dren clears his throat and composes himself before he answers the question from Rovena.

"Nothing to worry about; I'm just watching you prepare the cup of coffee." He explained, the smile a little bit.

Rovena folded her arms across her chest, frowned, and looked directly into his eyes.

Because of that, Dren feels shy, so he lowers his head and pretends that he is checking some messages on his phone to find an excuse. He can't look directly into her eyes. He doesn't know why he feels shy in front of Rovena. Rovena is the only woman who made him lose self confidence.

If he was in front of another woman, he didn't feel and behave like that because he knew that they can't resist him because he knows he is good looking . But Rovena is different. As if she doesn't even notice how good looking he is.

Dren continues to pretend that he is really reading some messages on his phone. He just looks up when Rovena gives him the cup of coffee. He slipped his phone inside his pocket.

Rovena sits on the chair beside the small dining table after giving him a cup of coffee. She started drinking her coffee.

"Drink your coffee, Sir,before it gets cold, " Rovena said, looking at Dren.

"Alright," Dren said, then he started drinking his coffee. When he tasted the coffee that Rovena made, He remember his ex-girlfriend, whose name is Lara. Whenever he visits Lara, she always makes him a cup of coffee. And how she mixed the coffee tasted like what Rovena gave him right now. Lara is his very first girlfriend but not his first love. He just took pity on Lara before because of her concern for him. But because he takes his career seriously and he got so busy with work and always no time for her he lost Lara. Lara broke up with him and married another man. Now Lara is living a poor life because the man she married is a lazy one. Yes he has ample time to devote to her but Lara is the one who works to earn a living.

Dren misses Lara sometimes. There are times he helps Lara because he took pity on her but he stops when it causes rumors that Lara and him have an affair. Last week he had a business trip to Linz, Austria. He got a chance to see Lara again. Since Lara got married she moved to Linz where her husband's hometown is.

Because he remembered Lara, he didn't notice that he had pulled the necklace that she gave to him when they were still in a relationship. He is still wearing it, but he hides it under his clothes. Whenever he remembers Lara, he holds that necklace.

Dren noticed that Rovena was looking at him again. He just smiled at her a bit. Then he continued drinking his coffee. He heard Rovena talking to him;

"Your necklace looks nice..."

"Thanks," Dren said ,hiding his necklace again.

Chapter 8

While Dren is drinking his coffee he is in deep thoughts. He remembers all the memories of how Lara and him met in the past...

It's the year 2010 at Vienna, Austria school campus. It is 2:00 pm in the afternoon. One more subject to attend before Dren can go home. It's his breaktime so like what he used to do he will buy food at the canteen and sit on the bench near the school playground while eating. Watching the students sitting, standing, chatting, playing, studying around the school campus.

One of the students who is sitting on another bench in the school yard catches his attention. He thinks she is a transferee. She is a pretty girl. He can't take his eyes off her. She is wearing a faded uniform and old shoes. She looks so poor. He saw her walking towards the trash can near the place where he sits. She is going to put an empty food plastic in the trash can. When she looks at him he smiles at her. She smiles back at him. So he stood up from the bench and walked towards her to ask her name.

"Hi. Your name please?"

"I'm Lara."

"Oh ,nice name. I'm Dren."

"Nice meeting you Dren."

"Nice meeting you. Are you a new student here?"

"Ah yes. I started to study here last week."

"Transferee?"

"Yeah. My employer transferred me here. I work in her flower shop in the morning and in her late night restaurant in the evening . I attend classes in the afternoon here. I'm a working student."

"Alright so where do you live?"

"I live at my employer's house, which is at the corner of the next street from this school."

"Oh okay. So you stay in her house?"

"Yes."

"That's nice I can visit you after my classes."

"No you can't."

"Why not? You don't like me as a friend?"

"That's not what I mean."

"So why can't I visit you?"

"Because I still have work after my classes?"

" What?!!"

"You heard it right. I still have work after this. As I was saying I work at her late night restaurant..."

"Oh. So when can I visit you?"

"I don't know Dren. I need to work. I don't have much free time."

"How about Saturday or Sunday?"

"Maybe. If I don't go to the flower shop on weekends."

"Ahm, as if you don't know how to rest."

"Because I will run out of money to support my studies if I don't work."

"Oh I see."

" By the way, I have to go. I still have classes.."

"Okay. See you around. "

"Alright".

Then Lara walked away going to the classroom on the first floor of the three storey school building while Dren started walking to his classroom to attend classes on his last subject.

Dren was back in reality when he nearly lost grip on the cup of coffee in his hands. He noticed that Rovena started cooking breakfast.

Rovena started cooking breakfast instead of going to sleep. He feels sleepy but he can't just go to sleep because Dren is still there in her apartment. He can't just leave because he is drunk. In addition to that, the weather is bad. The road is full of snow. So it's not safe for him to drive home.

Rovena noticed that Dren is lost in deep thoughts but back to reality when he nearly lost grip on his cup of coffee. He looked at her for a while but didn't speak. She just continued cooking and pretended that she didn't notice him.

Rovena feels glad that Dren comes around. She can't deny the fact that she is attracted to Dren. But she knows the feeling that she feels right now is not right. She is just nothing while Dren is a billionaire. She knows status in life matters.

And she thinks that it is impossible that Dren and her become more than just friends. She knows she is not the type of a woman he will like. She remembered what Dren's employees were talking about and what type of woman he liked.

According to his employee, he has a classmate named Trina whom he likes so much. Dren admired Trina so much before. Trina is a well behaved and modest girl. She acts so feminine. She has an angelic voice and face; sophisticated and brainy. When Dren and her are still a student most of the boys in their campus including Dren are dreaming of becoming Trina's fiance. But Trina chose Florian to become her fiance because Florian belongs to a rich and influential family. Aside from that he is brainy, an athlete and a fashion model. His family owns a brand of clothing line.

Rovena heard that Florian was embarrassed Dren before because Dren tried to get close to Trina and revealed his feelings for her. Dren got embarrassed in front of many students because of Florian. The situation happened near the school canteen so there are many students who are watching and hearing it.

It's late in the afternoon. It's Dren and Trina's breaktime before their last subject. They both buy food in the canteen. They walk outside the canteen while talking to each other. Then they sat down on a bench under a tree on the opposite side of the canteen. Dren revealed that she has feelings for Trina. And he is sincere about that. He hopes that Trina will give him a chance to prove it to her but Trina feels sorry for Dren because Dren is late in letting her know about his feelings. Florian and her are already in a relationship. When Florian saw them talking to each other he walked towards Dren and Trina together with his friends and classmates. And intentionally speak in a loud voice to embarrass Dren in front of other students. He accused Dren of trying to get noticed by Trina. He said to all the students around them that Dren is nothing but an orphan who has no money while he belongs to a rich and influential family. Then he asked Dren if he thinks that Trina will choose Dren over him. Because of that all the students who happened to hear what Florian said laughed out loud while Trina stood up and got close to Florian. She holds on to Florian's arms. Dren just lowers his head for a while but later looks up to Florian and utters a threat. He said that he gave up his feelings for Trina. But it never just ends like that. After class, outside this campus Dren and Florian had a fight. Lara, who is Dren's friend, saw Dren start the fight against Florian and his friends. Dren and Florian exchange kicks and punches. Dren seems to win the fight against Florian but Florian's friends help Florian to fight against Dren. They assaulted Dren. Lara saw that Dren was defeated but still Florian's friends didn't stop assaulting him, Lara decided to help Dren.

Lara approached Florian's friend to stop them from beating Dren. But they didn't listen to Lara, instead they started to assault Lara also. Lara has no choice but to fight back. She is a mixed martial arts player in their school so she knows she can defeat them. And she is not mistaken winning the fight over them. Florian and his friends retreat. Dren thanks Lara for her concern. And from that day on Dren just decided to focus his attention on Lara. And because of what Lara did to him they got in a relationship.

According to Dren's employees, Lara is Dren's first girlfriend but Trina is his first love. But Lara in the long run succeeded in winning Dren's heart. But in the end Lara left Dren when they finished studying because Dren got busy with his businesses and almost no time for her.

That's all the rumors and stories about Dren that Rovena heard from Dren's employees while she was working in his company for one week.

Dren noticed that Rovena was finished cooking breakfast. The smell of the food makes him feel hungry. All of the sudden he felt his stomach rumbling.

He saw Rovena preparing the food on the small dining table. After she put the food on the table she talked to me.

"Sir Dren, let's eat breakfast."

When Dren heard her he stood up and dragged the single sofa where he was sitting near the small dining table to join her eating breakfast.

"Alright. I'm sorry if I disturbed you a lot."

"It is okay, Sir. No worries.

"Thank you."

For several minutes Rovena and Dren stop talking and just continue eating breakfast. But Dren talks again to Rovena a few minutes later.

"Rovena , do you have a fiance?"

When Rovena heard his question she just laughed out loud.

"Why did you laugh? Is there something funny about my question?"

"Sorry, Sir if I laughed at your question. I don't have a fiance. I am still busy with my studies. I want to finish college before I get into a relationship. I want to have a good job. And getting into a relationship right now is not my priority."

"Seriously?"

"Of course. How about you, do you have a girlfriend at present?"

"I'm single and available. So if you want to pass your resume, I'm accepting applicants."

When Rovena heard what he had said she just laughed again. She looks more beautiful when laughing. Dren can't stop himself from staring at her.

"You're laughing again. Do I look like a clown?"

"No ,Sir. I just don't believe what you have said."

"It's true. I don't have a girlfriend."

"Really? But why?"

"Maybe because I'm waiting for you."

"Waiting for me? Stop kidding me, Sir"

"I'm not kidding."

"I bet that is only the effect of being drunk on you. How many glasses of beer did you drink?"

"A lot. But still I know what I am talking about."

"Sir, I suggest you go to sleep first. And let's see if you will say the same thing when you wake up."

Dren laughed when he heard what Rovena said. He starts telling his feelings about her but he thinks she will not believe in him.He thinks that maybe she just wants him as a friend only. But he will try to tell her that what he feels for her is more than friends if he is not drunk. And he hopes she will believe in him.

"Alright. Can I sleep here in your place just for today?"

"Yes you can. Why not? I don't want to bother with my conscience if I let you go home while the weather is bad.

"Thanks for your concern to me Rovena.

"No worries, Sir. "

Dren smiles at her. Rovena smiles back at him while she starts getting some beddings and throws it on the single bed that is in this room. Then Dren heard her talk to him;

"Sir, You can sleep there now." Rovena said while pointing to the bed.

"Thanks." Dren said. Then he stood up and went to bed.

He really felt so sleepy so he didn't think twice about lying on her bed immediately. He saw Rovena occupying the long sofa. She will sleep there. While he is lying on Rovena's bed, she can smell her perfume on the pillow. She is using the same brand of perfume that she used before when she first met her.

Chapter 9

It's 12:00 p.m. and the bad weather went well. But Dren is still in Rovena's apartment sleeping.

Rovena has finished washing clothes, cooking lunch but Dren is still sleeping. She just decided to do her school projects and assignments while waiting for him to wake up.

She was solving a difficult math problem for her accounting subject when she heard Dren's phone ring. Dren's phone was on the bed. He didn't wake up even though his phone was ringing beside him.

Because his phone rings again and again and Rovena was disturbed with solving the equation that she is trying to solve, she decided to look for who is calling. She saw a woman's name on the screen of his phone. ' Lara'

Rovena is curious who Lara is? Is she Dren's ex-girlfriend? Those questions are running through her mind while staring at the screen of Dren's phone. The phone stopped ringing. Then she saw a message flashes on the screen from Lara;

"Hi, Where are you? I've already arrived from Linz. You promised we will see each other when I arrive this Sunday. See you tonight."

Rovena doesn't know why she feels annoyed after she reads such a message. She was not in the mood now to finish her assignment. Unintentionally she threw the book that she was holding on the table but unfortunately the book hit the glass of water that was on the table.

The glass fell on the floor and shattered. It made a loud sound that made Dren awake from his deep sleep. He got up from bed immediately to check what happened.

"Rovena, what are you doing?"

"Sorry If I woke you up, Sir. It's just a glass of water that falls on the floor."

"Alright. What time is it? Sorry I slept too long here."

"It's past 12:00 o'clock. It's okay."

"I have to go. Thank you for accommodating me here."

"No worries."

"So I can still go back here?"

"Ah, It's up to you."

"Alright."

Dren is about to go home when his phone rings again. He answered the call. Since it is on loudspeaker Rovena was able to hear the conversation between Dren and the caller.

"Hello, Lara?"

"Hello. So where are you? I called you a while ago but you didn't answer my call."

"Sorry. I'm sleeping. What's the matter?"

"You forgot your promise?"

"What promise?"

"I thought we would see each other this Sunday?"

"Oh sorry I forgot."

"You didn't mean it. I understand.

" So what's the matter?"

"I need your help!"

"Okay. What help do you need from me?"

"I'm pregnant..."

"I'm sure I'm not the father of that child." Dren teases Lara.

"Yes. You are not. You know how lazy my husband is. He tried to look for a job but he was terminated after a month because he failed to do his job."

"What?! So what do you want me to do? Give him a job?"

"If you can't give him a job. Please tell me can I borrow money from you?"

"Sure! Why not?"

"Thank you, Dren."

"No worries. By the way, what are you going to do with the money? For business?"

"Dren, I need money to give birth to this child. For sure my husband will find it hard to look for another job."

" Okay. I'll give you all the money you need but please let's stop seeing each other. It's quite not right that we still see each other despite the rumor that arises that we have an affair."

"Alright. Thank you Dren."

"Wait a minute, I will send it to your bank account right now."

"Oh really?"

"Yeah. I'm doing it."

Rovena was standing near Dren so she saw him transfer money from his bank account to Lara's bank account using his phone while he was talking with Lara. He gave her a million dollars .Then she heard Lara speak on the line.

"Hello, Dren, are you still there? I got the money. Thank you."

"Alright. I hope you won't bother me anymore."

"What do you mean by this Dren? We can't be friends?"

"Sorry we can't.Let's stop communicating with each other."

"Alright. If that is what you want."

"I'm sorry about this Lara,...but I think it's time for us to forget each other. I need to get over you."

"I understand. Bye Dren.

"Goodbye,Lara."

Then Dren turned off his phone. Rovena saw sadness in his eyes. She felt pity on him while she still wondered where her ex-girlfriend got the courage to ask help something like that to Dren .

Dren sat down on the long sofa. Rovena can see anger burning in Dren's eyes. He clenched his fist then he hit the sofa with his fist. The aura of his face changed from kind to cold. He lowered his head while covering his face with both hands.

When Rovena saw his reaction she suddenly felt afraid. It seems to her that Dren had a psychological condition that when being triggered manifested. It seems to her that Dren behaves differently.

Dren noticed that Rovena was looking at him. She seems afraid of him. At first, Dren was hesitant to tell me what was happening to him. But because Rovena gained his trust, Dren confessed to her all his deepest secrets that he had never revealed to any of his friends;

"Rovena I want to tell you something..." Dren said in a hesitant manner.

"What is it, Sir?"

"When I was 12 years old, I was diagnosed with a personality disorder. A split personality disorder. Only the doctor and Uncle Ivano as well as his wife knew about it. And now you know it. You are the only woman who knows my deepest secret. I hope you don't spill my secret to anyone. "

"I swear I will never tell anyone."

"Thanks, Rovena."

Rovena understands what condition Dren had for she works before as a maidservant to a family whose daughter has that kind psychological disorder.

She understands that if Dren gets in a situation that hurts his feelings he tends to shift from one personality to another personality. Maybe to guard his feelings from being hurt. Splitting is his defense mechanism. From being kind, patient and friendly, he will become arrogant, moody and distant from other people.

And she will not wonder if one of these days she will see Dren talking to himself in the mirror; will act as two different people sometimes; and the way he dresses, the way he talks and behaves varies.

Rovena was awake from deep thoughts when Dren speak to her;

"Rovena what are you thinking of? I noticed that your look is so far away."

"Nothing, Sir!"

"Don't worry about me. I'm okay. The relationship that Lara and I had ended a long time ago. I just don't understand why he keeps bothering me. It was her idea to end that bullsh*t relationship but she keeps on coming back. I swear this will be the last time I will entertain her."

"Do you still love her?"

"Nope. Since the day she cheated and left me, all my feelings for her were gone."

"Alright."

"Anyway. You have no work today right?"

"Yes. It's my day off today in your company and at the late night-restaurant where I am working."

"Uhm, that's good. Can you go with me?"

"Where?"

"At the mansion where I am staying. I will introduce you to Uncle Ivano and to his wife. It's Sunday so they are there in the mansion."

"But..."

"No buts, Rovena please? I want to introduce you to him. I mentioned to them that you are the woman who drove me home last time when I was drunk..."

"Alright. I will go with you."

"Glad to hear that."

"I will just change my clothes so please wait for me outside ..."

"Oh okay. I will wait for you outside."

When Dren went outside her room she changed her clothes immediately. She doesn't want to go with him to the mansion because she feels shy. She saw how elegant and big his mansion is. And she has never been inside that kind of place before. But she knows Dren will just insist on what he wants like what he did the last time. So she decided to accompany him.

After changing her clothes she grabs his phone and wallet. Then she went outside the room. She saw Dren standing outside scrolling through his phone. But when he noticed that she went outside the room he turned his eyes on her and he talked to her.

"Can we go now?"

"Yes, Sir."

Rovena and Dren walked towards Dren's car which was parked outside on the opposite side of the road. While they were walking to his car he held her hands.

Rovena wants to pull her hand away from Dren. She feels awkward because she is attracted to him. But she has to hide her feelings because she knows it is not right to fall for him. Dren is her boss.

When they reached the car, he opened the door for her to get inside on the passenger seat in front. Then he got inside his car and fastened her seatbelt. Then he started driving to his home. While driving he looks at her from time to time then he smiles. Rovena wonders why.

In a short period of time of driving Dren reached the mansion. He drove so fast that made Rovena feel nervous. As if the car is flying on the road. She wants to remind him but she chooses to keep silent. She knows he is not in the mood right now because of Lara. Aside from that he is her boss so she doesn't want him to get annoyed at her.

When they reached the mansion, he parked his car in the basement parking area. Then they went up the staircase from the basement going to the garden area.

In the garden Rovena saw a middle aged man sitting in one of the chairs of the garden set. When the old man saw them he smiled. Rovena guesses he is Dren's Uncle.

When they get near the old man Dren talked to him;

"Uncle Ivano, she is Rovena. The woman I'm talking about." Dren said while smiling at his uncle in a weird manner as if he is conveying something to his uncle. Rovena knows the old man gets what Dren wants to say so he answers Dren.

"Oh. Alright. It's good that you meet each other again. And I'm glad that you took my advice seriously."

"Of course Uncle that's why I want to introduce Rovena to you."

"I know. Nice meeting you Rovena. How are you?"

"I'm fine, Sir. Nice meeting you too."

"You can call me Uncle Ivano like Dren does."

"But Sir...I..I'm just an employee of Sir Dren..."

"It doesn't matter if you are just his employee, Rovena. You know destiny is out of control. What if you become Dren's wife someday." Ivano said and smiled while he made a short glance at Dren.

Dren laughed softly while Rovena lowered her head when she heard Dren's laugh. But she looked up when she heard a voice of a woman. When she looked up she saw a tall and slender woman the same age as Dren's Uncle Ivano.

"Dren, why don't you tour your girlfriend around the mansion? I am so glad you have a new girlfriend. My dream to have a grandchild will come true." The woman said, feeling so excited while smiling.

"Yes Aunt Mila. I will do that really."

"Nice meeting you,Madam but I'm not Sir Dren's girlfriend..."

"Oh, nice meeting you, I thought you were...

but I think you will be...soon...right, Dren?"

Dren just smiles in response to his Aunt Mila while Ivano clears his throat. Rovena lowers her head again.

"Why are you just smiling Dren? Aren't you like her? She is beautiful..."

"Yes she is beautiful. Aunt Mila, Uncle Ivano, please excuse us. We will get inside the mansion."

"Alright, Dren..."

"Thanks ,Uncle."

"Go ahead. I will ask a maidservant to prepare food for you and for ...oh what's your name young lady?

"I'm Rovena, Madam..."

"Alright."

"Thanks, Aunt Mila."

"No worries."

Dren and Rovena get inside the mansion. Dren started to tour her around the mansion. The mansion house is huge. Everything inside is elegant and beautiful. It is also equipped with modern facilities.

Dren brought her to a huge room which contained his collections of different items coming from different places which he visited.

And there is a box of jewelry which belongs to a woman. Every piece is too beautiful and looks too expensive.

Rovena wonders why Dren has that kind of collection in this room. Dren is not a woman who will collect such kinds of things. There are many questions running through her mind. 'Who is the owner of that? Is Dren a gay? or

Does he have a girlfriend and that jewelry belongs to her?'

'What if Dren has a girlfriend that he never told her about and suddenly comes and gets angry with her?'

'What will she do if that happens?'

Chapter 10

Dren noticed that Rovena was lost in deep thought when she saw the jewelry on the box. Dren wonders what she is thinking of. Those are jewelry that he bought last year when he had a business trip outside the country. When he saw it in a gift shop he bought it. He wanted to give it to the woman who will become his next girlfriend.

Even though he knows that is impossible because it's been more than several years that he dates a woman. It is unexpected that he gets attracted to a woman this time this much again. After a series of unsuccessful relationships that lasted only for a few months he stopped dating a woman. He focuses on his businesses.

Dren walked towards the beautiful box that held the jewelry. He held it. He just decided to give it to her so he talked to Rovena.

"Rovena this is for you!" he said to Rovena while walking towards her.

"For me?" Rovena was shocked.

"Yes, I bought it last year. Even though I don't know to whom I will give all these. And now that you are here I will give it to you." He said to Rovena looking straight into her eyes.

" Sir, I can't accept that." Rovena said as she looked away from him. She doesn't want to accept those jewelry because she thinks of what other people would say if they knew that she accepts such expensive items from Dren. She doesn't want to be labeled as a gold digger.

Dren laughed softly before he talk to her;

"Uhm, why?"

"Those are expensive... sorry I can't accept that..."

When Dren heard what Rovena said he couldn't believe her reasons. Most of the women he dates accepted expensive gifts from him even in their first meetings.

"You don't have to say sorry."Dren said and smiled at her.

Rovena forced herself to smile. Dren is about to touch Rovena's face to tell his feelings about her but he stops when he sees one of the maid servants is coming.

"Excuse me, Sir. The daughter of your Aunt's visitor is looking for you and I think she will come here." The maidservant said.

Dren feels annoyed. And he can't hide it when he talk;

"Who is she?"

"Your ex-,girlfriend, Sir. She, her mother and some of your Aunt's Mila arrived a while ago, " The maid servant said. And looked at the door when she heard footsteps.

"Alright. Aunt Mila told you to prepare a snack for me and Rovena in the dining area, right?" Dren asked the maid servant while he put down the jewelry box on the place where he got it.

"Yes, Sir. But the visitors are already in the dining room eating the food..." The maid servant said in a hesitant voice.

"It is alright. Just prepare some on the terrace. Okay? " Dren said to the maidservant,

"All right, Sir." The maidservant agreed and left.

From the doorway Dren sees Melissa is coming. She is holding a set of documents in a folder. He can see how Rovena looks at her as if she is mesmerized by the beauty of Melissa. Yes, Melissa is very beautiful. She is the most beautiful among his ex-girlfriends.

Melissa really looks like a fashion model in her light pink above the knee dress with matching pointed high heels sandals. Her long and straight hair is tied up in a bun. She has a white skin complexion that is so flawless. And most of all she is tall and has a perfect body shape.

Melissa is his ex-girlfriend. He and Melissa broke up three years ago. She broke up with him because according to her he is moody, possessive, always feels insecure and jealous with other men whenever she and him are attending social gatherings or events when it happens that some men talk to her. Or in some situations, she entertains men.

But Melissa was wrong. Dren never feels insecure or jealous of them. He just can't take how those men look at her. Their look was full of lust. And their words show their lustful desire towards her. He always warned Melissa about that but instead of listening to him she always accused him of being insecure and jealous of them. And when she broke up with him for those reasons he just let her go because he just can't take her accusations. His pride and ego was touched too much. He was just concerned about her before but she didn't see it. Instead she always misinterprets him.

Well, That was three years ago and Dren had no regrets about that break up. It is clear to him why Melissa is still talking to him, making friends with him after she and him broke up. He knows all she needs from him is his money. That's why she accepted him immediately to be her fiance when he told her his feelings about her before. And he will never be wrong about it because she keeps on pestering him at present whenever she, her friends, her relatives or her colleagues need investors in their new businesses.

Dren wants to stop communicating with her but she keeps on bothering him whenever she has a problem with their businesses. She is the daughter of Lady Lira. One of Dren's Aunt Mila's friends and business partners. So whenever his Aunt Mila asks him to help her he can't just say no. He doesn't want his Aunt Mila to get disappointed if he acts immature if he doesn't help her just because Melissa and him were ex-lovers.

But he feels too annoyed at this moment with her because he doesn't want to attend to whatever her problem is. He wanted to spend the whole day with Rovena. He couldn't stop himself from frowning when she approached him.

"Hi, Dren. How are you?"Melissa said while getting close to him and pushed Rovena aside. Rovena is standing in front of Dren while looking at her so she pushes aside when she talks to him.

Rovena got embarrassed for what she did. So she walked a little bit away from Dren and Melissa. Just pull out her phone from her pocket and scroll through it. Dren is talking to Melissa but his eyes is on Rovena;

"I'm fine. What can I do for you, Melissa?"

"I just want to give you these documents. Can you please consider investing in my friend's businesses again? They are looking for investors." Melissa said while she handed him the documents that she was holding.

"Okay. I will study these first. Then later I will decide if I should invest or not." Dren said after accepting the documents.

"Oh, thank you Dren. By the way, who is she? An applicant for a maid servant position? Could you please tell her to give respect to your visitors instead of acting like that." Melissa said while looking at Rovena from head to foot.

"Melissa, please leave her alone. She is not a maidservant." Dren answered Mellissa in an irritated voice.

"Oh, I'm sorry about that. I thought she was. Don't tell me that she is your new girlfriend. My God, Dren..." Melissa said but Dren suddenly talked so she was not able to finish what she was going to say.

"So what if she is my new girlfriend. It's none of your business, Melissa." Dren said to her because he felt too irritated by her attitude. She is belittling Rovena.

"What?!! Are you serious about that? Is she really your new one? Come on, Dren. I know she is not the type of woman you like." Melissa said in disbelief.

"What makes you think that she is not the type of woman I like?" Dren asked her. Then he laughed softly.

"But look at her. She looks so poor and not classy. I can't imagine that a billionaire like you will just get a girlfriend like her. For sure she only wants your money."

"Just like what you want from me, Melissa?"

He said to Melissa in a sarcastic manner.

"Dren!" Melissa couldn't say anything aside from his name when she heard what he said.

Rovena hear what Melissa said so she gets near her and talk to her;

"Excuse me Ma'am. I don't ask for money from Sir Dren aside from my salary from his company. I'm working in his company."

"Shut up. I'm not talking to you. And don't pretend that you are not a gold digger." Melissa said to Rovena in an angry manner.

"But Ma'am I'm not..." Rovena said but Dren stopped her.

"Rovena, Please stop. You don't have to explain yourself to her." Dren said to Rovena warning her to stop talking to Melissa because it's nonsense to talk to her.

"Alright, Sir Dren. I'm sorry." Rovena said, bit her lower lip and lowered her head.

When Dren heard what Rovena said he didn't answer her instead he talk to Melissa;

"If you don't need anything aside from giving me these documents. You can go now. This is the weekend so I want to rest." Dren said to Melissa. He is hoping that Melissa will leave immediately. He doesn't want to talk to her anymore.

"As if you want me to leave immediately?" Melissa said in a sad voice making a drama again.

"So do you need anything aside from what you asked earlier? Do you need to discuss these documents with me?" Dren asked Melissa in an irritable manner. He couldn't hide his annoyance at her so he frowned.

"Yes, Dren. Please?" Melissa said and smiled sweetly.

"Today is Sunday. I'm off to work. Come to my office tomorrow so that we can discuss this matter. Not now." Dren said to Melissa in an irritated tone.

"Please, Dren? I have other appointments tomorrow..." Melissa said but she was not able to finish what she was going to say because Dren suddenly spoke.

"As I was saying, let's talk about this matter tomorrow in my office." Dren said to her, his voice raised slightly because she keeps on pestering him.

Dren hates her. it 's just because of his Aunt Mila that's why he acts civil to her. But this time when he lost his temper he couldn't hide his anger.

Rovena and Melissa saw the anger in his eyes that he cannot hide so they both suddenly felt afraid of him. His angelic face now seems like a devil because of the sharp look in my eyes. As if he will kill a person if they provoke him.

Rovena knows what they are seeing is the different side of Dren because he really lost his temper.

Dren almost shout when he speak again;

"Leave me alone before I totally piss off."

Because of that both Rovena and Melissa want to leave the room immediately. But Dren called Rovena's name before the two of them could leave the room.

"Rovena!"

Rovena held her breath and stopped walking but didn't want to turn around to look at him . While Melissa talks in a soft voice to Rovena. As if she doesn't want Dren to hear what she is saying to Rovena.

"Go back before he gets totally mad at you. He is calling you if you hear that." Melissa said to Rovena. As if she is scaring Rovena more.

Rovena answered her in a soft voice also,"It's your fault, Ma'am, that's why he got angry."

Melissa answered her almost in whisper but Dren could still hear her. He stood still on the spot where they left him. He crossed his arms on his chest while looking at them.

"I know but could you please go back and talk to him? And pacify his anger before he trashes all the documents that I gave him. Those documents are all important. My friends need investors. And only Dren could give a solution to their problem. If Dren trashes those documents, it's your fault." Melissa said to Rovena blackmailing her.

"What?!! How come?" Rovena asked. She has decided to leave the room and doesn't want to be left.

"Look. Stop asking questions, Miss. Go back. I'll go ahead." Melissa said and rushed out the door.

Rovena and Dren were left alone in the room again. Rovena still didn't move in the place where Melissa left her. Dren knows she felt afraid of him so he tried to compose himself. After a few minutes his angry feeling subsides. He gets near Rovena and talks to her as sweetly as he can so that her fears at him subsides.

"Rovena, I'm so sorry I didn't mean it. It's just that Melissa provoked me, that's why I lost my temper. I really am not in the mood to work right now. I know discussing the matters about these documents can be done tomorrow but she keeps on pestering me." Dren explained to Rovena.

After Dren explained to her, Rovena looked at his face. She looks worried. Dren knows what she is thinking. It's about his personality disorder that manifests if some situation triggers it.

Rovena talks to him. Forcing herself to smile;

"I understand, Sir Dren. You don't have to explain..."

Dren knows she still feels afraid of him, that's why she acts like that. So he tried his best to show her that she has nothing to be afraid of.

"Ahm, You know this mansion has a small art gallery aside from this collection room that is full of my collections of different souvenirs from the places where I've been." Dren told Rovena, trying to make conversation with her.

"Alright, Sir." Rovena said and forced a smile.

"Let's go there." Dren said and smiled back at her and held her hands while they were walking to the art gallery.

Dren knows Rovena wants to pull her hands away from him but she never does, maybe because she is afraid that if she embarrasses him he will get angry.

Chapter 11

Rovena was lost in deep thoughts while Dren and her were walking towards the art gallery located inside this huge mansion.

She is thinking about the behavior of Dren a while ago. Even though she knows what's the secret that he's been hiding, she still feels afraid of him. But she is trying her best not to show it to him but she knows he still notices it. She knows Dren is trying his best to calm himself so that the fear that she felt for him a while ago subsides.

Even though Rovena knows the reason why Dren acted like that, she still feels afraid of him. She knows the different side of his personality is manifesting. She noticed it because his mood suddenly shifted. Maybe because of his bad experiences connected to his ex-girlfriend triggers it. So it shows. Splitting is his defense mechanism. He is just trying to guard his feelings from being hurt. So from an angel like attitude he suddenly shifts into a person with a devil like attitude. She knows his personality is splitting. His emotion is splitting. She knows this will last for hours or even days before he goes back to normal. He will go back to normal when he realizes which of his two personalities needs to exist in his present situation. 'Reality is the middle ground.'

But Dren can handle himself still in spite of his psychological disorder. He can handle himself better. But still he is mentally unwell. That is one of the reasons why the relationships that he had ended all in break up.

Rovena was awake in deep thoughts when Dren and her reached the art gallery. He opens the door of the gallery. They walked inside.

His art gallery has many beautiful paintings.

Dren talked to Roven when they were inside;

"Rovena, this is my art gallery. I bought most of the paintings from outside the country."

"Your painting collection is all beautiful, Sir!"

"Do you like them?"

"Yes, Sir. You know how to paint isn't it?"

"Yeah. And I'm doing it whenever I have free time. Some of them are my paintings." Dren said shyly.

Dren is still holding her hands. She wants to pull her hands away but she just can't. What if he suddenly gets angry again.

She just focused my attention on the beautiful paintings that hang around on the walls of the gallery.

She noticed Dren is looking at a painting of a woman whose clothes are like the one I always wear. The woman is wearing a unisex black t-shirt, ripped jeans and old rubber shoes. But she has no face. As if it is not yet finished. It's not hanging on the wall but still on a stand that is commonly used for painting.

She got curious so she ask Dren about the painting;

"Sir, Is that one of your paintings?"

"Yeah." Dren said and he let go of her hands. Then he got painting materials. She felt relieved when he let go of her hands.

She asked him again;

"Who is she? Why does she have no face?"

Dren answered her while he was still looking at the painting.

"Just my imagination...Wait. I will just finish painting her. Now I know what her face looks like."

"Oh Alright."

"Now her name is Rovena..."

"Rovena?... Why?"

Dren laugh softly before he answered her;

"Because this woman in my painting looks like you..."

"Me?" That is the only words she was able to say when she heard his answer.

Dren answered her while he started painting the face of the woman on the painting. He is not kidding, he is really painting her face.

"Yes. This is you. I have been painting this since like five years ago." Dren said in a sad voice.

"Five years ago? That long?" Rovena asked in a curious voice.

Dren answers her while he continue painting;

"Yes. I don't know how to finish it because I don't know what face I should paint. So I'm waiting for the time that I will meet a woman similar to her to finish painting her face."

"Seriously?! Why do you paint me?" She asks him because she is wondering.

She was surprised by what he said. She can't believe that he is wasting his time waiting for a woman that looks like the woman on the painting just to finish it.

"Of course. I paint you because you look similar to her."

When she heard what he said she just kept silent because she didn't know what to say.

Dren looked glad when he finished painting her face. He is good at painting. The woman in his painting really looks like Rovena.

After he finished his painting he looked at her. He got near her when he didn't receive a response from her. He looked at her face but she didn't look back. She pretends her attention is focused on looking at his painting. She doesn't want to look at him. She is scared that if she looks into his eyes he will see that she is attracted to him. She doesn't want Dren to notice it. She doesn't want their relationship as employee and boss to be ruined because of her feelings for him.

Her heart beats so loud when she heard Dren asking question to her;

"Rovena, have you fallen in love before?" Dren asked her while he stood in front of her ,blocking his painting now to get her attention.

Now to avoid looking at him she dropped her phone on the floor, got it and stood beside him before she answered his question.

"Ah yes, but that was long ago. I never saw him again." She said without looking at him. She focused her eyes on the painting hanging on the wall.

Rovena heard Dren answer, "I have this feeling that you don't want to look at me." Dren said , then he stood in front of her again. He noticed that she didn't want to look at his face or in his eyes.

"Oh no, Sir. Only that there are lots of beautiful paintings here that catches my attention. I can stop myself from looking at them." Rovena tried to deny it but she knows Dren is not a fool to believe her easily.

Dren laughed softly when she heard what she said. Then he touched something on one of the paintings near him and all of the lights at the gallery turned off. She can't see the painting on the wall anymore. And the only place that has light is the spot where he and her are standing. She can't believe this.

Now Dren is standing in front of her touching her on both shoulders, looking straight into her eyes while talking to her;

"So now that you can't see all those paintings, no distractions at all. Probably you may be able to focus your eyes on me, right?"

"Sir?" That's the only word she was able to say because of fear.

Then she heard him talk again;

"I want to be honest with you, Rovena. I felt attracted to you.. And I'm hoping you feel the same way for me. Can we be more than just friends?"

When what he said syncs her mind. She doesn't know if she will take it seriously or not. What if he just wants to know her real feelings about him. She would rather not reveal her true feelings about him.

She answered him;

"Stop kidding me, Sir! This is not good."

Dren answered her in a serious manner again. He is still holding both of her shoulders. She wants to remove his hands on her shoulders but she feels like she was frozen to where she is standing.

"I'm not kidding, Rovena. I repeat my question. Can we be more than just friends?"

She answered him;

"Sir Dren, will you please stop asking me that question?" She said to him while she was finding the courage to look in his eyes.

Dren answered me;

"But why? You don't like me because you know my deepest secret?"

She explained to him immediately. She doesn't want him to feel annoyed again.

"It's not what I mean, Sir. I just want to remain as your friend rather than..."

She was not able to finish what she is going to say when Dren suddenly spoke;

"Rovena we can't be just friends. As I was saying, I want our relationship to be more than just friends. Is it hard to understand?"

Dren was hurt when she said that she just wanted to remain just as a friend of his. Rovena saw it in his behavior. So since she has feelings for him she decided to admit it rather than continue denying it. She knows the probable effect of this to Dren if she continues hurting his feelings.

"Alright." But that's the only word that she can say to him to admit her feelings.

When Dren heard what she said the smile crossed his angelic face.

"Rovena, you mean you agreed with me?" Dren asked, still looking into her eyes.

"Okay."

"Seriously?"

"Yes."

"Thank you, Rovena. You made me feel so happy." Dren said, feeling so glad.

She didn't expect Dren would hug her. She can't just hug him back. She feels shy because she knows that she agreed with Dren even though she knows that it's wrong that she and him will have a relationship. She doesn't belong to where he belongs. He is a billionaire, a wealthy man that belongs to upper class society while she is not. She knows status in life matters.

But what will he do if she doesn't agree with him? She will just hurt his feelings. If she does that she knows it has a bad effect on him. She knows that he is mentally unwell and she doesn't want his condition to become worse.

Few minutes had passed but it seems Dren still didn't let her go. She doesn't want this thing to go further so she is thinking of possible excuses so that he would let her go from his hug but none comes to her mind.

But she decided to talk to him when she felt that he was about to kiss her. She tells him that she wants to go home.

"Sir Dren, can I go home now? I need to finish some of my school work. " She asked. She does that to stop him from doing what he wants to do.

"Could you please stay here at the mansion a little bit longer? I promise I'll drive you home before evening comes."

"Alright but..."

"No more but please? Let's go to the terrace. I asked the maid servant to prepare some food for us there, right?"

"Alright."

They left his art gallery and proceeded to the terrace. The terrace is also spacious.

Dren led her to the dining table and pulled a chair for her to sit down. Then he pulled a chair for himself on the opposite side of the dining table and sat.

"Ahm, Rovena let's eat." Dren said then he began to hand her some food to put on her plate.

They are eating silently. Dren is lost in deep thoughts while Rovena keep silent because there are many questions running on her mind like;

'What other people can tell Dren if she will be his girlfriend?'

'Will his uncle not get angry if Dren and her have a relationship?'

'And will Dren 's feelings for her last longer? or will she become his ex-girlfriend after a few weeks?'

She took a deep breath because of those thoughts in her head. Dren noticed it and asked her why.

"Why? You don't like the food? Wait. I will ask the maid servant to bring what you want to eat."

"The food is delicious. No need to ask the maid servant. I'm just thinking about my school project, that's why." She said to Dren so that he would not be bothered.

"Alright. Don't worry, I will help you do your projects, okay?." Dren said and smiled at her

She smiled back at him and said,"Thank you."

Chapter 12

Dren is glad that Rovena gave him a chance to prove his feelings for her even though she is hesitant as far as he can see. She is hesitant because of their status in life and because of the deepest secret of him that she already knew.

She is just giving him a chance because she doesn't want him to become upset. She feels pity for him. She is thinking if she hurts his feelings it will have a bad effect on his mental condition.

Dren notices all that but it doesn't matter to him if she just feels pity on him. It doesn't matter to him because at least she gave him a chance. He swears he will do his best to be a good relationship partner to her.

' And he hopes that his bullshit personality disorder won't betray him. He hopes he can handle it. He can't afford to lose Rovena because of it. This is his greatest fear.

He noticed that Rovena took a deep breath. She is thinking about her school project so Dren decided to help her with it. He will drive her home after they finish eating their food. When he saw that she finished eating her food he talked to her;

"Rovena, I will drive you home now. As I was saying, I will help you with your school projects."

"Thank you, Dren. But don't worry about it. I can do it alone."

"I insist. Let's go?"

"Alright."

Dren looked for his uncle first to tell him that Rovena and him were leaving. He saw him sitting in the study room. He saw he had a visitor.

Dren and Aleksa entered the study room. Dren talked to him.

"Uncle Ivano, I will just drive Rovena back home." Dren called his attention because he didn't notice that he and Rovena entered the room.

He cleared his throat before he answer me;

"Oh why too early? She just came an hour ago."

"She still has work to do. She needs to go home."

"Alright."

Dren noticed that Uncle Haris is holding some old photos of a house;

"Uncle, what is that?"

Ivano took a deep breath before he answers Dren;

"This is the inheritance of Vena. My friend's child."

Dren was surprised. He cannot hide the curiosity in his voice when she asks him again.

"Your friend's child? Whose friend?

"Arman. "

"What I know is that he didn't have any fiance before when you were working at my father's company. I have known you and him since I was a little child."

Ivano smiled at Dren before he spoke.

"I have told you about Lina, right? She is the mother of his child."

"But as you have told me she married another man..."

"Lina and him had a one night stand before Lina's marriage was arranged to someone else. But he was too cowardly before to fight for her. He chose to let her go rather than to fight for her. Because he thinks her future will be better if he married that guy rather than him. Lina's fiance belongs to a wealthy and rich family there in Tirana, Albania. Arman is not a citizen of her country and has no money and almost nothing to eat at that time. Your father just helped him. That's why his status in life changed, right?

"Yes,but according to you Lina and her husband always had a fight because Lina was not capable of having a child?"

"Yeah that is true.She is not capable of having a child after a car accident that happened to her. But before that accident happened to her she already gave birth to her daughter. Before Lina got married she went to another country to hide from her parents that she was pregnant. She was able to give birth to her child secretly since the date of her marriage will be held for the next two years. After giving birth to herbchild she went back to Albania to obey her parents to marry her late husband. She gave her child to her former personal assistant to hide the child's identity. But as time goes by Lina and her personal assistant lose contact and she can't find her anywhere. Lina lost his daughter."

"Alright. So you know now where to find his daughter? And is that confirmed that she is really his daughter? Who told you about these?" Dren asked him a series of questions because he felt worried when something came into his mind.

Ivano didn't answer him yet. He first gathered some documents that he
wanted to show him

Dren wants an answer from him to those questions of him to stop himself from being worried. He is happy that his uncle finds his friend's daughter
who will inherit all the property of his late friend. But what is sad is for sure
he will ask him to marry his friend's daughter if he is able to find her. He will
ask that for sure for the sake of his promise to his friend before his friend dies
that he will look for her daughter and give all her inheritance. Worst of all
Dren's marriage was arranged to his friend's daughter. Dren just doesn't take
it seriously because he didn't expect that his uncle will really find the long
lost daughter of his friend. It seems like finding a single needle in the middle
of the ocean but he was wrong, his uncle was really determined to find his
friend's child.

If that happens Dren doesn't know what will happen to him and Rovena.
He started telling Rovena about his real feelings and he didn't want to hurt
her feelings. He knows he can't say no to his uncle if he will ask him to marry
his friend's daughter. He doesn't want him to think that he is ungrateful if he
refuses on what he will ask him in the future.

He needs to solve this matter before he will be put into a situation where
he needs to choose between Rovena and his friend's daughter.

Dren hear his uncle talking to him again;

"Yes, it is confirmed that he is Arman's daughter. Look at these documents from the orphanage where she grew up. The private investigator
brought these documents to me. Ivano said in a glad voice.

Dren took a deep breath while reading the documents and listening to
Ivano. It is confirmed. This Vena is the daughter of his uncle's friend.

Rovena is right, she and Dren need to remain just friends. The situation
gave him a headache and sad feelings.

Dren gave back the documents to Ivano and looked at Rovena who was
just standing behind him. She hears all what his uncle and him are talking
about.

Dren wonders what is running through her mind right now. He sees her
eyes are fixed on the photo of Vena which is on the top of the table of Ivano.

Dren talked to Ivano again after he gave back the documents;

"Alright. So when will you go to Albania to meet the administrator of that orphanage?"

"After the conference meeting tomorrow I will travel to Albania. And I have something to tell you. You need to know this early." Ivano said in an authoritative voice.

That makes Dren hold his breath because he knows what he is going to tell him. And he will tell in the presence of Rovena?

To confirm it Dren asked him;

"What is it, Uncle?"

Ivano takes a deep breath before he speaks;

"You need to marry my friend's daughter if I find her. I know you already knew the reason why, Dren. I hope you understand, son."

Dren feels like dying. He was not able to answer him immediately but he forced himself to give him an answer.

"Yes, Uncle. I understand."

"Thank you, Dren."

Dren took a deep breath and held Rovena's hand as he asked his uncle for permission that he will drive Rovena back home.

"Alright. I will just drive Rovena back home."

"Alright. The two of you take care. But wait, Can we talk for a while, Rovena?" Ivano said before Rovena and Dren could leave the study room.

Rovena answered him;

"Yes, Sir."

Ivano asked her a question that surprise Dren;

"Are you from Albania?"

"Yes, from Tirana, Albania Sir."

"That's good. Maybe you can help me find my friend's child?"

Dren heard Rovena agreed to help him and he was shocked by what Rovena revealed to his uncle. But Dren just keeps silent while Rovena and his uncle are talking to each other.

"I will see what I can do. Honestly I grew up in that orphanage too. And I know who Vena is, Sir.

Ivano's face lit up when she heard what Rovena said.

"Really? So do you know where I can find Vena at present?"

"Yes. And the administrator of that orphanage knows also where to find her. So they can give you the information you need."

"Alright. So I will just talk to the administrator of that institution."

"Alright, Sir. I'll go home now if you don't need anything." Aleksa said, asking permission of Ivano that she will go home.

"Alright. Thank you for this information. That will help me a lot to find Vena. So if you need help with your studies or anything don't hesitate to come here or to my office to ask, " Ivano said in a glad voice.

"Thank you, Sir."

"You're welcome."

After their conversation Rovena and Dren walked towards the basement parking area. They rode in Dren's car. He started to drive. He kept silent while driving. He felt ashamed at Rovena about what happened.

He reveals his feelings for her unknowingly that he needs to marry someone else in the future. But he really likes Rovena and he wants to fight his feelings about her but he needs to obey his uncle . He wants to keep Rovena. But it's not that simple to keep Rovena if the relationship is more than friends. He wants Rovena badly more than just friends but he needs to face his destiny. And he needs to accept the truth that they are not meant to be.

'No, this can't be as I really want Rovena.' Dren said in his mind.

He wished he had another choice. And have the solution for his problem.

He decided to talk to his uncle about that arranged marriage again when he came home. He will convince him. He will tell him that he and Rovena are already in a relationship and he doesn't want to go for that arranged marriage. He is hoping that his uncle will convince.

Chapter 13

Dren keeps silent while driving. Rovena didn't dare to talk to him. She just focused her eyes on the road while thinking about what happened a while ago.

She is still thinking about what he discovers about her parents. According to the documents that she saw on Ivano's table both her parents are dead. She reads on the last will of his father that her father's property will be inherited by her.

She wants to tell him that she is Vena but she stops herself from doing so. She will let the administrator of the orphanage tell him about her.

According to Ivano , Dren is going to marry her and Dren said yes. So his silence means to her that he is thinking what he is going to say to her. Unknowingly, she is Vena.

Rovena didn't notice that Dren and her arrived in front of her apartment. Dren stopped his car and stepped outside. He opens the door for her to go outside the car.

Dren still goes with her inside the apartment to the room where she is renting. When they got inside her room he sat down on the single sofa. Then he talked to her;

"So,show me your school projects and let's start doing it, sweetheart."

Rovena noticed that Dren didn't call her Rovena. Rovena thinks he is kidding again. So he just ignored what he called her instead she got all his school projects and showed it to him.

"Here. It's about my accounting subjects. I find it hard to finish."

Dren looked at the folder that Rovena showed him. He smiled after reading it. Then he talk to her again;

"Don't worry, I will do it for you."

"Thank you, Dren."

"No worries, sweetheart."

Dren called her "sweetheart" for the second time around. She is not used to it so she decided to ask him to stop calling her that way.

"Sir Dren, can you please just call me by my name. I'm not used to hearing you call me that way."

Dren laughed softly when he heard what she said. Then he talks while his eyes are fixed reading his school project.

"Why? What's wrong with that?"

She answered him;

"As I was saying I am not used to hearing you calling me that way."

Dren smiles before he answers her;

"From now on be used to it because I want to call you that way."

"Stop kidding me, Dren. This is not good.

"Why? Because I and Vena will get married if Uncle Ivano finds her... Don't take that seriously, Rovena. I have a solution for that. I will talk to Uncle Ivano as soon as I arrive at the mansion."

I'm confused about what he is talking about so I asked him;

"What do you mean, Dren?"

Dren looked at me this time. He looked into my eyes.

"I will not marry Vena.

Rovena was shocked when he heard what Dren said. She can't believe he is planning to do that.

"What??!"

Dren take a deep breath before he speak;

"I'm not doing this just for nothing. I want to be with you, Rovena. I don't wanna lose you."

Dren is really determined to do that. I can sense it in his statements;

"As I was saying I will be doing that because I want to be with you.

"But Dren, It is better to obey your Uncle than to do that..."

Dren frowned before he speak;

"For a chance to be with you, I'll try to risk it all, Rovena. Is it hard to understand? or you just don't like me that's why you are pushing me to marry Vena?"

Based on what he said she can't change his mind so he just keeps silent and never answers him. He also didn't talk for more than several minutes. He focused his attention editing the draft of her school projects.

Since he is not talking to her, she stood up and left him for a while just to make a cup of coffee. She wants to drink coffee because she feels too cold because it's winter and there's no fireplace in her room. In her apartment only big rooms have a fireplace. She can't afford to rent such a room.

After making two cups of coffee she gave one to Dren. Dren smiled at her when he accepted the cup of coffee but still didn't speak. She sat on the chair near the table to finish some of her assignments. There's a deep silence in the room while Dren and her are doing her school work. Both Dren and her doesn't try to open a conversation

After Dren finish her project he talked to her;

"Rovena, I finished with the draft of your project."

"Thank you, Dren. I really find it hard to finish that one."

"No worries. You can always ask me to do some of your school projects that you find it hard to do. I will help you."

Rovena smiled shyly at Dren before she speak;

"Thank you."

Dren smiled back at her.Then he drank his coffee before he talked to her again;

"Rovena, I will make a request to the HR department to transfer your work assignment to my office. I need an office staff to arrange all my files in my private office."

Rovena was confused about what he is talking about so she asked him;.

"But you have a secretary, right?"

Dren crossed his arms on his chest before he answered her question;

"Yes, but I didn't allow my secretary to touch my personal files in my office. I trust no one when it comes to that."

What he said made her more confused so she asked another question;

"You trust no one but you will ask the HR to transfer my work assignment to your office to arrange that."

Dren smirked before he speak;

"Except you. I know I can trust you.

" You still trust me? We have just met each other for just a few weeks , right?"

Dren laughs softly before he speak;

"Of course. I still trust in you. So expect that your work assignment will change."

But Rovena thinks there's a conflict on schedule and number of hours of work if he will be transferred to Dren's office. So she tells Dren.

"But Dren, I think there is a conflict in the working schedule. Your office hours start at 8:00 am and end at 4:00 pm. I can come to work at your company at 10:00 am because I have classes."

Dren smiled at me, and gave me an assurance;

"Don't worry about that. It's okay. You can start working around 10:00 am."

I lower my head and said shyly;

"Alright. Thank you."

Dren answered me while he was scrolling through his phone;

"Alright, I want to stay here a little bit longer. Because I feel so bored at the mansion. Don't want to go home early. Hope it is okay with you."

"Of course you're always welcome here. Anyway I will just cook food for dinner."

"Alright. Let me help you."

"It's okay, I can do it alone."

Rovena said to Dren and she went to the small kitchen area of her room. Since it is nearly evening she decided to cook food for dinner. She started preparing the ingredients.

She saw Dren stand up then he followed her in the kitchen. Dren volunteered to help her chop some of it.

After several minutes Dren and Rovena were finished chopping the ingredients. So Rovena heated the pan and started cooking the meal.

When she started cooking Dren was talking to her while he was standing leaning on the wall with arms folded on his chest.

"You know I want to have a wife who knows how to cook."

She answered without looking at him. Her attention is focused on what she is cooking;

"Why?"

She heard Dren answered her;

"I just want to. Now that I found you, I think my wish will come true."

She doesn't know what to say to him so she just keeps silent. She heard him asking her;

"Why don't you answer me? As if you don't want me to be your husband?"

Rovena looked at him to see if he was kidding or what but what she saw is Dren looked sad while looking at her. As if he was hurt when she didn't respond to what he was saying. She took a deep breath and comforted him.

"I never said that , right? Why not if you are really sincere about it."

She said to him, His face lit up. Then he talk again;

"Of course I'm sincere about it, Rovena. I want to marry you in the future. Let me prove that to you."

She took a deep breath before she answered him.

"Alright."

Rovena finished cooking the food. She finished cooking the food exactly when it's time to eat dinner. She prepares it on the table. They started eating dinner. Dren likes the food. He eats silently while his attention is fixed on the food that he is eating.

After spending another hour in her apartment Dren told her that he will go home.

" Rovena, I need to go home now. I received a text from Uncle Ivano. He wants to talk to me about some important matters."

"Alright, Dren. Take care."

"I will, Aleksa. Bye." Dren said. Then he hugged her and kissed her before he went outside the door.

Rovena was surprised by his actions. That's why she felt like she was frozen in the place where he left her .

She will not allow Dren to act like that towards her next time to make sure that nothing will happen between him and her.

She is afraid of the possible things that will happen between them. He is a man and she is a woman. Even though she wants to trust him still she can't stop herself from doubting him.

What if the feelings that he felt for her is just lust. And what if after something happens between them, he will realize that she is not the woman he wanted to marry. Even though she knew that their marriage was arranged.

"No! Those things will never happen to me. I swear. Yes I have feelings for Dren but I know the limits."

Rovena mumbles.

Chapter 14

Dren arrived at the mansion. He proceeded to Ivano and Mila's room because a maidservant told him that he was already in his room. He knocks on the door of Ivano's room.

"Knock! knock! knock! Uncle, this is Dren!"

"Come in, Dren!"

Dren heard Ivano say so he pushed the door and got inside. He saw Ivano sitting on his bed now. Ivano gets up and sits on his bed when he sees Dren while Mila is sitting in front of a mirror brushing her long hair.

"Good evening, Dren!"

"Good evening, Aunt Mila."

Dren sit on the chair beside the bed and talked to his uncle,"I received your text message. What are you going to tell me? You said it's about Vena."

Ivano get a bunch of folder on bedside table and handed it to Dren before he speak;

"I have a surprise for you. It's about Vena. I know you will be happy about this."

Dren felt nervous when he heard what Ivano said. Everything about Vena seems like a problem to him. He wants to marry Rovena, not Vena. He needs to tell his uncle about that immediately before it's too late.

So he continue talking to him and ask a series of questions;

"Ahm, what do you want to tell me about Vena? You found her? I mean you know where she is?"

Ivano removed his eyes glasses and laughed softly before he answered Dren;

"Yes. I talked to the orphanage over the phone after you and Rovena left this afternoon. Fortunately I was able to talk to the administrator who knows where Vena is.

What Ivano said made Dren hold his breath. He listens carefully when Ivano continues talking about Vena.

"The administrator told me where she is and emailed her photo to me. I ask your Aunt Mila to print her photo for you to see."

Ivano stops talking while getting something on the drawer of the bedside table. The information he told Dren makes Dren's heart beat so loud. He doesn't know where to start telling him that he doesn't want to marry Vena without making him feel disappointed about him. But he need to tell him because he doesn't want to disappoint and hurt Rovena's feeling. He feels he is caught in the middle.

Dren heard Ivano talked to her again while giving him some photos;

"Here. Look at these, Dren.These are Vena's photos."

Dren gets the photos from Ivano. When he looks at Vena's photos he wants to jump. He feels too glad. He didn't expect that he wouldn't need to tell his uncle that he didn't want to marry her, instead he wanted to schedule the wedding as soon as possible because Vena is Rovena.

The wide smile crossed into Dren's face. He talked to Ivano,"So when will be the date of the wedding of Vena and me, Uncle?"

Ivano coughed and laughed when he heard what Dren said. Then he talk to him;

"I told you. I have a surprise for you. But honestly ,Dren, I don't know how I will tell Rovena that she is Arman's daughter. I hope she will not hate her parents."

"Don't worry, Uncle. I will help you explain the situation to Rovena. I know Rovena will understand it."

"Thank you, Dren."

"No worries Uncle. And I think Rovena already knew. She was here when we talked about her parents, right?

"Alright, But why she haven't told us that she is Vena in spite of knowing that I was looking for her?"

"Maybe she just wants the administrator to reveal the truth about her. Maybe she is hesitant that we will believe her easily if she will be the one who reveals the truth."

"Alright, You have a point. I think I have nothing to worry about. Since it's late at night.You can take a rest."

"Yeah,Uncle I will. I'll go ahead. Goodnight."

"Alright. Goodnight."

"Aunt Mila, I'll go ahead. Goodnight!

"Alright, Dren. Goodnight!"

After their conversation Dren proceeded to his own room. He lay on his bed with the thoughts in his head about Rovena.

Dren felt so glad about what happened. She didn't expect that Rovena is also Vena. So he has nothing to worry about. No need to convince Rovena to be his fiance. Whether she likes it or not she is now his fiance and will become his wife. Rovena will belong to him soon.

He doesn't understand himself right now why he is feeling so attracted to Rovena. He can't control his feelings towards her. He wants Rovena badly. He just can't tell right now if what he feels for her is really love or lust.

As far as he can see Rovena's trust in him is slowly fading. He doesn't want that to happen but the other side of him keeps on betraying him. It pushes him to do something not appropriate like acting so intimate towards Rovena.

Just like what he did before he left her and went home. He didn't mean to hug and kiss her but he just found himself doing it. When he was back in reality he felt regrets when he see Rovena's reaction to what he did. As if she was frozen in the place where he left her. As if she is afraid.

He wants to send a message to her to say sorry but he feels ashamed to open that topic to her. So he just sent a goodnight message to her.

"Goodnight, Vena." His message was sent.

After a few minutes he received a reply from Rovena;

"Goodnight, Dren. May I remind you,I'm Rovena."

He can't stop himself from smiling. He sent that intentionally because he wanted her to give a clue that he already knows the truth that she is Vena.

He decided to reply to Rovena;

"Oh, sorry about that"

He received a reply from her;

"So you said you don't want to marry her but she is on your mind at this moment."

Dren decided to tease her;

"Because I saw a photo of Vena. She is beautiful in her photo. Uncle knows where she is at present because the orphanage told him.

He got a reply from her that made him laugh;

"So are you going to marry Vena because you see that she is beautiful in her photo? Whew! What if she is ugly in person?"

He replied to her to tease her more;

"I will still marry her so that I will have a personal assistant!"

He got another reply from her. And still he can't stop himself from laughing;

"Seriously?! I am just a personal assistant to you? If that would be the case I will not marry you!"

He replied at her while still laughing;

"I'm just kidding. Uncle and I talked about it already. You are Vena so I have nothing to worry about. Everything is okay now.

She replied at him;

"Alright. ."

He sent another message to her.

"Go to sleep now, Rovena. You have classes and work tomorrow. Goodnight, sweetheart."

"Goodnight,"

After their conversation Dren decided to go to sleep.

Rovena can say that the attraction that Dren feels towards her is unusual. Sometimes she feels afraid whenever she notices the burning desire in his eyes. She still believes that Dren won't do anything bad to her. But what if the darker side of his personality pushes him to do so. She knows that is possible to happen.

But even though Dren is mentally unwell Rovena hopes he can still control himself.

As far as she can see he can handle himself and he is able to hide it from others. His psychiatrist, his Uncle , his Aunt and her are the only people who knew his deepest secret.

When Rovena notices that it is past midnight she decides to go to sleep. He lay on her bed but she couldn't go to sleep. Her mind is still full of thoughts about her parents.

Her heart beats so loud. She can stop herself from being happy that her parents left her inheritance because she is feeling so tired of living as poor as a rat. Almost always has nothing to eat, has an empty wallet and is working like a slave for every job that she has just to earn money for a living.

She remembers the days when she was a child and living in an orphanage. She hates her parents a lot those times, hating them for being irresponsible parents who left her in the orphanage that causes her sufferings. But now she knows what happened to them so she is ready to forgive them.

Chapter 15

It's 8:00 am, Monday. Dren is in his private office at DW Manufacturing & Distributing Company

He started reviewing some of the documents on his table that need his approval. After signing some of them he decided to make a request letter to the HR department to transfer the working assignment of Rovena to his office.

Since she is Vena and will soon be his wife he wants to train her in handling the businesses that he has. And he will start to train her here in his office.

After making the request he asked his secretary to give it to Hr Department.

"Selma, please give this letter to the Hr Department. Tell them I expect Miss Rovena Mehic to report in my office as soon as she arrives."

"Yes, Sir. I will tell them. Is she going to work here in your office?" Selma answers him and asks a question.

She smiles as sweetly as possible and stands in a way that she will look sexy in front of Dren. She has been doing that ever since she works here as his secretary. She is a niece of one of the maid servants at the mansion who asked for a recommendation from Dren's Aunt Mila so that Selma could work here at his company.

Dren has hated her actions ever since. Yes she is beautiful but she is not the type of a woman he will like. He hates flirts. The common thing that most of the women he met have except Rovena. The common reasons why he broke up with some of his previous girlfriends.

He answered Selma as soon as possible so that she can leave before he get pissed off to her;

"Yes. Here in my private office only as an all around clerk. So she is not under your supervision. Your work responsibility remains as is. And you are not allowed to send her any errands. Okay?"

"Okay, Sir. I will inform her to go in here as soon as she arrives. "

"Alright. Thank you.You may go."

"Okay, Sir. You're welcome. I'll go ahead."

After his secretary left the room he continued working on a file of the documents on his table while he patiently waited for Rovena.

Because of too many things to do he didn't notice that it was already 10:00am. So since it's 10:00 am he is expecting Rovena to arrive.

Few minutes later he heard a knock on the door.

"Knock! knock! knock!"

"Please come in. "

He said when he heard the knock on the door. The door of his private office swings open and Rovena enters the room. She greets him when he gets near him.She just stood up beside his office table and didn't take a seat.

"Goodmorning, Sir." Rovena said that made him laugh.

"Sir? Why are you calling me that way?" He asked her while looking at her.

"You are the CEO in this company and I am your employee." Rovena said in a serious manner.

"Just call me Dren, Okay?" He said to her, Then he smiled at her.

"But what if other employees hear me say that I am just calling you in your name? I'm worried about what they will tell me." Rovena said. He knows she is worried about what other employees might think about her . He can see it in her eyes.

"Don't worry about that, Rovena. You can just call me by my name. I will not hide that there is something between you and me. Dren said to Rovena, giving her an assurance.

"Look, Sir, you don't understand. I don't want other employees to judge me. I know they will think something bad about me if you do that. You are the CEO of this company and I'm just a poor employee. Do you think they will just accept such ideas without judging me that I do something just to be noticed by you?" Rovena said, still worried.

"So what do you want me to do? To deny in front of them that you are my fiancee? Dren asked Rovena while he raised his eyebrows.

"I'm your fiance?"

"Yes I will claim that you are my fiance from now on. And we have been in a relationship since yesterday, Okay?" Dren said to clarify it to Rovena so that all her doubts and confusion will go away.

"How come? You never told me yesterday. " Rovena said, wondering.

"Our marriage was arranged.We kissed yesterday, right? Isn't that enough reason to claim that you are my fiance?" Dren said to Rovena. When she heard it she blushed and lowered her head. She can't look into his eyes. Maybe she feels uncomfortable about that topic. But he heard she answers him;

"We didn't. You're the only one who did it." Rovena said without looking at him.

Yes, she is right. He did it without her consent. Though it is easy to pretend in front of Rovena that he did that without any regrets, deep inside he feels ashamed for what he did to her yesterday. He took a deep breath before he talked to her again.

"Okay. Fine. But we are in a relationship now as I was saying so I don't agree that you will call me sir."

"Please, I will still call you that way in front of other employees."

"Alright. I agree with you if that is what you want and will give you peace of mind. But without the presence of other people here in the company just call me Dren and not Sir, okay?"

"Alright.Thank you." Rovena said while taking a deep breath. As if she felt relieved because her face lit up.

"No worries. And will you please take a seat?"

Dren said to her asking her to sit down because she has remained standing since she arrived.

Rovena sit down on swivel chair beside his office table and talk to him;

"Can you please tell me what my work is so that I can start doing it." Rovena said while looking at him.

"Just start arranging those bunch of files on the other table and put it on that filing cabinet on the left side of the table. " He said to her then he smiled as sweetly as possible.

"Alright." Rovena said while she smiled back at him. Then she proceeds to do her work.

While Rovena is arranging the file on the other table he can't concentrate on what he is doing. He looks at her from time to time. He can't concentrate because of her presence while she is just doing her work continuously without even bothering to look at him even for a short glance.

Based on Rovena's behavior , he wonders if she really likes him as a relationship partner or not. As if she isn't even affected by his presence. That is weird. Based on his experience no woman can resist his presence like that.

He admits he really chose to wear the best business outfit that makes him look more good looking not because he will conduct a board meeting today but because he wants to be noticed by Rovena but it seems that it has no appeal to her. He took a deep breath. He just comforts himself by thinking that maybe she notices it but she just doesn't bother to comment about it.

He has to leave Rovena for a while here in his office because he will need to attend a board meeting. It will not take long hours so they can still eat lunch together.

He calls her attention when he is about to leave his private office to tell her that he is going to the board room.

"Rovena, I leave you here first. But I will be back after half an hour. Can you please wait for me before you take a lunch break? Let's eat lunch together." He said to her hoping she would wait for him.

"Alright, Dren. I will wait for you." Rovena said and looked at him just for a second and focused her eyes again on the files on her hand.

"Alright." He said to her then he walked outside his private office.

When she is alone in Dren's office she gets lost in deep thoughts. Thoughts about Dren.

She can't believe that Dren is her fiancee now. He said it officially. She really feels worried about what other employees will tell her. She knows they will accuse her of being a social climber, flirt, opportunist, gold digger etc.

Rovena was back in reality when the door of Dren's office swung open. She saw his beautiful secretary enter. She is frowning at her. She walks towards Dren's office table and puts some folders. Even though she frown at her she choose to greet her;

"Hi." Rovena said to her in a soft voice. Because she greeted her she got near her but didn't just greet her back but instead she received an insult from her.

"So the CEO requested to transfer your work assignment to his private office. I wonder what you did to convince him. As far as I can see you are just new in this company and just once met him at the production area. You're a

great seducer I guess." Selma said to her while raising her eyebrow and looking at her from head to foot.

"Ma'am Selma, I didn't do anything like that. I knew Sir Dren before I
worked in this company." Rovena said to her in a polite manner even though
she felt insulted by what she said.

"Oh really? My friend on Hr department showed me your files. You have
other part time jobs aside from this. And you work at night. Maybe you are
working in a nightclub as a stripper or the like and Sir Dren meets you there."
Selma said. Then she smirked and folded her arms on her chest.

"No, I'm not working in a nightclub! And I'm not a stripper! "

She can't bear Selma's accusations so she can't stop herself from shouting
at her.

Selma insulted her again because of that;

"Watch your manners. That's evidence that you are a low class bitch. I'm
not shouting at you but you did shouting at me. Come on . I don't believe in
you that you know Sir Dren before you work her. Me and all other employees
here will make sure you will be terminated in this company. We hate social
climbers and gold diggers like you. Me and his employees are just concerned
to the CEO so we will throw you out of this place."

Rovena can stop her tears from falling when she hears what Selma said to
her . She needs her job to survive in her studies. If that happens she needs to
find another part time job. So she begged Selma.

"Ma'am Selma, please let me work here. I will not do anything against Sir
Dren. I'm telling the truth. I need this job." Rovena said to Selma and held
Selma's arms but she pushed Rovena away.

"Don't touch me. And don't get near me. I don't like my skin being
touched by trash." Selma told her and walked away going outside the office.

More tears fell from her eyes because of that. She is poor, that's why she
called her trash. She can stop herself from crying. But she dried her eyes immediately when she saw Dren was coming. She doesn't want Dren to notice
that she is crying .

When he gets near her he smiles and talks to her;

"Sorry if I make you wait longer. I know you feel hungry now so let's eat
lunch."

"Alright, Dren." She answered Dren while putting the file folders on the filing cabinet.

"Rovena, don't mind Selma. I know you felt insulted and hurt by what she said. And you were crying before I arrived. Don't worry I will transfer her as a head supervisor in the production area and request a new secretary."

Rovena felt shocked when she heard what Dren said. She wondered why he knew all that while he just arrived. She guesses there is a hidden camera in this office. So she asked Dren.

"How did you know that, Dren?"

"Well. There is a hidden camera connected to my cell phone. No one knows about that. I installed those cameras here by myself."

"Alright, I understand now." She answered him.

"So let's go to the nearby restaurant and eat lunch."

"Alright, Dren"

They walk outside the office to ride on the elevator. At the corner of her eyes she saw Selma frowning at her when Dren and her passed by the reception area of Dren's office. The office of Dren is huge. It consists of a waiting area, a meeting room and his private room. It is located almost on the top of the building of his company next to the penthouse. The penthouse is the last floor of his company.

Chapter 16

Rovena and Dren went back to the office after lunch break. Dren noticed that Rovena was worried and upset. And he knows the very reason for that. It's because of Selma. He thinks Rovena still thinks those accusations of Selma to her.

Dren felt so annoyed when he heard Selma was saying something not good to Rovena. He can't take what he heard she said to Rovena. Rovena is not working in a nightclub and not a stripper. She is working at a late night restaurant in the city as a cashier. Selma's behavior is somewhat unforgivable. She even called Rovena a trash. She doesn't even know who Rovena is. She had no right to talk to Rovena like that.

Because of that Dren wants Selma to get lost in his office as soon as possible. Instead of giving her a warning about what she did to Rovena, Dren is planning that he will talk to the head of the HR department to transfer Selma to any department that lacks an employee. So she will be transferred to the production area as a supervisor. Then Dren will ask the Hr to assign a new secretary in his office. And he wants this to be done by tomorrow.

Dren received a message from his Aunt Mila. She is asking him to stop Rovena from working at the late night restaurant where she is working at present. She doesn't want Rovena seeing working so late at night and almost no time for sleep. Dren agreed with her. So Dren talked to Rovena. He needs to convince her.

Dren saw Rovena dusting the filing cabinet. He decided to call her first and talk to her;

" Rovena, please stop what you are doing. Let's talk first. I want to tell you something."

Rovena answered him while she put some alcohol on her hands before she gots near to his office table and sat down on the chair beside the table.

"Alright. What is it all about?"

Dren looked at her and answered her question.

"Why not work in this company as a full time employee? And stop working at that late night restaurant where you work at present."

Rovena didn't agree with what he said. She cited her reasons;

"Dren , I can't be a full time employee here. I'm attending classes. The schedule is complicated. And I can't just drop my work in the restaurant. I need additional income for food and rent."

"Rovena you forgot. There is a nightshift in my company in the production area. If you want additional income you can have overtime in the production area until 10:00 pm. Please consider my offer. Or I will give you an allowance for you to stop working at..."

Dren was not able to finish what he is going to say when Rovena suddenly talk;

"Okay, I will consider your offer to work as a full time employee rather than you giving me an allowance. That's not right . "

Dren was surprised by Rovena's reaction.

He doesn't know what's wrong if he gives her some money because she is his fiance. He did that to his ex girlfriends and those women gladly grabbed his offer. And some of them voluntarily asked for it.

Out of curiosity Dren asked Rovena why;

"Rovena, what's wrong if I gave you some money? You are my fiance so you can ask for that from me."

Rovena took a deep breath before she speak;

"I am just your fiance but not your wife. Why should I ask such a thing from you?"

Dren laughed softly when he heard her reasons. He is thinking about what kind of woman Rovena is. She is so different from others he met.

"Alright if you don't like that idea I will not insist but you can ask me about that if you have a change of mind."

"Thank you, Dren. So when can I start working overtime?"

"You can start by tomorrow. Don't go to work at the restaurant tonight, Rovena,okay?"

"Okay, Dren. Thank you. I'm going back to work."

"Alright. Can you please get me a cup of coffee?"

"Alright."

"Thank you."

"No worries."

As soon as Rovena left to get a cup of coffee outside Dren's private office Dren called his Aunt Mila.

"Hello, Dren!"

"Hello. Aunt Mila, I was able to convince Rovena. She will not go to work at the late night restaurant instead she will work here as a full time employee. She will work here at my office from 10:00 am to 4:00 pm, then she will just work overtime at the production area after my office hours. I just allowed her to work until 10:00 pm every night shift. She can't extend her overtime beyond that time."

"Alright, Dren. But have you offered her an allowance or the like?"

"Yes, Aunt Mila. But she didn't like the idea. So I did not insist on it. Don't worry I will find ways so that she will accept some money from us. Or we have other choices than that. You know what I mean. Let's give her her inheritance from her father.

"Dren, We can't do that easily. Me and your uncle are still processing the documents. You know that her father's step sister, Lydia won't give the property and Rovena's share in the company easily. We need to provide some documents that she wants to see before she gives it to Rovena. You know that Lydia is the one who managed the business of Arman when Arman died. You are also aware that she hinders all the information that will lead to finding Rovena so that she will own the property and business of Arman totally. We are only fortunate that we found Rovena already.

"Don't worry, Aunt Mila. I will help you with that."

"Thank you, Dren."

"No worries. By the way, she is coming. I just ask her to get me some coffee so that I can call you without being heard by her."

"Alright. Alright. Turn off the phone. Bye."

"Bye, Aunt Mila."

Rovena arrived exactly after the conversation between me and Uncle Haris was over.

"Dren , here is your coffee."

Rovena said to Dren while she put the coffee on Dren's office table.

"Thank you."

Dren smiled at her as sweetly as possible.

"You're welcome."

Rovena smiled back at Dren.

Rovena goes back to work after giving Dren the coffee while Dren goes to the waiting area of his office to meet some clients.

Rovena is worried because when Dren asked her to get him a coffee, when she passed on Selma's desk, Selma raised her eyebrow and looked at her from head to foot. Because of that she can't help but wish that Selma will be transferred to another department.

Rovena knows Dren will do that if she will just ask him but she also knows that Selma needs her job. So she chose to keep silent rather than to ask Dren.

Rovena looked at the door when she heard the office door swing often. She saw Dren and a sophisticated, pretty woman entered the room.

Dren goes directly to his office table and sits down. The woman follows him and occupies the swivel chair in front of Dren's office table. Then the woman put down the folder that she is holding. Dren gets the white folder and reads. And ask a question to the woman about the content.

"So, Ms. Swan, your distributing company needs a supplier of chocolates products but lacks funds to avail the volume which is required by my company to purchase before you can be a distributor of all its products?

"Yes Mr. Wolf so I made that proposal. I'm hoping you will consider it."

Ms. Swan smiled at Dren. Her beautiful white teeth show and a dimple on her left cheek appears . That makes her more pretty.

Ms. Swan is wearing a black business suit that reveals her beautiful body figure. She looks so sexy in her outfit. She is wearing a miniskirt so her beautiful long legs are shown when she sits on the swivel chair crossed leg. She intentionally showed it to Dren. Dren notices what she is doing so his eyebrows form in one line and frown slightly.

Dren speaks to Ms. Swan again with that frown in his face. While Ms. Swan maintains her beautiful smile on her face.

"Okay. I'll give you some papers to show to the purchasing department and everything will be okay."

Dren is getting documents from one of the folders in his table. He signed it and gave it to Ms. Swan.

"Oh, Thank you, Mr. Wolf."

Ms. Swan said while receiving the paper.

"No worries."

Dren said in a serious tone and never smiled through their whole conversation.

"Mr. Wolf, are you not going to accompany me to the purchasing department? This company building is huge. I'm afraid I'll be lost. "

"Sorry about that, I have guards and other employees here who can guide you. That's not a part of my job here. Please ask my secretary for directions on going there, Okay?"

"Alright. Thank you once again. Maybe I'll visit you again here in your office some other time. Or can I get your personal number? I just want to invite you to my birthday party next week."

"You're welcome. You can call me directly here in my office. For sure I can answer your call."

"But what if you are not around here in your office when I call you..."

"Don't worry. Just tell it to my secretary or look to Rovena. Rovena is a clerk here in my office and she will tell me when she receives your call. Right, Rovena?"

Dren called Rovena's attention to give Ms. Swan and assurance. Rovena answered him;

"Yes , Sir I will tell you."

"Good. You heard that Ms. Swan. So you can go to the purchasing department to give those documents that I gave you today before the office hours end today. Okay?"

"Oh okay, Mr. Wolf."

"And I think you need to go because there's only one hour more to go before the office hour ends."

"Oh, Okay. I need to go. I'll go ahead Mr. Wolf. Bye."

Ms. Swan hurriedly walks out of Dren's private office to go to the purchasing department. She needs to be quick before it closes.

"Bye."

Dren said while he shrugged his shoulders.

Roven sees Dren get his phone and scroll through it while pushing the swivel chair where he is sitting away from his table. Then he put his booth feet on his office table.

Dren feels too tired sitting at his table in a dignified position and now that it is almost the end of office hours he wants to stretch and sit in a relaxed position. That is a disadvantage of being a CEO, you always need to act dignified and you cannot just act improperly in front of your clients and employees.

Chapter 17

It's 4:00 pm. End of the office hour. Dren feels exhausted. He wants to go home as early as possible. He sees Rovena is preparing to go home. She picks her backpack and walks towards him. When she gets near him he heard her talking to him

"Dren, Can I go home now?"

Dren didn't answer her immediately because he is thinking if he will ask her to eat dinner at a restaurant or ask her to come to the mansion and together they will cook dinner. He didn't look at her, instead he continued scrolling through his cell phone. Because he is not responding to her she talk to him again;

"Dren, I said, can I go home?"

This time Dren looks at her and smiles. Then he said to her,"No."

Rovena look back at him and asked;

"Why is there something else that I need to do here in your office? Please tell me so that I can finish it."

Dren shrugged his shoulders and smirks before he answer her;

"I mean. Please go with me to the mansion. Let's cook dinner. And please just sleep over at the mansion after dinner."

"I can go with you to your mansion and cook dinner but I can't sleep there. You forgot? I have classes tomorrow early in the morning."

"Don't worry. I will drive you to the university early in the morning."

"But..."

"Rovena, please? May I know why you don't like to sleep over at the mansion? Are you afraid of me?"

"No, Dren. I'm not afraid of you."

" So what's your reason?"

"I'm worried about what people around us will tell me if I will sleep there."

"What?! What's wrong if you sleep over at the mansion? You are my fiancee and soon you will be my wife."

"But people around us will not understand that, Dren."

"My God Rovena. Why do you keep listening to those people? Don't mind them. It's none of their business if we ...Ah! Never mind, let's go home."

Dren stood up from the swivel chair. He held her hand and led her out of his private office to go to the elevator down in the basement parking area.

Rovena doesn't understand what Dren meant by his last statement. But she keeps silent. She doesn't want to ask him. What if he wants to say something censored. That's why he didn't continue to say it in front of her.

Rovena gets inside the car when Dren opens the door for her. Then Dren went to the driver seat and started the car engine. But he fastened her seatbelt before he drove away from the company.

After 25 minutes of driving he reached the mansion. He parked the car in the basement.

They stepped outside the car and walked upstairs to the garden and entered the mansion.

When they were on the living room Dren talks to Rovena;

"Rovena, I will just change my clothes before we cook food for dinner. You can do the same."

"How will I do that ? I don't have clothes here."

"Come with me. I will show you something."

Rovena follows him silently when he goes upstairs. Then he stopped in front of a huge room. That is his room. He entered and got something from a large drawer. Rovena remained standing outside the doorway. Dren goes out of the room again. Now he is holding a key.

He talks to her again;

"Rovena, that is my room but let's get inside the opposite room."

"Alright."

Dren opens the door of the opposite room.

"Rovena lets get inside. You can use all the clothes and things inside those cabinets."

Rovena sees what is inside the room is all for a woman. She wonders whose room it is. Mila has prepared the room for her the last few days because she feels too excited when Dren said that he will invite Rovena the next few days to sleep over at the mansion.

Dren continued talking when he didn't get any response from Rovena;

"What is inside this room all belongs to you."

"How come?

"Aunt Mila prepared this room for you because I said to her that I'm planning to invite you here for a sleepover."

"Thank you, Dren."

"No worries. You can change your clothes now. I will go to my own room first and go back here after several minutes, okay?"

"Alright."

Dren smiles at her and goes outside the room. While she opens one of the cabinets and gets some clothes and change.

After several minutes Rovena heard a knock on the door. She opened the door to go outside. She saw Dren standing in the doorway. He is now wearing a sleeveless shirt and jeans shorts. He looks so handsome. His shirt almost revealed his 6 pack abs because he is wearing a dropped armhole tank top.

Dren smiled at her when he noticed she stared at him for a while and looked away after. Rovena looks too ashamed when he notices it even though he made no comments.

"Can we go to the kitchen now and start cooking dinner?"

"Yes. Let's go."

"Alright."

They went to the kitchen. Dren suggested some food recipes to cook. Rovena starts preparing the ingredients. She started chopping it.

Rovena started cooking the food while Dren watched her. He can't stop himself from imagining that maybe this will always be the scene if they are married.

Even though there are maid servants and cooks here at the mansion, he asked her to do this because he wanted Rovena to be here.

Less than half an hour later, Rovena finished cooking all the food for dinner. Dren called a maidservant to prepare the food in the dining area.

Since Mila and Ivano went to Linz to meet Mila's cousin who arrived from another country, only Aleksa and I will eat dinner.

The maidservant finished serving the dinner in the dining area. So they went to the dining area.

While eating dinner, Dren noticed that she always focuses her attention on her food. She kept silent like when she was cooking her attention was on the food ingredients. She didn't look at him.

He is curious why she behaves like that. He thinks maybe because of the clothes that he is wearing and she was affected by seeing him wearing that kind of clothes.

Rovena is not used to seeing him like that. He is wearing a dropped arm-hole tank top that almost reveals his body. And ripped off jeans shorts. His clothes matter to her.

Dren can't stop smiling. He is still wearing clothes but she behaves like that, she can't even look at him. He thinks, what if she sees him totally naked? Maybe she will disappear in front of him if that is the case.

Dren has no intentions to show his body to Rovena. He only used to wear clothes like that if he was at the mansion when he was off to work because he wanted to free himself from wearing the formal suits that he wore all day long. So he only wears clothes like that after work.

Because of Rovena's behavior Dren feels a little bit ashamed. He decided next time he will wear a turtleneck with long sleeve shirts with matching pants.

"What?!! Is that really necessary?" Shouted the different side of him in his mind.

"Maybe yes or else Rovena will feel uncomfortable all throughout the time she and I have been together."

Dren is talking to himself.

"As far as I can see that is not necessary. Sooner or later she will become your wife. She needs to be used to seeing you like that!"

"Will you please stop?"

"I'm just telling the truth. Why don't you want to hear me? You're playing like a gentleman while you are burning with desire to have her. So this is your chance... "

"I said stopppp!!!"

Dren was back in reality when he heard Rovena talking to him;

"Dren, you don't like the taste of the food? You're just staring at the plate and not eating."

"I like the food. Don't worry. I'm just recalling something that I forgot to do in my office."

Dren made an excuse. He is afraid that Rovena will notice that he is not himself a while ago.

Dren thought he was able to overcome talking to himself like that, seeing himself as a different person talking to him. But still he is battling with himself again.

Dren feels annoyed at himself. He wants Rovena to see him as Dren who is a gentleman, a dignified one, a well behaved man and harmless. Not the other side of him who is rude, with a devil-like attitude, and tempted at her.

He doesn't want to play like a man who will build her up and let her down. He doesn't want Rovena to see that he is not the man who is best for her. He sees it coming so he should start controlling himself before she doubts him.

Dren hears Rovena talking to him again;

"Dren, tell me the truth, what is happening to you? I will understand if you..."

Rovena was not able to finish what she wanted to say because Dren talked suddenly to explain to her. He gets what she meant to say, she noticed what was happening to him. Dren is drowning in fear because what if she breaks up with him in the next few days because of that, like what his previous relationship partners did.

"Rovena, I'm okay. Please trust in me. I will not do anything to hurt you. Please don't be afraid of me."

Dren is almost begging her.

"Don't worry. I trust in you. If I don't trust in you."

"Thank you, Rovena."

Dren felt relieved when he heard what Rovena said. He is trying with all his might to stop the tears that want to fall from his eyes. He doesn't want to cry in front of Rovena. He doesn't want Rovena to think that he is weak.

"No worries. Eat your food. It's getting cold." Rovena said. Then she smiles at him.

"Alright."

Dren smiled back at her before he started eating the food on his plate.

He's a little unwell again. Rovena knows that. She can see the changes happening in his eyes while he is staring at his plate a while ago. She knows he is talking to himself. Seeing himself as a different person talking to him. That behavior of Dren is not new to her. Yes she feels afraid of him but she doesn't want to leave Dren because of that. She feels that Dren is important to her now.

They are in a relationship but Rovena admits that still she is not used to it. Yes sometimes she admires his physical appearance but it stops on that. It never comes to her mind that they will end up doing something which a normal couple do.

Chapter 18

It's early in the morning. Dren drove Rovena to the university where she is studying because he was able to convince her to sleep over at the mansion last night.

Then he proceeded to his company after he drove her. He started doing his work in his office but his mind is still occupied with the thoughts about Rovena.

What had happened to him and Rovena last night still lingers in his mind. That's not supposed to happen but he was betrayed by his psychological disorder. He found himself doing it to Rovena.

Rovena was too afraid.She just gave me all I wanted from her because she was not able to stop him.

When Dren was back in his right mind, he was full of regrets for what he did. He apologized to Rovena. Even though she said that she understands what is happening to him, Dren knows her trust in him has already been lost. He can't bring it back no matter what he does.

Dren was awake in deep thoughts when his phone rang. He received a call from Ivano. He answered the phone.

"Hello, Uncle."

"Hello. I just want to inform you that I and your Aunt Mila can't go back there at the mansion for one week. We decided to extend our stay here at her cousin's place."

"Alright, Uncle. I'm glad that you and her will be taking a vacation."

"Yes, we do. It's been so long since she and I have a vacation."

"Alright Uncle."

"Thank you, I got to go for now. Take care."

"Alright, Uncle. No worries."

"Alright."

"Okay, Bye."

"Bye, Uncle."

Dren is feeling guilty. Ivano trusts his friend's daughter with him. He promised to Ivano that he will take care of his friend's daughter but he can't even protect her from himself. He took a deep breath because of those thoughts.

Few minutes later, Dren is hearing the voice of his alter again, he is not in his right mind again.

"What is your problem, Dren?"

"I'm feeling guilty for what you did."

"Oh, Dren. You shouldn't feel that way. Rovena will understand. You are in a relationship, right? So it is expected that things will happen between you and her from time to time."

"You know I want you to get lost. You keep on betraying me. I hate you."

"I know that, Dren! But I am part of you that you can't erase. And you know that also. Why not choose to be me instead of eliminating me?!"

"Bullshit!!! I swear one of these days I can totally remove you from my system. And you will no longer exist. I will never want to be you totally. You are a devil inside of me that needs to vanish!"

"Ahaha, You can't win over me. You are weak without me. You want to be trampled by other people again? It's me who saves you Dren from being hurt by other people, both physical and emotional. You are a strong and dignified man in the eyes of others because of me. Don't hate me, Dren!"

"I agree but because of you I became mentally unwell!! Leave me alone. Get lost."

Dren was back in reality when the door of his office swings open. When the door swung open, he saw Rovena enter. She rushed near him when she noticed that there was blood running on his hands. It was because the pen with a knife inside that he was holding broke because of his strong grip on it.

"Rovena?"

"What are you doing, Dren?"

Dren feels like he is frozen on his chair. He made no reaction when Rovena removed the broken pen out of his hands. Then Rovena gets a medicine kit. She gets some alcohol and cleans the blood that flows from his wound. He doesn't know what he will say to Rovena. So he kept silent while Rovena put medicine on his wound.

Dren heard Rovena talking;

"Dren, what's wrong with you? You hurt yourself. Is it about last night? I accept your apology, right? So please stop thinking about it."

"Thank you for understanding me."

"Alright."

"Maybe I need to see my doctor again. Before your trust in me totally lost..."

"I still trust in you. I know I can trust you."

"I'm really sorry, Rovena. I swear I will set our wedding date as soon as possible."

"No worries. Are you really determined about that matter or do you just feel guilty about what happened to us last night?"

"Both. By the way may I know if I really become my alter, will you still accept me?"

"Dren, stop seeing yourself as two different people. You don't have to choose between the two. You need to accept both. It's both part of you. Learn to accept the darkside of your personality, Every person has a bad and good side. A good person can be bad sometimes. And a bad person can be good."

"I'll try. I'll do it for you. "

"Alright."

Rovena smiles at him. Then she proceeds to do her work. Deep inside Rovena is drowning in fear but she doesn't want to show it to Dren because she knows it will only make his condition worse.

While she is doing her work at Dren's office, she can't stop thinking about what happened between them last night.

She can't totally get angry with Dren. She knows that if Dren is in his right mind he will not touch her. Dren will not hurt her. And since she didn't want to get hurt too much last night she chose to give what he wanted.

She knew he was not in the right mind last night. She also knows that he keeps on battling with his alter that keeps pushing him to do so because he apologized to her when he was back in reality, full of regrets. She accepted his apology but she didn't know that he kept on thinking what happened. Still have guilty feelings. She hopes Dren will overcome those feelings.

The guilty feeling of Dren slowly subsides after the conversation between him and Rovena because Rovena shows to him that she is not blaming him or getting angry with him. She said she still trusts him.

Because Dren's mind is busy he didn't notice that it was almost lunch break. He decided to ask Rovena to eat lunch. He calls her name to get her attention.

"Rovena!"

"Yes. Do you need something?"

Rovena answered him but he noticed she kept scrolling on her cell phone. I wonder what she is doing. So he stood up and got close to her. He stands behind her to see what she is doing on her phone.

Dren read that she sent a message to a man named Travis. In her message.
" I'm at work, so I call you later,"

Dren gets jealous. Rovena is talking to another man. He calms himself. He doesn't want to overthink it. But before he could ask Rovena a question about Travis she talked to him. Showing the photo of Travis.

"This is Travis. He is my adoptive parents' nephew. He is like a cousin to me. Please don't get jealous.

Dren felt relieved even though he knew that he was not a real cousin of Rovena.

"Alright. You mean you have adoptive parents?"

"Ah yes. When I was 9 years old I was adopted by a businesswoman named Lara who happened to give charity to the orphanage where I am. She likes me very much but unfortunately she was sick. She has cancer and it is nearly in the last stage. She died when I was 14 years old. She left me an inheritance but Travis' mother, Aunt Lina, took all of that because according to her I have no right to her sister's hard earned money for I am not a real daughter of her sister Lara."

"Sad to hear that. Don't worry. About your inheritance from your real father, I promised I will talk to your father's stepsister, Lydia so that she will give it to you..."

"Thank you, Dren.

"Okay. So let's go. It's lunch break. Let's eat lunch."

"Alright."

As they walk to the lobby to go to the nearby restaurant outside the company, all the eyes of Dren's employees are on Rovena. Rovena saw some of them frowning at her. She heard some of them whispering.

"She is a Flirt.."

"She is a social climber..."

"She is a gold digger..."

"She is an opportunist..."

"She seduced the CEO..."

"She is a sex worker..."

Rovens feels like dying while hearing those accusations of other employees towards her. She wants to disappear in front of them so that they can't see her anymore.

Dren heard all of that also. So he frowned and clenched his fist in anger. Then he told Rovena;

"Don't mind them, Rovena. If they only know who you are. They will get embarrassed."

Rovena doesn't understand what he means to say. That's why I ask for an explanation

"What do you mean, Dren?"

"I mean you are my fiancee. And soon to be Mrs. Dren Wolf."

"Alright."

They reached the restaurant where they will eat lunch. They sat on the table at the corner of the restaurant. Dren ordered some food. They began eating lunch when a woman who was holding a baby approached Dren.

"Hi, Dren."

"Trixie?"

"Yeah. It's me."

"What about the child who is his father? Am I ?"

Rovena doesn't know if Dren is just kidding on that woman or what. Rovena can't stop herself from being annoyed. She heard the woman laughing.

"What if I said yes. What will you do? Are you going to marry me?"

Dren laughs softly and gets the child from Trixie. He cuddles the child.

Is it possible he is a son of Dren? Rovena asks herself.

Rovena feels so jealous. I want to snatch the child from Dren and throw it in the face of his woman. Rovena can't stop herself from shouting at Dren.

"This can't be! He is not your son, right?"

Rovena said while holding back her tears with all her might. The mother of the child feels shocked because of Rovena's behavior.

Dren looked at Rovena. His eyebrows formed in one line. Rovena was about to stand up and leave but Dren grabbed her hand and never let her go. Then he talked to her;

"Rovena, Please calm down. Yes Trixie is my ex-girlfriend but this child is not my son. This is the son of Elvin. One of my friends. He is now Trixie's husband."

Rovena feels embarrassed about her actions. So she immediately apologized to both of them.

"I'm sorry. I didn't mean it."

"It's okay. Don't worry." Trixie said while smiling at her.

Rovena notices Dren is trying his best to hold his laugh while still cuddling the child. She doesn't know if he wants to laugh at the child's behavior towards him. Or he is laughing at her childish behavior.

Rovena heard Trixie talking to her;

"You're too possessive about Dren. For your information, you cannot own him. He is difficult to handle and most of all a womanizer."

Rovena looked at Trixie but she didn't answer her. When Rovena looked at Dren he just shrugged his shoulders. Then talk without looking at Rovena. His eyes were focused on Trixie's son.

"Don't worry, Rovena, I'm yours. No other woman can have me now that you are here." He said seriously.

Rovena can't answer him. She doesn't know what she will say to him. But Trixie made a comment on what Dren said.

"Is she the one, Dren? The woman you want to marry?"

"Yeah, she is. She is my fiance. And sooner or later she and I will get married."

"Seriously?! I'm happy for you. Now that you found the woman you want to marry. So your search is over."

"Yeah. That's true."

Chapter 19

They went back to the company after lunch break. Dren needs to attend a board meeting at 2:00 pm at the nearby establishment. He has a 50% share of stock in that company. So his presence is badly needed.

Before Dren left his office he gave Rovena instructions to continue typing some documents that he started. Then he proceeded to the nearby company. It's a beverage manufacturing company.

Before the board meeting, one of the board members approached Dren;

"Good afternoon, Dren. Can we talk in your office after the board meeting?"

Dren frowned when he answer him;

"For what reason?"

Even though Dren frowned at him he continued smiling and talking to Dren,"Of course it is about investment. It's about my brother's company in Linz."

Dren is not in the mood to talk to him so he just agreed that he should just come to his office;

"Alright. Just go to my office."

"Thank you, Dren."

"Alright."

Dren said and made an excuse that he needs to talk to someone on the phone so that he won't bother him.

He is Glenn. One of Dren's classmates in college. A son of one of Ivano's friends.

Glenn and Dren are not friends. They have always been in competition ever since.

Glenn is also the reason why Talya and Dren broke up. Talya is one of Dren's ex girlfriends. But among all his previous relationship partners Talya is the one he likes the most. He is planning to make a marriage proposal to her at the time that he caught Glenn and her having an affair. Dren will never forget that night when he caught Talya and Glenn in bed.

When the next day came Dren broke up with Talya. Then one month later he got the news that Talya and Glenn will be getting married because Talya was pregnant and the father of the child is Glenn.

At present Talya and Glenn are having a happy married life with their children.

That was four years ago since Talya and Dren broke up. That bitterness passed and Dren didn't want to remember the pain that he felt in his heart because of that.

Since he is in the world of business, he'd rather choose to be professional if he came across those people who caused pain in him.

He still talks to them if they come to him and asks him to invest in their company.

That is how Dren's alter ego, the different side of him, makes them pay for the pain they cause him. That is how he takes revenge on them. Because of his alter ego Dren survives in difficult situations. His alter ego protects him from other people who want to trample on him. But what Dren doesn't like about his alter ego is that it is heartless, wicked and moody that creates fear in the hearts of those who work for him.

Several minutes later, the board meeting started. Dren sat in the last seat. There are just seven people inside the boardroom. The CEO of the company started the meeting. It's about the annual profit of the company. The CEO of this company is newly appointed. She replaced the position of his old grandfather.

Half an hour later. The meeting adjourned.

During the meeting Dren noticed that the CEO's eyes were always on him. Maybe because this is the first time she saw him attend a board meeting in her company but he was wrong. She has other intentions.

After the board meeting she approached Dren.

"Are you a son of Sir Ivano?" she asked sweetly.

"Adopted son."

Dren said without looking at her because he is scrolling through his phone sending a message to Rovena.

"Oh, you have a fiance?"

She asked Dren while looking at him. She held in his arms as if they had known each other for a long time.

Dren feels irritated by the way she looks at him. He hates the way she talks to him. She is overly sweet. He removed her hands on his arms while talking to her,"Yeah, I have a fiance. One of Uncle Ivano's friend's daughters. "

"Just a fiance and still not her husband. So you can still go with another woman. I just want to invite you for dinner tonight."

"Sorry about that, I can't go with you, Miss. I'm busy."

"Oh really?! Come on. But it's beyond office hours..."

"Yeah but there are more investment proposals that I need to read."

"Seriously?! Or are you just afraid of your fiancee?"

"Think whatever you want to think about me but it won't change my mind. I won't go with you. As I was saying, I'm busy. Thanks for the invitation by the way. I'll go ahead."

"Ahaha, What kind of man are you? Can you resist a beautiful woman like me who is inviting you? Are you gay? What a pity! You look so handsome..."

"Miss, will you please stop insulting me? Just because I don't go with you and was able to resist your temptation you're accusing me that I am a gay. I just don't like women who overly think that she is too beautiful. Goodbye!"

"What the hell?!!!"

Dren heard she got angry but he didn't waste time making an apology. He got out of her company without looking back at her. It is she who insulted him first so he doesn't have to apologize. She doesn't behave properly so that is her prize for insulting him.

While he is driving back to his own company he hears the voice of his alter ego talking to him,"Nice, Dren. I don't like to go with that kind of woman either. All I want is Rovena from the start. Since we met her. I feel glad that we both have the same feelings for Rovena, "

Dren talks to himself;

"Our feelings for her are not the same."

"How do you say that?"

"What I feel for Rovena is love, yours is lust."

"Oh come on Dren, Don't tell me that you don't feel the same pleasure that I felt last night when..."

"Will you please stop?!!!

"Why should I?"

"Don't you know how I felt guilty because of what you did."

Dren was back in reality when he heard the loud blow of horn by a ten wheeler truck on the intersection which he is about to cross. He stopped his car for a while and let the truck pass by.

Several minutes later he reached his company. He parked his car and proceeded to his private office.

It's past 4:00 pm when he reached the office. Rovena was no longer in his office. His new secretary told him that Rovena goes to the production area for overtime.

He decided to go to the production area too even though it's beyond his office hours. It is because there are some clients who arrived and asked for a tour to see the actual processing of the milk products in his company. He allowed such clients' requests to show to them that the products in his company are of good quality and clean.

When the purchasing department head saw that Dren was in the production area, he introduced Dren to the clients. So Dren walked around the production area together with him and the clients.

Dren saw Rovena operating a machine as part of her overtime. He and the purchasing department head as well as the clients are walking towards Rovena's working station.

Dren saw Rovena get a gallon of liquid milk products to process in her working station. To make it sterilized milk and refill it in a can. Rovena's supervisor is standing beside her as well as the quality assurance supervisor.

The supervisors greet Dren as well as the clients when they stop on Rovena's working station.

Dren was walking towards Rovena when he saw her suddenly spill the liquid milk products on the floor.

Unfortunately Dren slipped on the floor when he accidentally stepped on the milk mess. He was too embarrassed because of that. He was down on the floor and his black business suit was soaked in the milk but Rovena just stared at him and never got near him to apologize.

Dren stood up immediately when he was able to compose himself with his head held high. Pretended that it didn't matter to him. He smiles at everyone and makes a dignified exit. But deep inside he felt too ashamed.

He left the production area and proceeded to the penthouse at the top of his office to take a bath and change his dirty clothes.

When he was in the bathroom of the penthouse he let the cool water splash on him from the shower while thinking why Rovena did that to him.

"What is her problem? Is she angry with me?"

Few minutes later, he is not in his right mind. He hears the voice of his alter ego. He tries not to listen to him. He hears his alter ego is too angry with Rovena and wants to punish her for what she did. But Dren loves Rovena too much. He can't hurt her. He kept battling on his alter ego for several minutes.

"Whether you like it or not Dren , I will punish her. She deserves to be punished!"

"Please don't, she didn't mean it. She needs her job. I can't terminate her like what you wanted."

"Allright. Let's not terminate her but I will inflict punishment on her every day."

Dren tried his very best to win over his alter ego but he lost. He felt like his alter ego locked him in a cell. And he can't escape.

His alter ego is now manipulating everything while he can do nothing against it. He can't stop it. He feels so weak. Then he lost consciousness.When he awakened his alter ego wins. He is now behaving on what his alter ego is dictating him to do. He is not in his right mind so he feels hate at Rovena.

Dren changed clothes and went back to his office even though it's beyond office hours. He will wait for Rovena if she will show up at his office. He concluded that Rovena intentionally did that because of what he did to her last night. She was angry.

Dren is talking to himself as his alter ego.

I don't deserve such embarrassment. I will make her pay. I hate her. I can't forgive her for making me embarrassed in front of the clients and my employees. I teach her a lesson that she deserves.

I will never marry her. I'm not really ready for a married life. I still want to enjoy being single. Play with a woman I like.

Dren's alter ego is the reason behind Dren's break ups. It made his previous relationship unstable until his previous girlfriends broke up with him. They felt like Dren is not ready to enter a serious relationship.

After a few minutes of staying in his office he heard a knock on the door. For sure who was knocking was Rovena. He cleared his throat before he answered. He needs to maintain the sound of his voice. He doesn't want anyone to know that he is unwell at the moment. He needs to pretend that he is alright before Ivano sends him to a doctor again.

"Please come in."

The door opens. Rovena enters the room and walks towards him. He smirked. She talked to him when she got near him;

"Can we talk?"

"Oh we're talking, right? What do you want to tell me?"

"I'm sorry. I didn't mean it. The production supervisor wants to terminate me. Dren, please? I need this job. I can't go back to the restaurant where I'm working part time because they already hired a replacement for me. And finding a new job is not that easy. I'm begging you."

"Alright, sweetheart. No worries. I will not terminate you as long as you are willing to do all that I want. Just promise you will obey me all the time."

"I will, Dren. I'm really sorry."

"Sorry is not enough for what you did to me. I feel too embarrassed in front of my clients and employees."

"I didn't mean it. Please believe me. I will explain why that happens."

"I don't need your explanation. Just agree to all the errands I will ask you."

"Alright. What will I do so that you can forgive me?"

"Good question! Go with me at the mansion. Cook me dinner tonight. And after dinner you will know what will happen next. Is that okay?"

"But, Dren..."

"Oh I thought you were asking for an apology to me but it seems not. I'm just wasting my time talking to you. I'll go ahead and I will ask the Hr department to terminate you..."

"No! Please don't. I'll go with you to the mansion and ..."

"Good. Glad to hear that. So let's go..."

Rovena follows behind him silently while I walk to the elevator to proceed to the basement parking area.

While going to the parking area Dren is battling with himself again. His emotion is splitting as his personality is splitting. His hate and love for Rovena collides.

Chapter 20

Rovena goes with Dren to the mansion to show that she wants to apologize to him about what happened. She didn't mean it.

She was lost in deep thoughts while they were on their way to the mansion. She is thinking about how that incident happened.

She is operating a machine in the production area when Dren and his clients stop at her workstation. The load of the machine was empty. So she gets another gallon of liquid milk products to refill on the machine.

She was about to refill the liquid milk on the mixer but she saw Dren was walking towards her so she stopped for a while and looked at Dren but her supervisor, Miss Penny, got angry when she stopped refilling the mixer. Miss Penny pushed her. As a result she lost grip on the container of milk and it all spilled on the floor.

Because Dren was almost in front of her and was not able to step back when the milk spilled on the floor. He stepped on the mess. Because the liquid made the floor slippery, Dren slipped.

When Dren slipped down on the floor Rovena wanted to get near him immediately to help him stand up but I felt someone cause her uniform to be tangled on the machine. If she moves quickly, both her uniform and clothes will be ruined! She will definitely be in the nude if she makes a wrong move!

She wanted to explain that to Dren but he never let her explain. She understood why he felt so angry with her and didn't want to hear her explanation because It was the most embarrassing moment that could happen to a CEO like him.

She knows Dren hates her right now. She is thankful that he didn't terminate her. But she is expecting that he will punish her each and every day while she is working at his office.

She is willing to accept all his punishment until he forgives her. She hopes Dren will listen to her explanation one of these days and forgive her.

After 25 minutes of driving Dren reached the mansion. He stopped the car in front of the gate and arrogantly asked the guards to park it in the basement parking area.

The guards were all surprised because Dren didn't do such things. Dren noticed the guards' reactions so he decided next time he will park the car by himself before they tell Ivano about the difference between his actions at this moment. For sure Ivano will bring him to his

therapist. And he doesn't want that to happen.

When Rovena and he were inside the mansion he pulled her to the kitchen and asked her to cook dinner for him.He sat on the chair in the kitchen and watched her while she was cooking the food for dinner.

Rovena looks haggard because she felt too tired. But she is still beautiful in Dren's eyes. Dren smirked when Rovena looked at him. Then he asked her to get him some cans of beer.

"Give me some cans of beer, Rovena."

"Alright."

Rovena gets some cans of beer in the fridge. Then she gave it to him . Dren touched her hands when she gave him the beer. She wants to pull her hands away from him but she never did because she doesn't want him to get angry. He talks to her while he is still holding her hands.

"Cook the food immediately. I want to rest. Give me a body massage after dinner."

"Alright. I will."

"Good."

Twenty minutes later Rovena finished cooking the dinner. She serves it to the dining area. Dren eats dinner while she is just serving him. Dren knows she is starving but he didn't invite her for dinner.

Dren is still battling with himself. He wants to stop punishing Rovena. But he still hates her so just continue punishing her. And he wants to inflict more punishments on her.

After eating dinner Dren decided to go up to his room. But before he left the dining area he reminded Rovena to follow in his room immediately;

"Clean this mess on the table in 5 minutes. And follow me in my room. As I was saying, I need a body massage. Is that clear, Rovena?"

"Yes.I will."

Rovena is full of hesitation but she chooses to agree with him. Dren walks away from the dining area after reminding Rovena. He went upstairs to his room. He took off all his clothes when he reached his room. He just wears a robe. He lay on the bed.

Five minutes later Rovena came in. She calls Dren's name,"Dren."

He answered her,"Come here. Start giving me a body massage."

"Alright."

Rovena gets near him. She started giving him a massage. Dren feels so relaxed while burning with desire for Rovena every time she touches him.

After Rovena finished massaging his whole body she asked permission that she will go home but he didn't allow her to go home. Instead he told her to sleep over at his room because he is planning something hellish to Rovena.

His emotion is splitting. He is trying to stop himself, but his hate pushes him to start doing his devilish plan to Rovena.

Rovena groans in pain at every touch of Dren. He inflicted more and more pain on her while doing nasty things to her. He is planning to do it repeatedly on her until night is over.

Rovena cries but never begs him to stop from what he is doing because she really wants to apologize to him.

Dren stopped what he was doing to her when he felt satisfied. And seeing her too tired and weak. Of course he doesn't want her to die so he stops and lets her sleep. But he will make sure that she will receive more pain than this the next time.

Dren hates her for making him embarrassed in front of his clients and employees. He is not ready to forgive her right now.

Several hours later. The night is over.

It's early in the morning. Rovena is already at the university. Her classes have started but his mind is not on the lessons that his professors are discussing.

What had happened last night at the mansion still lingers in her mind. Because of that I know that Dren is so angry with her. She felt it in his every touch last night. And She knows he is just getting started to punish her.

Rovena is determined to endure all his punishment that he will give from day to day so that his angry feeling on her subsides.

She just can't believe that Dren could hurt her like that. What he did left marks on her body. She can still feel the pain both physically and emotionally. But she understands why Dren did that to her. She let him down. She knew that the embarrassment he got yesterday was too much.

Even though Dren was able to compose himself in front of his clients and employees, the embarrassment that he got is too much. He maintained his dignified act in spite of what happened. As if nothing happened to him when he faced the people around him. He managed to smile and exit the production area without showing any act of unprofessionalism.

Rovena doesn't know how long Dren will feel angry with her. She hopes it will not take forever. She will do her best so that he can forgive her.

Her classes ended but she doesn't remember any lesson that his professor discussed. She left her classroom. He started walking outside the university going to the place where Dren's company is located. She will go to work.

After twenty minutes of walking fast she reached the company. She goes up immediately to Dren's office. Dren's new secretary greeted her. She is Lila. Lila is different from other employees. She is kind to her.

"Hi. Rovena. How are you?"

"Hi. I'm fine."

"By the way, please make a cup of coffee first before going inside Sir Dren's office. He told me to ask you to bring him a cup of coffee when you arrived."

"Alright, Lila. I will."

"Okay."

She goes to the coffee table and makes Dren a cup of coffee. She will bring it inside his office. After she made a cup of coffee for Dren she walked towards his office.

She knocks on the door of his private office. She heard he is giving her permission to enter his office.

"Come in."

She opens the door and enters the room. She saw a visitor in his office when she entered the room. A woman with an angel-like face with long straight hair and a perfect sexy body dressed in an elegant business suit. She looks modest and sophisticated. She heard her talking to Dren. Her voice sounds so sweet like it's coming from the lips of an angel. The woman looks so beautiful and soft spoken.

Rovena thinks she is just nothing compared to her.

Rovena thinks the woman's age is the same as Dren's age. As far as she can see Dren is enjoying the woman's company. She sees how he smiles while talking to her.

Rovena felt like she was frozen to where she was standing. She doesn't know if she will bring the coffee that he is holding to Dren or what.

Rovena saw Dren look at her and frowned. She looks back at him. She wants to talk to him but she feels like she has lost her tongue. She can't find the words to say. She remained standing near the door still holding the cup of coffee.

Rovena heard the woman ask Dren about her;

"Who is she?"

Dren answered her. And his answer hurt Rovena's feelings too much;

"She is my ex-girlfriend. But she is working as a clerk in this office, that's why she is here. Just don't mind her. And about your question if we can go out tonight. Yes we can. I also want to know you further, like what you want from me."

"Seriously? Thank you, Dren. I just need someone to talk to. Honestly Leo and I were just cool off. But if you ask me to be your girlfriend, I'm more than willing to be yours."

"Really. Let me think about it."

Dren said and they both laughed softly. Upon looking at them Rovena realized that they will be a good couple. They look like two angels talking to each other.

When Rovena heard from Dren that she is now his ex-girlfriend and just working as a clerk in this office she slowly walked to her table and put the coffee that he made for Dren. He started doing some work without minding them while talking to each other.

She thinks Dren felt too disappointed in her because of the incident that happened yesterday. He doesn't want her to be his fiance anymore. But it is okay for her because at least he still gives her a chance to work in his company. He never terminated her

She needs her job badly in order to survive. She can't easily find a job like this that will support her expenses. She is not a citizen in this country so finding a good job will be difficult for her.

She needs her job so that she can finish her studies. She is getting old. And she doesn't want to remain like an uneducated trash just what others regard her.

She will just swallow her pride while working in Dren's office. She will just accept all the punishment that Dren will be given to her. She needs to finish her studies first before she will make a decision to leave Dren's company.

She feels sad about the incident that happened yesterday. Because of that she lost Dren. What hurts the most is he is just being so close and she has too much to say but she can't tell him. There is nothing she can do but set him free.

Half an hour later. Dren's visitor is about to leave. They've finished discussing the investment proposal that she presented to Dren. She learned that her name is Eloisa. She is a CEO of one of the companies that is about to fall for bankruptcy. She is asking Dren to save her company.

She heard her telling Dren that she is about to leave;

"By the way Dren, I have to go. I need to finish some work in my office. Thank you for giving me the favor to save my company. I really enjoy talking to you. I'm hoping we have more moments like this."

"Alright. See you tonight."

" Okay. I'll expect that. Bye,Dren, see you later."

Eloisa said to Dren while making a graceful exit from this office.

Chapter 21

When Eloisa left Dren's private office, the smile on Dren's face vanished. His eyes are full of anger while looking at the direction of the door where Eloisa exits. Rovena heard him talking;

"Flirt! Do you think you can fool me, Eloisa? I know the very reason why you are flirting with me. You just need me to save your businesses."

Rovena can't stop herself from turning around and looking at Dren. When Dren notices that Rovena is looking at him, he feels annoyed. He scolded her;

"Rovena, Are you staring at me? What are you thinking of?"

"Nothing. Sorry."

"Nothing? Or are you thinking that I will really go out with Eloisa tonight? Let me clear this matter to you. I'm not interested in her. I hate flirts and liars. Do you understand?"

"Yes."

"Good. Bring that coffee to me."

"Alright."

Rovena gets the coffee from her desk and brings it to Dren's table. While she is putting the coffee on the table she feels afraid of Dren. Especially when Dren stood up and wrapped his arms around her waist. She feels his hands almost touching the private parts of her body. While he was doing that he asked her to order food for lunch.

"It is almost lunch break ,Rovena. I'm not in the mood to eat at the restaurant so you need to order some food for us." Rovena felt his breath on her ears while he was talking.

What Dren is doing to her right now is so annoying but she can't just push him away. She knows his hatred towards her will just add up if she does that. She just waits for him to stop by himself.

She pulled out her cell phone from her pocket and dialed the number of the restaurant nearby and ordered the same food that they ate for lunch break yesterday. She finished ordering some food but Dren still didn't stop from what he was doing. As if Mirza will not stop because he is enjoying what he is doing.

Rovena takes all her courage to stop him. She didn't expect Dren to behave like that towards her even though they are in his office. She calls his name and begs.

"Dren! Please stop..."

Dren heard her but he only laughed and never stopped. Then he talked to her a few minutes later.

" I'm just making you realize that I don't need Eloisa. Why should I need that bitch? While you are here with me. Don't worry this is the only thing I will do to you for now. I still have my manners . I won't do the things that I did to you at the mansion here in my office."

Dren said and let her go. She walked away from him immediately when he let her go. She goes to her desk and continues doing her work without looking at him. She is drowning in fear. She thinks Dren is out of his mind again. It is his alter ego who is manifesting. She knows Dren will not behave like that in this kind of place if he is in his real self.

Rovena knows his personality is splitting again. And she knows it's because of what happened yesterday. She notices that Dren's choice of clothes since yesterday is different. The way he talks is different as well as his behavior towards her.

Aside from that, Dren always keeps her hair in a man bun and never lets it lose like what he did today.

She wants to tell Ivano about this. But how can she contact him? She knows he is not in his office. She doesn't even know his personal number.

She knows Dren is looking at her right now. So she just pretended that she didn't notice him. But she heard him talk to her so she needed to look at him again.

"Rovena ,it's the weekend. So we will take a two day vacation at my resthouse in Bosnia. We will travel after office hours."

Dren drank his coffee after talking to Rovena. Rovena knows she can't say no. So he answered him,"Alright but I still have to work at the production department after office hours..."

"You will no longer work there starting today..."

"But Dren I need extra money for..."

"I will just give you money."

"But I'm not your fiance anymore. I can't accept money from you..."

"What did you say? You are not my fiance?

Who told you?"

"What do you mean, Dren? You told Eloisa that I'm your ex..."

"I told Eloisa but I never told you, right? So just shut up and accept my offer"

"You mean I'm still your..."

"Of course. You are still my fiance. It will never change whether I like it or not."

"Why Dren? Are you really taking that arranged marriage seriously?"

Rovena asked him but he never answered her. He walked towards the door but she talked to him again before he could go outside the door.

"I am begging you please tell me the truth."

Dren turned around. Folded his arms on his chest and speak;

"Stop asking me, Okay? I'm not a search engine that if you type your question there is always an answer."

"But Dren..."

Dren only shrugged his shoulders in response to her. Then he turns back and walks outside the door. So she followed him and asked;

"Where are you going, Dren?"

Dren stops walking and answers without looking at her,"At the penthouse. Bring the food that you ordered there when it arrives." After talking to her he walks towards the elevator.

When Dren rode on the elevator Rovena did not go back inside Dren's private office. She will only wait for the food delivery outside the office.

Few minutes later the food delivery arrived. She brought the food to the penthouse. When she arrived at the penthouse she saw Dren sitting on the long sofa drinking wine.

Dren talks to her when he saw that she arrived;

"Serve the food on the dining table."

"Alright."

She goes to the dining area and prepares the food on the dining table. Afterwards, she finished preparing the food. They started eating lunch.

While They are eating lunch Dren is talking to her.

"I think it's better that you live in the mansion, Rovena."

Rovena can't answer him immediately. She doesn't know what to say to him. She doesn't like the idea. Why should she stay in his mansion? She is still not his wife.

"After we have been in Bosnia you will move into the mansion..."

"But Dren, I'm not your wife, why should I move to the mansion?"

"It is not necessary that you will become my wife before you move there."

Rovena didn't respond to him. She is full of hesitation to obey Dren. She knows he is making that offer to inflict more punishment to her. And she feels afraid because of those thoughts.

Dren talks to her again when he doesn't receive any response from her;

"Why don't I hear any response from you, Rovena?"

"I don't like to live in your mansion..."

"As I was saying, you will move into the mansion. And don't even think of telling Uncle Ivano and Aunt Mila of what I did last night to you. If you do so, I swear I will make your job harder each day."

"I...I will not tell them anything about that..."

"Good. Since sooner you will be my wife I will train you starting next week to handle all the businesses that I have. So I'm expecting total obedience from you. Is that clear, Rovena?"

"As I was saying I don't want to..."

"Bullsh*t! As I have said, you need to move into the mansion whether you like it or not!"

Dren shouted at her and hit the dining table with his fist. His eyes are full of anger while looking at Rovena. Rovena feels so afraid of him so she agrees with him even though she doesn't like his offer.

"Alright."

"Good."

Dren kept silent until they finished eating lunch. Rovena still can't believe that he will behave like that.

Dren feels glad that Rovena agreed with him. So he doesn't need to ask her to go with him in the mansion whenever he needs her. That gives him a real favor because he is not finished giving punishment to her.

Dren hates Rovena but he needs to obey Ivano to marry her. Yes he will obey his uncle to marry her. Anyway he can have another woman if he wants to even if they will get married. He knows Rovena could do nothing if he will have a mistress after their wedding.

After eating lunch she asks Rovena to choose all the clothes that she wants to buy on the brochures from the known boutique in town . Then he will ask the boutique to deliver it at his office. He wants Rovena to look presentable in the eyes of those who knew him. Rovena is beautiful and Dren knows he only needs to teach her to dress properly.

He was sitting on the sofa when he called her. She is about to leave the penthouse and will go back to the office when he calls her.

"Wait, Rovena. Come here first. Look at these."

Rovena walks towards him;

"What is that Dren?"

"Look at these brochures. Tell me all the clothes that you will like. And we will buy it."

"Do I have to buy new clothes? Aunt Mila gave me many clothes last time when I slept over at the mansion..."

"Those are different from these. You need to buy business suits and formal dress. Come here. Sit beside me and choose."

Rovena sat beside him on the sofa and picked up the brochures. She started pointing out to Dren the clothes she wants but he doesn't like it for her to wear. The style is too old fashioned. He wants her to wear some clothes that are modern. So she ask her to choose again.

"Look, Rovena. The style of these clothes are too old fashioned. Choose clothes which will fit your age. You will look like a grandmother if you wear these."

"But other clothes here are too daring..."

"I said choose another style. I don't want to see you wearing those kinds..."

"What do you want me to wear? Those clothes that almost reveal my body..."

"Stop raising your voice at me Rovena. Do what I said."

"I told you I don't like to wear those clothes.."

"Okay. You are too stubborn. Let me help you decide what clothes you need to wear."

Dren doesn't like her attitude being disobedient to him so he chose the clothes he wants her to wear. Then he showed it to her. Rovena totally disagreed but when she saw Dren frowning and throwing away the brochures on the floor she just agreed.

Dren saw the fear in her eyes when she looked at him. As if she is seeing that he is unwell this time. For Dren that is not good. So he needs to do something to remove her doubt towards him before she tells her uncle about it.

Chapter 22

Rovena went back to Dren's private office to continue her work while Dren conducted a meeting among all the department heads about the new policies that he wants to implement.

Rovena feels afraid of Dren because his attitude towards her gets worse with each passing hour. She feels guilty because she is one of the reasons why Dren's personality disorder was triggered. But it's not all his fault. But he can't blame him. She knows his situation so she needs to understand and help him back to normal psychological conditions instead of fearing him.

Rovena hates the person who sabotages her in the production area. She swears she will look for that person who betrayed her in the production area. The person who ruined her image in the eyes of Dren. The reason why Dren hated her now. That person is really the cause of why that accident happened to Dren and not totally her. If that person did not sabotage her with that liquid milk that she accidentally spilled on the floor that caused Dren to slip on the floor in front of his clients and employees , Dren would not get angry with her.

Rovena can't stop her tears from falling thinking that Dren hates her now. And they can't go back just like before. She dried her tears immediately when she heard the door swing open. Dren arrived. She guessed the meeting was adjourned.

She did not look at him when he entered the room. She pretends her attention is focused on printing some documents that he asked her to print before she left the penthouse.

Dren walks towards Rovena instead of proceeding to his office table. He smiled at her when she looked at him. She is surprised about his behavior this time. He was so annoyed at her when she left him in the penthouse but now he is smiling at her. She finds it weird. Some questions are running through her mind;

'Did he notice that I'm planning to tell Sir Ivano about his condition? This is not good. I know his uncle can't convince him easily to see his doctor.'

Dren talked to her when he gets near her;

"How's the documents that I ask you to print?"

She answered him. And forced herself to smile at him;

"I will be able to finish it before the office hour ends."

"Thanks I need it on Monday but since it's Friday you need to finish that, okay?"

Dren smiles as sweetly as possible but Rovena notices that in his eyes that he hides his annoyance towards her. She is right, he just doesn't want to tell his uncle about his condition right now.

So she answered him and pretend that she believe in his pretense;

"Yes, Dren. Don't worry I will finish this today. I'm glad that you are in a good mood now."

"Yeah. You need to finish that early. We will fly to Bosnia immediately after office hours end. You can't extend beyond office hours."

"Alright."

"And since I don't want to drive long hours we will use a private jet going there."

"Alright. I will finish this early."

Rovena continues printing the documents while Dren proceeds to his office table and opens his laptop.

Five minutes later Rovena heard Dren calling her name;

"Rovena..."

She answered him immediately so that he won't get irritated at her;

"Why, Dren?"

"I am sending files to the desktop on your table, please make me a powerpoint presentation about it. You need to finish it today, okay?"

"Alright."

She opens the desktop and looks for the files he sends. She feels a little bit annoyed when she opens the files that he sends. How can she finish doing that in two hours left before the office hours end?

He sent many files containing pictures that she needed to put in some captions based on the documents that he sent. She needs to read it thoroughly so that she can put the right caption on each photo. And she is still not finished printing all the documents that he asked her to print. So she moves quickly so that she can do all this task that he gave her at the last minute.

Dren is not looking at her but Rovena sees that he keeps on smiling because he knows how difficult the tasks are that he gave her today. Rovena knows it is just part of his punishment.

Several minutes later Dren called her again and she heard him asking her to do some errands;

"Rovena, Please bring these files to each department that is on the folder label. But before you go, make me a cup of coffee first."

"Alright, Dren."

Rovena rushed to the coffee table and made him a cup of coffee. And put it on his table. Then she picks up the file folders that she needs to bring to 6 departments of his company. She left Dren's private office to go to the department head offices.

She spent almost 25 minutes distributing the files that he asked him to bring to each department. She walks as quickly as she can so that she can go back to Dren's office immediately and continue what he is asking her to do there.

When she arrived at his office she rushed to her desk to continue working on the slides on the powerpoint while printing the last few documents.

She didn't notice that it's already the end of the office hours if not for Dren telling her when he gets near her.

"It's already the end of the office hours. Are you finished doing that?" Dren asked her while standing in front of her, folding his arms on his chest.

"I am just finalizing the documents to send it back to you." Rovena answered without looking at him while she hurriedly edited some errors she made.

"I'll give you five minutes to finish that. Follow me on the rooftop after, I will just check the jet."

"Alright..."

Dren walks out the door while Rovena sends the files. After four minutes she finished doing it. So she grabbed her sling bag and walked from the office to follow Dren on the rooftop.

While she is walking she remembers that she doesn't have any clothes in her bag. She was not able to bring even one. And Dren told her that they will spend two days there in Bosnia. He didn't tell her last night so she is not prepared for that. She feels annoyed while thinking about what she will wear in the next two days.

She reached the rooftop. She saw Dren standing in front of his private jet frowning while he crossed his arms on his chest. When he saw her he talked to her;

"What took you so long? Let's go."

"I only took five minutes to get here."

Dren raised his eyebrows when he heard her reasoning. Then he goes up to the jet so she follows behind him. She doesn't see any pilot or crew.

Dren sat in the pilot seat. He will be the one who will make the private jet fly. Rovena wanted to ask some questions but she stopped herself. She can see that he is not in the mood again. She doesn't want to disturbed him. She is afraid that if she disturbed him and he made a mistake in making the private jet fly, both of them would die in a plane crash.

One hour later. Dren made the jet land on the rooftop of a building. Then both of them stepped out from the jet and went down from the rooftop.

Rovena realized that it is not a company building but a huge resthouse. The resthouse is too modern and elegant. They proceeded to a huge room when they were inside the resthouse.

Dren opened the door of the room and entered but Rovena didn't follow inside. She just remained standing on the doorway of the room. So Dren talked to her when he saw that she was full of hesitation to enter the room.

"We will occupy this room instead of occupying two separate rooms."

"Alright."

"Why are you still standing there? Get inside and take off your clothes and ..."

"What?!"

"What are you thinking of? Will you let me finish what I'm saying before making a reaction like that?"

"Sorry..."

"As I was saying you can take off your clothes and get some clothes to wear from that built-in closet to change your clothes. I'll wait for you outside this room. I'll give you 10 minutes."

"Alright."

Dren went outside the room and closed the door while Rovena hurriedly opened the closet to choose some clothes to wear. She saw that all the clothes from the cabinet are unisex. She chose a black shirt and jeans shorts.

She changed her clothes. Then she walked towards the door to open it. But I can't open the door. She tried to open the door while calling Dren's name.

"Dren!"

She heard him answered from outside the door;

"What is your problem?"

Rovena shout at him when he still not opening the door;

"Open the door. Don't lock me here!

She heard Dren's voice. He is annoyed.

"My God Rovena. Will you stop accusing me? You can go out by yourself by only topping the button placed near the knob."

She tried to follow what Dren said and the door opened immediately. She didn't notice this kind of lock. She felt ashamed when she was able to open the door by herself.

When she stepped out of the room she saw Dren looking at her frowning. She blushed because of embarrassment. She can't look at him. When Dren noticed that he shrugged his shoulders.Then he talk to her;

"Go to the kitchen and cook dinner instead of accusing me of locking you there. Why should I do that? Who will cook dinner if I do that?"

"I'm sorry, I didn't mean it..."

"Stop explaining. I don't need your explanation. Just go to the kitchen and do what I asked you to do."

"Dren..."

"You still have a problem? What is it?"

"Why don't you want to hear my explanation?"

"It's not necessary. Why should I waste my time listening?"

"But Dren, I want to tell you something about..."

"Rovena, it's better you cook dinner instead of nagging at me. I'm starving."

"Alright. I will cook."

"I'll wait in the living room."

"Okay"

She goes to the kitchen to cook dinner. While she is cooking dinner she can't stop herself from crying. Thinking that Dren really hates her and doesn't even want to hear her explanation makes her cry. It hurts her feelings so much that Dren hates her.

"Why are you crying, Rovena?"

She was surprised when she heard Dren's voice. She thought Dren was in the living room. She didn't know that he was following her and he was standing behind her.

She dried her eyes immediately before she faced him. Then she answered him;

"It's only because of onions."

"Because of onions? Do I look like an onion? or do I smell like onions?"

"Why are you asking me that?"

"Because I know I'm the reason why you are crying so I'm that onion."

Rovena didn't answer Dren. She only lowered my head and focused on slicing other ingredients. She couldn't look at him because she felt her tears falling from her eyes.

She felt Dren got close to her. He wrapped his arms in her waist while he was whispering in her ears.

"Stop making drama. Yes you are right. I hate you. But you can still have me, right? Just because your father and Uncle Ivano arranged our marriage. "

Rovena answered him while removing his arms on her waist. The she move away from him;

"I'm not making a drama. It just hurts me that you are hating me now."

"It's all your fault. You make me embarrassed in front of many people. You let me down..."

"Dren I didn't mean it..."

"You mean it. I know that..."

"Why should I do that..."

"It's because you are annoyed at me..."

"Why should I get annoyed at you..."

"Don't ask me. We both know the reason why."

"What do you mean? I don't get it..."

"It's just because I forced you to be in my bed when you slept over at the mansion. I know you get angry because of what I did ..."

"Dren, I don't get angry with you because of that. I understand why you were able to do that.."

"Seriously?!"

"Dren please listen, that incident happened in your company has nothing to do with that. It's because someone sabotaged me, that's why liquid milk spilled on the floor and when you stepped on it accidentally you slipped."

"Fine. You don't get angry because of what happened to us at the mansion? Then prove it to me. Maybe I can forgive you. If you prove me wrong."

After saying that Dren left the kitchen. When Rovena was left in the kitchen she was thinking what she will do to prove it to him so that he can forgive her.

Chapter 23

After eating dinner, Dren goes out. She doesn't know where he is going. She decided to go back to the room upstairs. She remembers Eloisa. So she is mumbling while walking upstairs.

"Is Mirza going to meet her here in Bosnia tonight? That's why he chose to stay here in Bosnia this weekend."

"If he is going to do that, why does he ask me to be with him here? Is this another part of his punishment? Make me jealous of other women? This is so annoying. "

"Ah! I wish someone could give me work in another company. I don't want to work at Dren's office anymore. It's better to leave him than to receive his punishment everyday. Maybe he can't really forgive me."

Since Dren left tonight and she doesn't know how long he will spend time outside she decided to go to sleep. But before I could lay on the bed she heard the sound of a car approaching.

So she went down from the bed and peered at the window. She saw Dren step out of his car with grocery bags in his hand and paper bags which she guessed were inside are women's clothes, footwear and accessories. Then he walked towards the main door and got inside the house.

Several minutes later. She heard his footsteps on the staircase. After a few minutes it stopped. She guesses he is outside the door. The door of the room is closed. She waited for him to knock but he didn't. Instead the door of the room suddenly opened. She felt too surprised because she didn't expect him to open the door without knocking.

He frowned at her when he saw her eyes widened when he entered the room while she was standing beside the window and the curtain almost covered her because the strong wind blew from outside the window.

"What are you doing, Rovena? Will close that window before the snowflakes enter our room."

"Nothing. Alright. I will close the window."

She closed the window immediately so that he would stop scolding her. When she looked at him again she saw him put the paper bags on the single sofa which is located at one of the corners of the room. Then he talked to her again.

"Get these. These are all for you."

"Thank you..."

"I bought that because we will attend a party tomorrow night. Don't even think that I forgiven you. I still hate you."

Rovena didn't answer him. She just lowered her head while standing beside the single sofa where he put the paper bags. While she saw Dren get a towel and go to the bathroom.

When Dren was inside the bathroom she looked inside the paper bag to see what was inside. She is thankful that the clothes he buys for her to wear at the party are not so daring. She put all the clothes and accessories in the closet.

Fifteen minutes later. Dren comes out of the bathroom. He just wrapped around the towel on the lower part of his body. She felt afraid when she saw him. But when she gets some clothes inside the closet and gets dressed she feels relieved.

Dren's former friend Alessandro invited him to his birthday party. Alessandro is one of his former friends. Because Alessandro betrayed him, he hates him. They don't communicate with each other for a long time.

Dren doesn't want to talk to him anymore. Alessandro was the one who talked to Dren when they saw each other tonight when Dren was buying some personal things from the nearby supermarket. Alessandro approached him. Apologized to him and even invited him to his birthday party tomorrow.

Dren accepted the invitation. He wanted to show him that he had moved on already. And Jesica is not that important to him.

Alessandro took Jesica away from Dren. Jesica is Dren's former girlfriend in his college days who thinks that Alessandro is a better man than Dren so she goes with Alessandro and breaks up with Dren. Now Alessandro and Jesica are husband and wife.

Jesica is not as sexy and beautiful as before during their college days. She really looks like a mother now because she and Alessandro have 4 children already.

Dren got the news that they almost suffered a financial crisis. And looking for investors to save their company. One of their companies had fallen to bankruptcy. So this is the chance for Dren to take revenge on them.

Dren plans to introduce Rovena to them to show to Jesica that he has a beautiful girlfriend at present than her.

Because of that she bought Rovena a party dress and accessories to wear. She knows Rovena will look so beautiful on that dress. She knows Jesica will feel insecure and envious.

When she arrived she went to the bathroom immediately to take a bath. He knows Rovena felt afraid when he saw him leave the bathroom wearing nothing. He just covered the lower part of his body with a white towel he wrapped around his waist. He knows she is thinking that something may happen between them again. But she felt relieved when she saw him put on his clothes.

Dren really wants to do such a thing to her but his real self keeps on stopping him. It bothers him from time to time. He thought it vanished totally but each passing hour he feels his alter ego becomes weak and he feels his real self is stronger than it again. But his real self did not win against his alter ego again. It vanishes again and his alter ego manifests.

He gets a comb and face in the mirror. In his mind he is talking to himself.

"Stop hurting Rovena. I forgiven her already. Why do you keep on punishing her?"

"She deserves that..."

"She doesn't deserve to suffer punishment in your hands. I know she didn't mean to cause such an accident that happened ..."

"She intentionally did that. Are you blind?"

"I'm not. You are the one who is always blinded with your anger towards people around us."

"Seriously?! Where do you think you belong right now if not because of me. Maybe you are a beggar and not a billionaire at present if I don't protect you from people around us."

"That's not true. I can still be what I am today even without you. Get lost..."

"You are ungrateful to me. After what I did to you, you want me to totally vanish."

"Because you are cruel to Rovena. I don't want Rovena to always get hurt because of you."

"Do you think you can win over me? Save Rovena from me tonight if you can. Watch what I do to her tonight while you can do nothing to save her. "

"Stop. Please don't hurt Rovena. "

He turned his back on the mirror and walked towards Rovena who was sitting on the sofa bed scrolling through her phone.

But before he could touch Rovena he was back in his real self. He managed to talk to Rovena.

"Rovena, go. Go back to Austria before he can hurt you again...?

Dren said to Rovena while kneeling in front of Rovena and touching her beautiful face with his both hands. Of course Rovena gets a little confused about what he is talking about. His alter ego pulls him away from Rovena to stop him from asking Rovena for help but it can't. It felt so weak and Dren almost didn't hear it again. And if Dren was able to take some medicine for sure it would vanish.

"What are you talking about, Dren? Who will hurt me?"

"Listen, Rovena. You need to talk to Uncle Ivano. I need to see my doctor again."

"Dren..."

"Please Rovena. Listen to me. Go back to the mansion. Here take this. My car keys, my wallet and my phone. You need to leave Rovena..."

"I can't leave you here.I will just call your uncle to tell him your condition..."

"Rovena you don't understand. I don't want to see you hurt again. So leave me here..."

"No Dren. I won't leave you."

Dren saw Aleksa stand up and get something from his bag. It's a sleeping pill. Then she gets a bottle of mineral water from the personal refrigerator placed at the corner of the room.

She walks towards him who is now sitting on the sofa holding his head with both hands because he keeps on battling with himself. Rovena talks to him;

" Dren, drink this for the meantime."

Dren looked at her, full of hesitation. But she follows what Rovena said to him. Few minutes later the pill takes effect on Dren. Dren feels sleepy and he can't hear his alter ego anymore. He talked to Rovena;

" Rovena, I'm feeling so sleepy."

Rovena made him lay down on the sofa bed while talking to him;

"Sleep now Dren. Tomorrow might be good."

She put a pillow under Dren's head.

Dren fell asleep. So she picked up his phone. She decided to call his uncle. She needs to talk to his uncle to tell his condition. She dialed his number. Few seconds later he answered the call;

"Hello, Dren"

"Hello. This is Rovena, Sir. I'm using Dren's phone."

"Rovena?"

" Yes Sir. I need your help. It's about Dren, that's why I call you."

"Why? Where is Dren? What happened?"

"Dren told me that he wants to see his doctor again. We are here in his resthouse in Bosnia. He asked me to accompany him to this place for a weekend vacation."

" Alright. What is happening to Dren right now?"

"He still acts normal when he is dealing with other people. I think he still knew that he would not ruin his image in the eyes of people around him. Even his alter ego, I think he will not allow that to happen. Only that he keeps on fighting his alter ego because of me..."

" Why? What did you do to Dren?"

"I didn't mean it. He hated me because of the incident that happened yesterday in his company. He was embarrassed in front of his

clients and employees. He slipped on the floor because of the liquid milk that I spilled on the floor because someone sabotaged me. I'm sorry about this for letting Dren down."

"Alright. It's not all your fault Rovena. Wait for me and my wife. We will go there. Take care. And please take care of Dren."

"Okay, Sir. I will."

After their conversation Ivano ended the call. Rovena sat beside Dren. She watched him sleep. Dren is too handsome. She feels sad while watching him sleep. She hopes Dren will be fine. She talk to him while he is sleeping;

"I'm sorry, Dren. I hope you can forgive me. I didn't mean what happened yesterday. I didn't mean to embarrass you in front of your clients and employees."

She can't stop herself from crying knowing Dren's condition. She knows Dren finds it hard to control his alter ego so he decided to see his doctor.

Some questions run through her mind while looking at Dren;

"Are they going to put Dren in a mental hospital?"

She doesn't want to see him inside of that kind of institution. She knows Dren is just a little bit unwell and not severe. She doesn't want to leave Dren just like what he said to her a while ago. Even though she feels afraid that he will hurt her again physically. She can bear the pain that he will inflict on her but she can't take if something bad happens to Dren because she leaves him in this kind of situation and saves herself.

Chapter 24

Ivano and Mila arrived early in the morning together with Dren's doctor. Rovena felt relieved when they arrived.

Dren was still sleeping when they arrived. So Mila decided to cook breakfast while waiting for Dren to wake up. Rovena accompanies her in the kitchen while Ivano and Doctor Elmir stay in the living room talking about Dren's condition.

Mila is a good cook. The food she is cooking smells so delicious. It makes Rovena's stomach rumble. She is starving. Mila makes her a cup of hot chocolate while she is cooking the food for breakfast.

Half an hour later Mila finished cooking the food. But they didn't start eating breakfast because they wanted to wait for Dren to wake up. Mila joined Ivano and Doctor Elmir while sitting in the living room.

Rovena goes back to the room where Dren is sleeping. When she entered the room. She saw Dren was already awake. He is sitting on the sofa bed. He looked towards the door when he felt that someone entered the room.

Dren looks at Rovena. His eyes are full of anger. Rovena remains standing near the door because she feels afraid. She knows he is not in his right mind again. She felt frozen from where she was standing when she saw Dren stand up and walk towards her.

When he gets near her he holds her arms too tight. She feels like the bone in her arms will break. Dren talked to her.

"Why is Doctor Elmir here? Did you tell my uncle that I'm going insane?"

Dren asked her in an angry low voice. As if he doesn't want someone to hear him. Rovena answer him while she is trying to bear the pain in her arms because he is holding her arms still too tight;

"Dren, you told me last night to do that, that's why they are here."

"Stop calling me Dren. I'm not Dren. From now on you won't see him anymore."

"What do you mean by that...? Ah! Please let go of my arms. It hurts too much."

"Stop asking too many questions, just follow what I am going to tell you if you don't want to get hurt badly."

"Alright. I will... I will obey you, Dren"

"How many times I'm going to tell you that I'm not Dren."

Dren said in an irritated voice. He touched her neck with his other hand while still holding her arms. She felt like her breath would stop because his grip on her neck was too tight. She can't speak or move while breathing heavily because of fear.

Dren gets closer to her and gives her a deep kiss which almost makes her breath stop.

His kiss is so familiar. I remember the guy named Ajdin. The guy whom she fell in love with when she was working as a cleaner in one of the hotels in Albania years ago.

But she was not able to see him again after her previous employer terminated her because her previous employer saw her always talking to Ajdin. Ajdin is their investor and her employer's daughter claims that Ajdin is dating her so she doesn't want her to get close to Ajdin. Her employer's daughter feels envy and jealous so she asks the HR department to terminate her.

From that day she was terminated from her job she never saw Ajdin again. Their paths never cross again. But she never forgets Ajdin. She is the very first guy she falls in love with.

Because I'm lost in deep thought I utter some words that makes Dren stop what he is doing to her;

"I miss you, Ajdin..."

When Dren heard what she said he let her go. Then he asked her a question that shocked her;

"How did you know that I am Ajdin?"

Rovena can't speak. She can believe Dren is also Ajdin. It means Ajdin is his alter ego. It means Dren is not in his real self that time. Rovena feels she was a fool that she was not able to recognize that Dren is Ajdin.

Dren repeat his question when Rovena didn't answer him;

"I'm asking you. How did you know that I am Ajdin? I never told that name to anyone except to the cleaner in one of the hotels in Albania where I made an investment five years ago. I like her very much that's why I approach her."

"What...are you doing there... five years ago?"

" Of course I'm visiting my parents tomb."

Dren went back to Albania that time to visit his parents' tomb. He stayed in that hotel after he made an investment there. Then he met Rovena unexpectedly when she was cleaning his room. He thinks Rovena fell in love with her after their several meetings but he was not able to see her because according to the owner of the hotel she resigned.

"I'm that cleaner."

"Seriously?!"

"Yes, Dren...I just didn't recognize you..."

" Stop calling me Dren! How lucky I am. I don't know that the woman I want to **** is just around the corner. Why did you just leave like that after making me want you badly?

Dren asked her and he smirked. Then he gets close to her again but she moves away from him. She will not allow him to touch her again. She doesn't want to get hurt.

Dren steps forward while she is stepping backward. She asks him to stop whatever he is planning to do. It is clear to her now that it is his alter ego who always betrays him.

Some questions are in her mind again. Dren did this also to his previous relationship partner, hurting them physically? That's why all his relationships always end in break up. Because they don't want to become a battered wife if they marry Dren. She feels too afraid. asking herself ; I am going to become a battered wife if I marry him?

Dren is still advancing towards her while she is stepping backward to avoid him. He had no plan to stop doing what he wanted to do to her. She needs to trick him to stop him. She take all her courage to talk to him;

"Are you doing this to all your ex-girlfriends that's why they left you?"

Dren laugh out loud before he answer her;

" I never touch them even once. I never forced any of them to lay in my bed."

"What do you mean?... You never slept with them even once."

" As I was saying, I never do that. That's how gentlemanly I am."

"Gentleman? Are you?"

"I am. But I don't know why I feel this way to you. I felt obsessed when I saw you in Albania six years ago. I want to continue what I failed to do with you in Albania..."

"Stop or I will tell them to send you ..."

"To a mental hospital? I doubt it. I know you would rather keep silent and give what I want than seeing me in that kind of institution. Do that if you are determined enough to ruin my image and reputation. But maybe you can do that because you made me embarrassed in front of my clients and employees right? Maybe you will do that because you don't want to marry me..."

"Stop accusing me. I love you..."

"You love me?! But why did you just leave me like that when we are in Albania? " Dren said in an angry voice.

" Because my employer terminated me and I don't even know where to find you, how to contact you. I 'm not allowed to go back to that hotel after they terminate me."

" Oh really?! Then prove to me now that you are telling the truth..."

She needs to stop Dren. It seems that he really needs to see his doctor. Dren needs to be treated again. She decided to agree with what he wants until he obeys to see his doctor. She needs to overcome her fear towards his alter ego so that she can help him back in reality.

She tried to talk to him again;

" Alright!"

"What do you mean?"

" I'm willing to give you what you want. But see your doctor after I allow you to do it."

"What?!" Why do I need to see him? I'm not insane."

" Then you need to tell them before they will send you to an institution to treat you. Do you understand?"

"Okay. Fine. I will obey you. Even though I know that you are tricking me only. And I hate you for doing that to me." Dren said in an angry manner.

Rovena felt too afraid when she heard that from Dren. She thought she was able to deceive him but she's not. She can't move to her place when he gets near her. When he starts touching her she flinches. Because of that he gets annoyed at her.

"I thought you were willing to give me what I wanted but what are you doing? Are you just deceiving me?"

Dren said in an irritated voice and he pulled her closer to him. She answered him even though she felt so scared at him;

"I'm not deceiving you. I just flinch because I feel pain in your every touch..."

"You know why because you keep on annoying me..."

"Alright...I won't annoy you anymore..."

Dren doesn't answer her anymore. He just frowned at her. She is trying her very best not to do something that will annoy him. Dren needs to see his doctor so she needs to do his best to make him obey.

She let him do all what he wanted until he got satisfied and let her go. After he's done he goes to the bathroom and takes a bath. When he gets inside the bathroom, She can't stop herself from crying. She felt so scared of him. But she knows she shouldn't be. He is just not in his right mind. She reminds herself of that.

When she saw the door of the bathroom open she dried her tears immediately. She doesn't want Dren to see her crying. She saw him go out from the bathroom and walk towards the built-in closet, get some clothes and wear them. Then he walked towards her. She is still sitting on the sofa bed where he left her. He talked to her when he got near her;

"Rovena, get dressed and let's go outside. I'm ready to meet Doctor Elmir. That is what you want me to do, right?"

When she heard what Dren said she answered him immediately;

" Ah, yes. I will just put on my clothes..."

" Make it faster before I change my mind.."

"Alright..."

She puts on her clothes immediately while Dren is standing in front of her. She doesn't care anymore if he is looking at her or what. He saw it all. She doesn't need to hide it from him. She saw Dren frown at her. She doesn't understand why. After she got dressed they left the room and went down to the living room to meet Dr. Elmir.

Dren walked towards the living room while Rovena was walking behind him.When Ivano saw Dren approaching the living room he greeted him. While Rovena stops walking and remains standing at the corner.

"Dren, how are you?"

"I'm fine, Uncle. Don't worry too much about me. I just want to see Dr. Elmir because I feel my anxiety attacks lately."

"Alright. I thought there's something worse happening to you..."

"Nothing, Uncle. It's just that. Trust me. Okay?"

"Alright. Alright."

"By the way, where is Dr. Elmir?"

"He just went outside for a while to answer his other patient call but he will go back in here immediately..."

"I am here now, Dren. How are you?"

"I'm fine. Dr. Elmir..."

"Guys, let's eat breakfast. I set the food in the dining area. Hello, Dren."

"Hi Aunt Mila. How are you?

"I'm fine. So guys let's go to the dining room and eat breakfast."

Mila said and they all went to the dining area. They all walked towards the dining table. Ivano sat beside Mila. Rovena sat opposite them. Dren sat beside her while Dr. Elmir sat opposite Dren next to Ivano.

They begin eating breakfast. Dr. Elmir talks to Dren from time to time. Dren answers him casually. He acts just normal as if it's not his alter ego who is manifesting right now. If you didn't know Dren you will never notice that his personality is splitting. You will never notice that he has a psychological disorder. Dren was able to hide his condition from other people for a long time. That is his dark and deepest secret. At first Ivano, Mila and his doctor knew it. But now Rovena knows it also. Just the four of them knew Dren's secret. And none of them will spill his secrets to anyone.

Chapter 25

After they finish eating breakfast Dren goes to the gym of this resthouse. He spent hours in the gym doing workouts.

While Dren is at the gym, Doctor Elmir tells Ivano something about Dren. Rovena just listens to their conversation while standing at the balcony looking at Dren down the gym near the big swimming pool. Mila is sitting beside Ivano and listening to Doctor Elmir.

Rovena heard Doctor Elmir said;

"He shifts in his alter ego, he is just deceiving us that he is in his real self."

" What will we do about this, Doc.?"

"I will suggest that you tell her fiance to avoid provoking him to get annoyed..."

" Does Rovena need to leave him?"

"Not necessary. He only felt confused about what he felt for her right now. Let him realize his real feelings for her."

"What do you mean Doc.?"

"As I observed, His emotion is splitting as his personality splits. His real self respects and loves his fiance while what he felt when he shifted in his alter ego was lust and hate for her. Maybe they met each other somewhere when he shifted into his alter ego. He is not in his real self when he feels obsessed with her. Then they don't see each other after a long time. And when they met each other again at present he felt the same. His obsession remains the same even though he doesn't know her as the same person he met before.

But at present maybe he felt that his fiance can't fully accept him when he shifted into his alter ego. That's why he felt the same hate that he felt before when they lived in separate ways. And there is an incident at present that was caused by his fiance that made him totally shift to his alter ego and totally hate his fiance.

"Alright, Doc. Let's confirm these things to Rovena so that we will know the solution for this."

"Yes. That would help."

"Rovena, will you please come here..."

"Yes, Sir..."

Rovena left the balcony and walked towards the living room where they were sitting when she heard that she was called by Ivano. When she a in the living room Ivano ask her;

"Maybe you heard what Doctor Elmir explained about Dren. Dren and you have met each other before, right?"

"Yes, Sir. That was six years ago. And I didn't know that he was Dren at that time. I didn't recognize him because his physical appearance changed a lot . Aside from that he told me a different name. He said his name is Ajdin."

"Alright. May I know what you did to Dren that time. Why does he hate you?"

" We had a mutual understanding before but not in a relationship. When I got terminated from my work on the hotel that he was staying because his business partner's daughter got jealous of me ,Dren thought that I only play games with his feelings because I got no chance to talk to him the day my employer terminated me because they didn't allowed me to talk to Dren anymore. I find no means to communicate with him again."

"I understand. So because of what happened you need to leave him before."

" Yes,Sir."

"I didn't know that because Dren never told me."

"I didn't mean to hurt his feelings before and even at present, Sir."

"It's alright. But I hope you are willing to take the risk?"

" Risk? What do you mean,Sir?"

" What I mean is it has a tendency that Dren will punish you because he hates you. There is a tendency that Dren will hurt you both physically or emotionally."

"I can take that but I don't know for how long . I still want to please Dren. I want to try again to ask an apology to him but if he really can't forgive me I leave him alone."

As soon as Rovena finished saying what she wanted to do ,Dren suddenly appeared at the doorway of the living room and entered. Rovena is hoping that Dren doesn't hear what she said.

When Dren gets near them he talked;

" What's happening here, guys? What did you say, Rovena?

Dren said while he sat on the single sofa looking at Rovena. None of them want to answer but they need to. Ivano answered Dren;

"It's just about the accident that happened to you at your company..."

"Forget about that Uncle since Rovena apologized to me already. Right, Rovena?

Rovena kept silent and lowered her head only when Dren asked him. She remembers that Dren warned him that she should not tell Ivano and Mila what he did to her.

" Alright. I hope the two of you can settle this matter."

"Yes, Uncle. Of course. Don't worry. By the way, I will only tour Rovena around the city since this is her first time here in Bosnia.

" Okay, Dren."

" Thanks. So let's go, Rovena?

"Dren, Why not just stay at home and rest ..."

" Aunt Mila let me show Rovena the different places here..."

"Oh, Okay, Dren. No problem. Let him Mila?"

"Alright, Ivano.

"So Rovena and I will go ahead. Doc. Elmir, thank you for visiting me here. See you at your clinic next week..."

"You're welcome , Dren. I expect you to be there. If you have any problem don't hesitate to call me okay?"

"Alright, Doc."

Dren holds Rovena's hands and pulls her away from them. He led her to the parking area. Then they ride in his black sports car. He drove away from his resthouse going to the city. While Rovena feels worried because Dren drives so fast.

But she knows she can still trust Dren because he is not totally insane. He still knows what he is doing. Only that he can't perceive his real self and his alter ego as one.

While Dren was driving to the capital city to look for a restaurant to dine in, Rovena can sense in his voice that he feels irritated at her.

"What did you tell them?"

Rovena didn't answer him even though she heard him asking her a question. She doesn't know what to say to him. She knows if he knows what she told them he will get angry. She just pretends that she falls asleep while they are traveling to the capital city.

When Dren saw that her eyes were closed he thought that she was really sleeping so he stopped asking her. Rovena is praying that he will not ask her again.

They reached the capital city. Dren parked his car in front of one of the popular malls in the city. They entered the mall to look for a restaurant.

After eating lunch they go to the nearby private resort. The resort is beautiful. There is a villa inside the private resort. There is a big swimming pool where clients can enjoy swimming. But Rovena doesn't like swimming because she doesn't know how to swim. Dren knew that but he still brought her to that private resort. She knows he will ask him to accompany him to swim so she needs to make an excuse so that he will not ask her to go swimming.

"Ajdin, can we sit down first." She called him Ajdin so that he would not get annoyed at her.

" Why?"

"I have a headache..."

" Fine. So instead of staying here in the pool let's get inside the villa."

"Why?"

"What do you think?"

" Ah my headache is not severe, we can stay here..."

" Don't fool me Rovena..."

" I'm telling the truth we can stay here..."

" I'm asking you to come with me there so that you can take a rest... What are you thinking of?"

"Nothing ..."

" So why don't you want to come with me inside that villa?"

"Alright, Alright let's go..."

Dren's attitude this time makes Rovena slightly annoyed. Rovena followed behind him while he was walking towards the villa. She can't stop herself from mumbling because she feels annoyed at him.

" You're so annoying.!"

"Same to you. Stop mumbling before I put masking tape on your mouth."

He said to Rovena without looking at her. Rovena really can't take his attitude this time.

When they were about to enter the villa, Rovena didn't notice the door-mat. She nearly slipped on the floor when she stumbled because of the door-mat. But Dren was able to catch her before she fell on the floor. Their position now is like they are dancing to sweet music and about to kiss.

Dren quickly lifted her in his arms instead of only helping her to stand up ;

"Put me down."

"Alright!"

"Dren said and put her down on the floor and made her lay down. He frowns and kneels down beside her. When he touches her face she immediately gets up , sits on the floor to move away from him to avoid his touch.

But Dren catches her immediately before she can move away. He pulled her closer to him by wrapping her arms around her waist. Her back bumps on his chest. Now she is sitting between his legs and leaning on his chest.

"Where do you think you're going, Rovena?"

Rovena can sense the hate in his voice towards her when he speaks. And she knows what will happen next. She is drowning in fear while Dren starts removing her jacket.

Now she is only wearing her sleeveless white tank tops and jeans. Dren started kissing her shoulder and touching her private parts. Rovena tried to push him away this time even though she knew that he was stronger than her.

She can bear no more. She still felt the pain in her lower body because of what he did to her early in the morning. This time he begs him to stop from what he is doing but he never listens to her. He acts like deaf and ignores her cry. He removes the remaining clothes on her body and pushes himself inside of her.

The more she cries, the more he seems satisfied. He derives pleasure from what he is doing while she cries in pain.

Rovena feels relief when he feels Dren stops his movements between her legs because he was able to satisfy himself. He pulled himself out of her.

Rovena thought he would stop totally but she was wrong. She drags her to the bathroom and continues to satisfy himself while the water from the shower runs on them.

After more than several minutes he totally stops when he feels Rovena's body is shaking because she feels too cold under the shower.

He pulled her away from the shower and threw her a bath towel then left her.

When Dren left the bathroom Rovena composed herself and went outside to look for her clothes. When she reached the living room she saw Dren already get dressed. He is now sitting on the single sofa drying his shoulder length long hair.

Rovena picks up her clothes on the floor one by one and gets dressed while Dren is looking at her frowning. When Dren saw her finish wearing all her clothes he talk to her;

"Let's get out of here. Let's explore the next city. "

Rovena didn't respond. She remained silent while standing at the corner in the living room. Dren get annoyed because of that so he continue talking to her;

"Will you stop your drama? As if you are not satisfied? Want me to do it again to give you more pleasure..."

" No! Please don't..."

"Alright. So if you don't want me to do it again, talk to me when I'm talking to you? Is that clear, Rovena."

"Yes."

"Alright. Let's go!"

Chapter 26

Dren and Rovena go outside the villa and get inside the car. Dren starts the car engine drives away from the private resort.

While they are on their trip to the next city Dren sees Rovena stretching her hands and arms. He talks to her while he combs his wet hair with his hand.

"So, what is happening to you? Do you feel body pain?"

"Why are you asking? Does it matter to you?"

" Of course not. I will add some more..."

"Why are you so cruel, Ajdin?"

"Because no one loves me, no one likes me..."

"It's not true, Ajdin..."

"How did you know?"

"Because I...I love..."

"You love me? Liar! If you really love me, why did you leave me six years ago..."

" Ajdin, I explained to you already..."

When Dren heard that he just looked at her and never said a word. He just concentrated on driving . Rovena gets close to the car window and just looks outside. Look far away.

Dren took a deep breath. He feels so bad. And he feels pain and it reflects in his eyes. The reason behind that pain and sadness is what Rovena said to him that she loves him. He doesn't want to believe that because Rovena is like an angel but always hurts his feelings.

Dren saw Rovena looking at him. It seems she wants to hug him to comfort him but she is afraid that he will get angry at her. So she just called his name;

"Ajdin..."

"What?!"

Dren noticed that Rovena didn't know what to say to him so she was not able to answer his question. She is just looking at him. Because of that Dren get annoyed at her again;

"If you have nothing to say don't call my name, okay?"

She just listened to what he said and hugged him tightly. He removed her arms immediately when she hugged him. He frowned at her and asked;

"What are you doing? Are you blind? Can't you see that I am driving? Do you want us to meet with an accident?

Because of his actions and harsh words she couldn't stop her tears when they started to fall from her eyes. When he saw that she was crying his eyebrow raised then he talk to her again;

" Stop annoying me, Rovena. Just tell me what do you want exactly..."

Dren's words and behavior each passing day towards her is unbearable. But he wants to punish her more and more. Dren think she wants to know if she still loves her or not so she asked him a question;

"Do you still love me, Dren?"

"How many times have I told you that I am Ajdin? And I never said that I love you..."

Rovena was not able to speak because what he said hurt her feelings so much. She looked away from him and cried.

Dren just glanced at her. But after a few minutes he stopped the car near a park . Then she touched her face with both hands and dried her tears.

She was surprised by what he did. After drying her tears he pulled her closer to him and hugged her. She doesn't understand why he is trying to comfort her after what he said to her. She is still crying. She can't stop herself from crying. So he talked to her;

"Stop crying Rovena. Yes, I never said that I love you but maybe I can love you someday...I just don't want to get hurt again so I don't want to fall in love again..."

She didn't answer him. Dren doesn't know what he is supposed to do now. How can she love her? There are valid reasons. That's why he hates her now. She made him embarrassed.

Dren doesn't know what's in her mind. She still didn't speak. She stopped crying. Then she hugged him back. He closed his eyes when she hugged him. She took a deep breath and thought of an excuse to move away from her because he feels that she is burning with desire again towards her. He needed to stop himself before he could hurt her again. So he talk to her;

" Let's get out of here and have some coffee."

"Alright."

She said and she let him go from her hug. He stepped outside the car immediately. He needs to get away from her immediately before he becomes consumed with his unrightful feelings towards her.

They entered the restaurant near the park. The warm atmosphere of the place makes them feel relaxed and have a good time. Dren chose a table and ordered coffee and lokum, a kind of Turkish delight treat.

The coffee is served in a copper-plated džezva pouring cup with an empty cup to decant your coffee into. On the tray, there is also water and sugar.

Dren spoons the cold water into the dezva to help the beans sink to the bottom. He uses the spoon to help create a creamy texture.

Then he adds a layer of the foam into the empty coffee cup with his spoon before pouring the body of the coffee from the džezva into the cup. He made two cups of coffee. He took one cup and gave the other one to Rovena.

Rovena doesn't know what is in his mind because he frowned and looked at her while drinking his coffee. She didn't want to look in his eyes, so she looked away and fixed her eyes outside the restaurant.

Rovena noticed that outside there are fine restaurants around the narrow streets and many small shops with souvenirs. All the stalls and shops were obviously geared towards tourist sales, but the merchandise ranged vastly from stall to stall. The vendors seemed polite, not pushy or rude, if someone passed by without purchasing anything.

While drinking her coffee, she enjoyed watching the scene outside. She glanced at Dren and she can say that he is enjoying the view outside also.When Dren catches her glancing at him, he talks to her;

"Rovena, let's walk outside. Let's see what souvenir items we can buy."

"Allright."

Then Dren stands up and walks outside, so Rovena follows him. They walk down a narrow street full of people hopping from one stall to another.

Dren decided to enter a lovely shop, different from other shops. Everything they sell is handmade and it's made by local artists. The shop is not that big, but it is worth seeing. They sell unique clothes made by local designers and handmade jewelry.

Dren looks at the jewelry. He picked some of them with lovely designs. When he found out that the jewelry was not expensive, he almost picked up all the designs that were available. He chose different sets of necklaces, rings, and bracelets. Then he brings it to the cashier to pay. While I was just stand-ing at the corner of the shop.

"I buy all of these? May I know how much it costs?"

The shop owner's eyes widened when he learned that Dren would buy all the designs of the set of jewelry that he picked.

"Sir, these all cost 5,089.80 Euros. Are you sure you are going to buy these?"

"Yes, of course."

"Oh, thank you very much, Sir. This means a lot to me. This is the highest sale I got from just one shopper today."

Dren just shrugged his shoulders in response to what the store owner said.

For Dren, the value of those jewels is not so expensive. But to the shop owner, the cost of all that is a huge amount of sales. The shop owner is so thankful to Dren when Dren pays for it. And why not? The amount of jew-elry that he bought for thousands of dollars is a large sum.

Aside from jewelry, Dren picks some books which are limited edition or rare and some look antique. Dren will add those books to his collections that are in the mansion's huge library.

While Dren is still looking for books to buy, the daughter of the shop owner approaches him and assists him in choosing some books that he want-ed to buy.

"Hello, Sir. I'm Janina. I'm the daughter of the shop owner. How may I help you?"

"Hi, I just want to buy some books. These old books got my interest. "

"Oh okay, let me help you choose."

"Thank you."

"It's my pleasure to assist you."

It seems that Janina is interested in knowing Dren further, so she assists Dren by herself without bothering to call their employee to assist him. Rove-na knows the reason why. Aside from being really good looking, Janina saw that Dren had a lot of money. This scene is not new to Rovena. It always hap-pens everywhere. There is always a woman who behaves like Janina.

Roven sees that Dren enjoys talking to Janina. He smiles often while talk-ing to her because Janina seems brainy and beautiful. She can tell Dren what the contents of those lots of books are. And she even mentioned some high-falutin English words that Rovena's mind could not grasp.

Their conversation lasted more than a few minutes before Dren decided to pay for the books.

"Are you going to buy all these?"

"Yes, please pack all these."

"Alright, Sir. Please wait for a few minutes."

Janina called someone to pack the books. Dren got money from his wallet and gave it to Janina as a payment for the books. Dten saw how Janina's eyes widened when she saw Dren's wallet.

Janina looks like a magnet that was attracted to Dren. She invited Dren for dinner at the nearby restaurant.

"Sir, can I invite you to eat dinner at a small restaurant nearby? I own it. "

"Where is it located?"

"A walking distance from here, five stalls away from here."

"Thank you. But I'm sorry I can't go with you. My wife needs to rest now. She and I need to go home. She is pregnant and it's not good for the baby if my wife gets too tired."

"Do you have a wife, Sir? "

"Yeah"

Where is she? I don't see any pregnant women here."

" Ah, she is just two weeks pregnant, so her tummy is not that big. She is the slender woman standing over there."

"Alright. Mr.,All I can say is thank you for buying lots of items from my family's shop."

"You're welcome. I'll go ahead.

"Bye Sir!"

"Bye."

Rovena is confused about what Dren is talking about. Some questions are in her mind.

'He had a wife and his wife is pregnant. When did that happen? Who is his wife? His wife is here inside this shop? Among the slender women here is his wife. Who among them?'

Rovena felt too jealous while looking at all the slender women here in the shop and thought who might be his possible wife among them.

While she glanced at all the slender women in the shop, Dren approached her. He cleared his throat before he talked to her. He notices that Rovena is angry but she is trying to hide it from him.

"Rovena, let's get out of here."

"Wait. Where are we going?"

"Let's go home."

Pak! Rovena slapped Dren in response to him. Dren touched his face where Rovena's palm landed while thinking about why she did that. Dren asked Rovena in an irritated voice.

"What's that slap for?!"

"Are you not going to approach your wife, Ajdin? You said she is here? Who among them is your wife? You already have a wife?"

Rovena raised her voice at him. Dren stops her from talking by putting his hands on her mouth.

"Shhh, you know I don't have a wife. I'm just making excuses so that Janina will stop inviting me for dinner."

Rovena sees Janina coming behind Dren. Janina gets the attention of Dren when she gets near Dren and Rovena.

"Sir, is she your wife?"

"Yeah. She is my wife."

Dren said, and wrapped around his arms on Rovena's shoulder. Rovena was shocked, so she was not able to say anything. Janina looked at her from head to foot and said.

"Well, she is beautiful but she doesn't know how to dress like a woman."

Dren cleared his throat and talk to Janina

" If you don't mind, me and my wife will go ahead."

"Alright Sir, Thank you for coming here."

"You're welcome."

They walked towards the car. When they reached the car, Dren opened the door in the passenger's seat. He pushed Rovena inside the car and closed the door immediately. Then he gets inside the car on the driver's seat and throws the things that he bought from the shop in the backseat. "

"Let's go home, Rovena."

"Why do you tell her that I'm your wife? I'm still not your ..."

"I know but sooner or later you will become my wife."

Dren started the engine and drove away. While on the trip going home, he kept silent. He focuses his eyes on the road while frowning. He is in a bad mood again. I know he wants to explore more shops in the bazaar, but because of Janina, he just decided to go home.

After a while, Dren began talking to her

"Rovena, we will attend a party tonight."

"I hope you have a change of mind. I don't want to attend any party.

He didn't answer her, instead he focused his eyes on the road.

Chapter 27

Dren wanted to stroll longer down to the Bazaar, but his enthusiasm was lost because of Janina. He thinks that if she sees him strolling around the bazaar, she will try to approach him again and again. It's better to go home than to get annoyed because of her.

After an hour, They arrived at the resthouse. The moment he parked the car in the parking area, Rovena stepped out of the car immediately. Dten did the same. When he stepped out of the car, he asked Rovena to cook food for dinner even though it was past dinner time.

"Rovena, cook some food for our dinner."

"Alright."

"After you finish cooking the food, inform me. I will just go to the study room. I will just finish some documents that I need on Monday."

"Okay,I will."

Before Dren went inside the house, he picked up the things that he bought from the shop in the capital city.Then gave the jewelry to Rovena. She is very hesitant to accept what he is giving her, but he insists she accept it.

"Rovena, take this jewelry. This is all for you." Dren said while he smiled at her.

" I can't take that."

"But why? Don't like the designs? "

"They are all beautiful. But what will I give you in exchange for that?"

"Nothing. Consider it as a gift from me."

"That gift is too expensive. I just can't take it."

"If you don't take it, I swear I will never forgive you. And you know this house of mine has a basement. I will lock you there so that you can't get away."

"Dren!"

"I'm not kidding, Rovena."

Dren said then he hold Rovena's arms and drag her going to the basement. Dren hates rejection, that's why he is doing that to her.

"Wait. Where are we going?"

"To the basement. You will stay there until you make up your mind to take all these."

"No! Let me go."

Rovena tried to pull her arms away from his grip, but he didn't let go of her arm. Until she said that she would take what he was giving to her.

Okay, I will take it. Just let me go."

"Good."

Dren let go of her arms and handed the boxes of jewelry to her. Rovena is catching her breath. She felt afraid of what he did.

"Thank you, Ajdin."

"You're welcome. You may go. Cook our food. I'm starving."

"Alright."

While Rovena is walking towards the backdoor to go to the kitchen, Dren uses the main door to go to the study room.

Rovena is still catching her breath while she is walking towards the kitchen. She felt too afraid of what Dren did. She thought he was just kidding when he said he would lock her in the basement if she would not accept those too-expensive jewelry. But he held her arms and he really meant to drag her to the basement. Even though she doesn't want to accept what he is giving her he leaves her no choice. She didn't want to be trapped in the basement of his resthouse, so she just accepted what he gave her. She doesn't know what is really happening to him. Why is he doing those things to her?

"He is really going crazy! Really crazy!'

Rovena reached the kitchen door. She opens it slowly and enters the kitchen. She started preparing meats, vegetables and bread to cook lunch.

While she is slicing the meat and chopping onions and garlic, she gets lost in deep thoughts. Dren hates her a lot. He always gives her punishment. To put an end to all of those things, Rovena wants to leave Dren . And when she leaves him she will never come back.

While she was chopping the onions, she accidentally cut her fingers.

'Ouch!'

Blood dripped from her fingers, so she was back to reality. She immediately washed her hands with running water to remove the blood on her finger.

After washing her hands, she began cooking the meat. She put seasoning on the meat and grilled it. Then she prepares the bread and some dessert.

After an hour, she finished cooking the food. She brought it all to the huge dining area and put it on the dining table. She decided to inform Dren that dinner is ready.

She goes out from the dining area and walks across the huge living room going to the large study room beside the large library.

She reached the front of the study room. The door is not closed and she clearly sees what Dren is doing. He didn't notice that she was standing in the doorway because he was too busy. She sees that he is preparing some documents, and he has put them in a black folder. And on his computer, She sees him open a page that seems like a bank account. She is not sure because she can't read it properly. She only saw a logo of one of the banks in Sarajevo and saw some numbers written on the screen of the computer.

Rovena sees Dren typing Eloisa's name. Then he types some numbers that are probably a bank account. She is not sure. But maybe he is transferring a large sum of money to Eloisa's name or bank account. Rovena can say that what Dren is doing right now is somewhat related to their conversation when Eloisa visited him in his office yesterday.

Rovena sees Dren open one of the drawers of the large dark brown cabinet beside a filing cabinet. She sees him get some bunch of documents. He looks like a devil with the face of an angel while frowning.

Rovena wants to run back to the kitchen because she doesn't want to talk to him. She really feels afraid. As she can see, he is still not in a good mood.

She slowly stepped backward to go back to the kitchen without making any noise so that Dren would not notice that she was standing there in the doorway. But unfortunately, she accidentally touched the door of the large study room. The door swung slightly and made a noisy sound.

When Dren heard the sound of the door, he looked at the door and before she could go away, he saw her. She notices that his brows have formed a single line. She is frozen in the place where she is standing. She felt too nervous. She put her hand inside his jeans pocket because she felt it was trembling with cold. She really felt afraid.

She saw Dren walking towards the door, but before he reached the doorway, he stopped in front of the study room table and put the bunch of documents that he was still holding on the top of the table.

Rovena wants to go but Dren has already seen her and he is walking towards her. She sees that he frowns a lot more than a while ago. She is really drowning in fear. She hears Dren call her name when he is getting near her.

"Rovena!"

She didn't answer because she felt too nervous. Now he is standing close to her. He looked at her face. Then anger crossed his handsome face. She heard him talk;

" What is happening to you? You look pale."

Rovena only looked at him without saying a word. She really doesn't know what to say. But a question is on her mind;

'Do I have to say that I am afraid of him?'

If she does that, he will get a clue that she has been standing there for more than several minutes and watching what he is doing. Before she can say anything, Dren touches both her shoulders. He is standing so close to her. She smelled his expensive perfume. He looked into her eyes and asked her again.

"I'm asking you what is happening to you? You look pale."

"Nothing, Ajdin. I'm just tired and hungry."

"Alright. So let's eat? Have you set the food in the dining area? " Dren asked her , while he was still holding both her shoulders.

"Yes, Please let go of me."

"Okay."

Rovena walked fast going to the dining area when Dren let her go. He was almost left behind. She wants to get away from him. She is really afraid of him. She heard Dren talk while they were walking towards the dining area.

"Are you running away from me, Rovena?"

"No, Ajdin. Why should I do that?"

"Because you're walking too fast."

"I'm sorry. I didn't mean it."

"Alright."

They reached the dining area. Dren gets near the dining table. He pulls a chair and sits down. Rovena can say that he likes the food that she cooked because he smiles slightly and gets the spoon and fork immediately after he sits down. Rovena is standing from a distance. She is standing close to the door. She is afraid to get close to him but he calls her.

"Rovena, let's eat. What are you doing there? I thought you were hungry?"

Rovena slowly walked towards the huge dining table and pulled a chair opposite to Dren. She sat down and put some food on her plate.

She heard Dren is talking to her;

"You know, I was really in a bad mood, but when I saw the food you cooked, my mood changed."

Rovena didn't say anything. When he got no answer from her , he continued talking.

"You know, I really want to have a wife like you, Rovena, because you know how to stand on your own. Who's independent. You can cook and do all the household chores without asking anyone to serve you. If you will be my wife, we can live our lives like this. Just the two of us in a house without the need for any maid servants. Don't get me wrong. You know, I can pay for the salary of a maid servant if we live apart from Uncle Ivano and Aunt Mila. But living with you alone without any people in the house is more comfortable for me. "

Rovena doesn't know if she would believe or just laugh at what Dren said to her but of course she can't laugh at him. What if he gets back into a bad mood if she laughs at him? Her nervousness is not totally gone, so she doesn't have the courage to laugh at him. She avoids glancing at him while she also continues eating her food. She can stop herself from being lost in deep thoughts. Some questions are running on her mind;

' He wants me to stay in his life but he hates me."

She was back in reality when she heard Dren talk again;

"I know you're thinking why would I want you to stay in my life while I hate you?

" Yes."

"Because of the lust that I feel for you. I can't just let you go."

Again, she was hurt emotionally. She lowered her head. Her eyes are fixed on the plate. She tried to finish eating her food, but she felt like she was choking every time she put some food in her mouth. What Dren said really hurts her feelings. She didn't expect it.

She heard Dren clear his throat. She saw him refilling the juice in the glass from the pitcher. He took one glass and gave the other to her.

Dren finishes his food and stands up. Then he walks away from the dining table.

"Wait! Where are you going?"

"To our room. I will sleep now. Since you don't want to go with me to the party I will not attend. "

"Alright.."

"After you finish cleaning the mess here. Follow me to our room."

"O..Okay."

Dren walks outside the dining area while she drinks the juice that he gave me because she feels thirsty. After she drinks the juice in her glass, She feels sleepy. She started cleaning the mess on the table. After several minutes, she finished cleaning up all the mess in the dining area.

She really feels sleepy all of a sudden so she decided to follow Dren. She also wants to go to sleep.

When she reached the room she saw Dren changing clothes as if he was leaving. He didn't go to sleep just like what he told her.

When she saw him looking at her , she pretended she had just arrived and never dared look back. She entered the room and she started cleaning some mess.

But when she saw Dren about to leave she took all her courage to ask him;

" Where are you going?"

"To a pub nearby. I will meet Melisa."

When she heard that he will meet a woman. She gets too jealous. She wants to stop him from leaving but she can't. All she can do is to ask who that woman is. She wants to know.

"Who is Melisa?"

"One of my ex girlfriends..."

"Alright."

When she heard what he said she turned away without letting him finish what he was going to say. She walks towards the bed and lies down. She hides her face on the pillow because she is about to cry.

Dren knows what is the meaning of Rovena's behavior. She felt jealous. He can't stop himself from smiling because of those thoughts.

Dren pretends that he left the room by slamming the door. But he didn't leave the room. He only hides behind the display cabinet in the room and watches Rovena.

When Rovena heard the loud sound of the slamming of the door she concluded that Dren really left. Since she thought she was alone in the room she started to cry out loud while hitting the pillow with her fist. She only stops when she feels tired. Then she curled in bed and embraced both her knees while she buried her face on the pillows.

Dren took a deep breath when he saw Rovena's behavior. He decided not to go to the pub to meet his friends. The truth is he will meet Melisa's husband and some of their friends.

Yes, Melisa is his ex girlfriend but she is married now to one of his friends. Melisa's husband texted Dren and invited him to the nearby pub since he learned Dren is also here in Bosnia taking weekend vacation just like them.

Dren texted him that he will not come to the pub to meet them. He hates Rovena but he can't take seeing her like that. After texting his friends Dren walks towards the bed and lays down beside Rovena.

Rovena feels so surprised when she feels someone lay beside her. She gets up to check who that is. She feels too embarrassed when he sees Dren.

" I thought you already left.."

"How can I leave, when you behave like that?"

Rovena looked away and didn't answer Dren. She can't believe that Dren tricked her only by slamming the door of the room. She feels relieved when she learns that Dren still cares for her.

" So since I obey you, will you stop your drama? Go to sleep before I have a change of mind."

Rovena keeps silent. She lies down again and prepares to go to sleep. She feels nervous when Dren gets up and touches her face. He only kissed her goodnight. Then he turned his back on her when he lay down and decided to go to sleep.

Chapter 28

Dren knows that Eloisa will not just stop flirting with him. She had two purposes for wanting him. She is physically attracted to him and she needs a huge amount of money to save their family business that will nearly fall to bankruptcy. Dren is her target because if she succeeds in seducing him, she will start asking him to save their businesses. Someone informed Dren about it through text message. That's what Eloisa is planning to do.

But Dren will not let that happen. Yes, Eloisa is beautiful, brainy, and sophisticated, but Dren is not a man who does not easily give up on temptation. She can not seduce him, no matter what she does. Dren plans to do something that makes Eloisa get away.

Dren didn't meet her last night like she and him agreed. He just said that yesterday to make Rovena jealous. To punish her. He thinks he succeeded.

He received a message from Eloisa today. She makes a follow up if the money that he sent yesterday in her bank account is his investment in one of her family's companies. So Dren told her that he changed his mind. Instead he will just buy one of her parent's properties that is located in Bosnia that is now for sale. The huge resort that is owned by Eloisa's parents is now for sale because they have no budget for the maintenance of it. But because of its expensive price no businessman wants to buy it at the price they want to sell it.

Dren once saw that resort and he likes its location and atmosphere so He is willing to buy it no matter how expensive it is. So he transferred a large sum of money to Eloisa's bank account yesterday as payment.

He decided to visit the resort in the late afternoon. He owns the resort now and he has no problem with Eloisa. He cast her away from him.

He went down the stairs to the living room. Then he called Rovena's attention who was sitting in the living room but she didn't notice him when he arrived because she was focused on watching a movie.

"Rovena! Go with me."

"Where?"

"We will visit my new property."

"Alright."

Rovena stood up from the single sofa where she was sitting and followed behind Dren to the parking area. When they reached the parking area, they got inside the car. Dren started the engine. Then he drove away.

After twenty-five minutes of driving, they are heading to Sarajevo, going to the resort that Dren bought from Eloisa.

After an hour of driving,

Dren reached the place where the resort is located. It was already evening when he found the place. It's a private resort which has a clubhouse inside. He approaches the security guard and asks him if Eloisa informed him that he is the new owner of the resort.

"Yes, Sir, you may come in. The club house is located 20 meters away from here. And the villa is 50 meters away from the clubhouse. "

"Okay. Thank you."

Dren immediately started the engine of his car again and drove away from the guardhouse, going inside the resort.

The moment Dren parked the car he stepped out immediately. Rovena did the same. When he stepped out of the car, he asked Rovena to prepare their dinner in the small elegant cottage near the swimming pool. He bought those foods from one of the restaurants on their way before they reached the resort.

"Rovena, Please prepare the food I bought on that table inside the cottage. Let's eat our dinner here outside instead of having it inside the villa."

"Alright."

"After you finish preparing the food for dinner, please inform me. I will just get inside the villa. I will just check what is inside."

"Okay,I will."

Before Dren went inside the villa, he picked up the food that he bought from the restaurant then gave it to Rovena

"Rovena, here is our food."

" Okay."

Rovena prepares their dinner on the table. While on the other hand, from inside the villa, Dren is watching what she is doing through the windows from time to time while he is checking what is inside the villa.

After several minutes he sees Rovena finish preparing the food. Rovena pulls her phone from her pocket and scrolls through it. Then after a few seconds he received a message from her;

"Dinner is ready..."

Dren replied;

" Okay. I'll be there... just a few minutes."

Then he checked on the restrooms. There are new swimwear and bath towels available. It is placed there for the use of the clients who will rent the resort.

Dren decided to change his clothes with swim wear because he wants to go swimming tonight. After he changed his clothes he grabbed a bath towel and went outside the room.

He goes to the bar counter and gets a bottle of whiskey and glasses that he saw available on the bar counter, Then he goes outside the villa and proceeds to the cottage where Rovena is waiting.

After Rovena reads Dren's reply she looks at the entrance of the villa. She sees Dren walking outside the villa going to where she is. Rovena's eyebrows raised when she saw that Dren is just wearing swimming trunks and has a bath towel hanging on his broad shoulders. Rovena's eyes were fixed on him. She can't deny that Dren is so attractive with his muscular body and angelic face. But in spite of the attraction that she felt towards him she is afraid of him because for her he is a sadist.

Rovena is back in reality when Dren reaches the cottage and puts the whiskey on the table and talks to her;

"Rovena, let's eat. What's the matter? Why are you staring at me?"

He sits opposite her. Rovena didn't say anything. She felt nervous. She doesn't have the courage to tell him the reason. She just avoids glancing at him while she puts food on her plate. But she hears Dren is talking to her so she looks at him for a while.

"I know what you are thinking ... you can have me if you will just say so..." Dren teases her then he smirks.

"What?!" Rovena exclaimed, while frowning at him

"You can't just deny the truth and lie to me." Dren continues teasing her.

Rovena feels annoyed so she answers in a way that Zamir didn't expect;

"How did you know? Even if I like you so much I will never wish to have an..."

She was not able to finish what she wanted to say when Dren spoke in an irritated voice.

"An intercourse with me? Really? I hate myself why I can't just let you go while I know I should have to. I hate you but I still need you because of the lust that I feel for you."

Because of what Dren said, Rovena kept silent. She lowered her head. Her eyes are fixed on his plate. She tried to finish eating her food, but she felt like she was choking every time she put some food in her mouth. What he said really hurts her feelings. She didn't expect it. She knows Dren hates her but it still hurts her feelings every time she hears it from him.

He heard Dren clear his throat. She glances at him shortly. She saw him refilling the whiskey in the glass from the bottle. He took one glass and gave the other to her.

Rovena doesn't know how to drink but because her feeling was hurt she takes the glass of whiskey that Dren gave to her. She wants to drink to forget her hurt feelings.

Dren finishes his food and stands up. Then he walks away from the dining table. He will go to the pool.

"Wait! Where are you going?" Rovena asks him, frowning at him.

"To the pool. I want to go swimming. Why are you asking? Do you want to join me?" Dren smirks.

"Of course not." Rovena raised her eyebrow.

"I thought you wanted to go with me, that's why you are asking. " Dren has a half smile on his lips.

He walks to the pool and dive while Rovena is drinking the whiskey that he put in her glass. She is watching Dren swim while she drinks. After several glasses of whiskey she felt sleepy. She started cleaning the mess on the table. After several minutes, She finished cleaning up all the mess in the dining table.

She really feels sleepy and dizzy all of a sudden, because of the whiskey that she drinks. She decided to take a nap where she is sitting. She rested her arms on the table and buried her face on her arms while Dren enjoyed swimming. After a few minutes she fell asleep.

Dren sees Rovena is sleeping so he goes up from the swimming pool and checks her. He thinks she is already drunk. He noticed the bottle of whiskey was nearly empty. Dren takes a deep breath. Then he ask her;

``Why do you drink too much? Get up. Let's get inside the villa."

"Inside the villa? I feel too sleepy, I'm feeling dizzy. I felt like I was about to fall on the ground..." Rovena stands up and walks , she is walking zigzagging on the way to the villa.

Before she totally fell down on the ground Dren lifted her and carried her in his arms. She is not conscious of what she is doing.

Dren frowns a lot but he carries Rovena in his arms and brings her inside the villa. He decided to bring her into one of the rooms to put her to sleep. She is really drunk.

He put Rovena in the king-size bed in the room and covered her with a blanket. He sits down for a while on the edge of the bed where Rovena is sleeping. He observed her for a while. He can't help but talk to her. He knows she can't hear him because she is sleeping so deeply.

"I thought I could hate you totally. But I just can't. I hate you but I don't want to let you go... " He is looking at her pretty face but he is not able to finish what he is going to say when he hears Jessica talking; she is not conscious or aware that he is there because of the effect of the alcohol that she drinks she lost in herself.

"I've been thinking that we were really meant to be but it's not... I thought you loved me but I was wrong...you only need me because of lust..."

Dren feels a little bit guilty but because of his alter ego his hate is not moved by what he hears from Rovena. He continued to listen to what she is saying;

"I still can't accept that you hate me now ...I loved you when I met you as Ajdin and even now I still love you but I feel afraid of you now... You hurt me so much...I hope... this is only a nightmare...and when I wake up I am forgiven... "

When Dren hears what she said his emotion is splitting he wants to forgive Rovena but his alter ego hinders what he wants to do.

He stands up and gets inside the bathroom and takes a shower to clear his mind. When he left the bathroom he looked for a shirt and shorts from his overnight bag, wore them and decided to sleep.

He turns off all the lights. He lay down beside Rovena and hugged her. He wants to comfort Rovena while inside his head he hears his alter ego speak, dictating him not to forgive Rovena.

Chapter 29

The night is almost over. Rovena is now sleeping soundly while Dren was not able to sleep. He is fighting his splitting emotions to make a sound decision. Aside from that he wanted to take Rovena once again. He is burning with desire for her but he doesn't want to hurt so he stopped himself.

When the clock struck at 4 o'clock am. Dren carried her to the car because he decided to go back to the resthouse. Because she is drunk and in deep sleep she is not conscious of what is happening to her.

After driving too fast Dren reached his resthouse. He reached his resthouse at 5 o'clock am. She carried Rovena to the room they were occupying then he left.

He decided to cook breakfast while Rovena was still sleeping. After half an hour he heard the door of the kitchen open. He looked at the door to check what happened. He saw Rovena standing in the doorway. He greeted her when she looked at him.

"Morning, Rovena."

"Morning, I'm sorry I woke up late..."

"Alright. Let's eat breakfast , let's go back to Austria after eating. Uncle Ivano and Aunt Mila went home already. They are now at the mansion today waiting for us."

"Allright, Dren."

After eating breakfast Dren walks towards the door of the dining area and goes outside while Rovena was left cleaning the mess in the dining area. After she finishes what she is doing she goes back to the room they are occupying to prepare for their trip back to Austria.

Dren is inside the bathroom when she enters the room. But the bathroom door opens after a few minutes. He goes outside the bathroom. He doesn't even bother to wear a bathrobe. He walked to the closet and looked for his clothes. He talks to Rovena when he saw her in the room;

" We will use the private jet when we go back to Vienna. "

"But the weather seems bad. I am afraid we will meet with an accident ..."

"We need to leave this morning before the weather gets worse and we get trapped here. I have an important meeting to attend in the next few days.

"But Dren..."

" I noticed that you are always calling me Dren instead of Ajdin. I'm sick and tired of hearing you calling me Dren while you know that my name is Ajdin!"

"But Ajdin and Dren are both your names."

"I made my choice..."

" What do you mean?"

"I'm Ajdin from now on...so forget about my name Dren..."

"This can't be... you must be kidding... "

"I'm not..."

Rovena just kept silent instead of answering him. Many questions run through her mind. Is Dren back in reality? His real self is Ajdin and not Dren. Is he okay now? If he is back to sanity why am I feeling so bad about this? Why can't I accept reality? Because it means that his cruelty towards me will continue. He will be rude to me as long as he hates me.

Does it mean what Dren feels towards me before is just a pure lust and he doesn't love me? Am I the only one who fell in love with him before? That's why he easily got angry at me when that incident happened in his company? And he can't easily forgive me, because he only needs me to satisfy his lust.

Because of that thought her tears began to fall. Reality hurts. When Dren notices that she is crying. He ask her in an irritated voice as usual;

"What is your problem? You know I really lost my patience towards you Rovena. If not because of Uncle Ivano I will no longer talk to you..."

"Fine. Then I will leave..."

"What?! And where do you think you're going? Our marriage was arranged. You can't go anywhere..."

"I will leave whenever I want. There's no sense to be with you. You will never forgive me no matter how I tried to apologize. "

"Stop making drama...!!!! Okay. Fine, call me Dren as long as you want. Maybe that is your problem...Now that I allowed you to call me by that name maybe you will stay?!!!"

Rovena feels shocked when Dren shouts and hits the full length mirror in front of him with his fist. But she shouted back at him when she was able to compose herself.

"Look at your attitude towards me! Isn't that enough reason for me to leave?!"

"Let's stop this Rovena...!!? Let's finish preparing for our trip so that we can leave as soon as possible.

"Okay.Fine!"

Several minutes later. They were able to change clothes and get their personal things. They didn't talk to each other until they walked to the rooftop where the private jet was.

They use the private jet to go back to Vienna. When they left the rest-house, snow started to fall heavily. As they went on their trip back to Vienna the sky began to get dark.

Unfortunately when they traveled farther, the private jet was not able to fly at its normal speed because of the thick snow that almost covered it. And it's dangerous to continue flying it. Dren can barely see their way because of his poor eyesight. He forgot to wear his contact lens. They might get into an accident if he continues to fly the private jet.

He looked for a possible place to land but because the weather was bad unfortunately a lightning struck the private jet. They had a crash landing. The private jet falls in a place far away from a city and has no houses at all.

It's inside a thicket. Fortunately they were able to get out of the private jet before it exploded.

Dren saw a small hut near the place where the jet crash landed. They decided to go to the small hut to shelter themselves from the bad weather. The weather was getting worse. It seems that the snow storm will get worse in the next few hours. Their clothes are already soaked in snowflakes.

When they got near the hut , Dren opened it. The hut seems abandoned. They decided to go inside the hut. Dren gets his phone from his pocket and checks the weather update. Fortunately, his phone still has a signal in spite of the bad weather.

"Rovena I think we will have to stay here until the bad weather is over."

"What?!"

"Are you a deaf? You heard me right? I didn't expect that the weather would turn bad today. "

"Okay, It seems that there is no fireplace here. It is too cold here. "

"Of course there is no fireplace here because it is just a hut."

Dren feels irritated at her so he is raising his voice at her.

"What will I do so that you will stop hating me?'

Dren didn't say a word. He just shrugged his shoulders in response to her. He stood up from where he was sitting, He got his traveling backpack and got a flashlight. Fortunately Dren was able to bring those things when they were struggling to get outside the private jet because it would nearly explode.

It's already evening and it's dark all over the place. Only the small flashlight gives light inside the hut.

"It's dinner time. But it seems that we can't cook dinner here. Let's just have soda and some potato chips. "

"A soda and potato chips ? Where do you get a soda and potato chips in the middle of this thicket? "

"I brought some...get it."

"Where ? You don't even tell me that you will bring it."

Dren smirked before he answer her;

"I put it inside that bag...just look for it."

Rovena scratched his head before answering him;

"Alright."

After a minute she found the soda and the chips. She gave it to Dren. They begin to eat. Dren begins to talk to her while he is eating.

"This is the very reason why I want you to become my wife even though I hate you a lot because if there are times like this, we can both easily adapt to the situation. "

"Don't give me that reason. Even other women can be able to adopt in this kind of situation if they have no choice."

"Okay, So what are the reasons you want to hear? "

"I don't know."

Dren doesn't talk anymore so the conversation between them ends. After eating her food, Rovena went near the window and peered out. Dren follows. He stands behind her and looks outside. When he looks outside the hut, He sees that the weather is worse than before.

They keep on watching the weather conditions outside. Few hours later, the whole place is almost covered with darkness. The light from the small flashlight slowly died down. The battery is already empty. Rovena wanted to go to sleep, but she noticed that the hut had no room nor bed.

He saw Dren yawn. Dren feels sleepy too while looking outside the window again. When he saw that the storm was getting worse he took a deep breath and started talking to Rovena.

"It is much better if we both go to sleep while waiting for the storm to calm. Tomorrow the weather might be good. I hope we can get out of here."

After talking to her, Dren sits on the ground. Rovena can't believe that he will decide to sleep on the ground.

"Let's go to sleep, Rovena."

"I will just stay here."

"You have no plans to go to sleep?"

"I have but there is no bed here and..."

"Is that a problem? Come here. Sleep beside me.

"But..."

"But the problem is, you don't trust me, so you won't sleep beside me here. Is that what you want to say?"

"No Dren, It's just the ground was cold."

"Cold? We have no choice. I will just hug you. Okay?"

Rovena doesn't answer Dren for a few minutes because she doesn't know what to say anymore.

"Rovena, you don't answer me anymore..."

"Thank you but..."

"Why? What are you thinking of? Are you afraid of me, Rovena?"

"No."

"So come here and let's sleep."

But Rovena is too hesitant to get close with him. Dren talks to her again. He lost his patience again so he raised his voice to Rovena again.

"Rovena, don't be too stubborn. I assure you I will not do anything wrong with you."

"I'm sorry."

Rovena slowly walked towards him and sat beside him. Dren hugged her. She leaned her head on Dren's chest and tried to go to sleep. After several minutes, Rovena didn't hear Dren talk again. Dren fell asleep.

Rovena feels afraid of the darkness that surrounds the house. She didn't move from her place because she felt she would disturb him if she moved. She can smell his perfume and hear his breath. She can see his face because of the light coming from the flashes of lightning. Mirza sleeps like an angel contrary to the attitude he shows towards her.

It's past midnight but Rovena can't go to sleep. She felt too cold even though Dren was still hugging her. She thinks the roof of the hut is now covered with thick snow. That's why it is too cold inside the hut.

The temperature was too cold. That made Dren wake up. He removed his jacket. Rovena felt too afraid. She pretends that she is sleeping. She wonders what he is doing. She thinks he will do something for her again, but she is embarrassed by what she is thinking when Dren only covers his jacket over her like a blanket. After doing that, he goes back to sleep.

Because of that, Rovena can say that Dren still has concern for her. She admitted that she was wrong when she accused Dren of feeling nothing but a lustful desire for her. But even so, she made up her mind to leave him. She doesn't want to spend his days living with a person who hates her.

Chapter 30

Morning came. The snowstorm was over. Dren got a good sleep, but he guessed Rovena did not. He knew she didn't sleep well last night. Maybe because of his presence beside her or because of the bad weather and darkness that surrounded the place last night. She was already awake when he woke up. She is just waiting for him to wake up.

He got up from the ground. He went to the window to check what happened outside for the whole night. He peered out the window. The cold morning wind blows on his face. He can see outside that the ground is still covered with snow. It means that it's hard to walk outside if the situation is like that. But they need to leave that place as soon as possible.

"Rovena, since the snowstorm has stopped we have to get out of here as soon as possible. I know it's hard to walk on the path way out in this thicket but we need to. "

"Alright, Dren."

"After we eat breakfast, we will go."

Dren said to Rovena while I'm getting some canned goods which were ready to eat from his bag and gave some to her.

Rovena didn't answer. Dren can see that she is not paying attention to what he is talking about. She still looks sleepy. Dren talked to her again when he didn't receive any answer from her.

"Rovena did you get enough sleep last night?"

"No."

"Why?"

"Because the whole place was too cold and dark. I'm still afraid of the dark sometimes."

Rovena had nyctophobia. She told Dren that before. It started when she was a child. Maybe because she became an orphan at an early age. She slept in the dark room with no one to comfort her when she felt afraid of the dark. Her fears become a phobia.

"You're still afraid even though you weren't alone here last night?"

"Yes."

"Why? Maybe you're not just afraid of the dark last night. You're also afraid of me, right?"

Rovena didn't answer again because what Dren said is true. She is afraid of him even though Dren was able to overcome the mild split personality syndrome that he is experiencing the past few days after talking to his doctor.After his doctor gave him some antidepressants he slowly came back to reality. Reality which is his middle ground.

But sad to say that he discovered that his real self is not the Dren that Rovena is expecting him to be. His behavior is really more of Ajdin now than the Dren she knew months ago.

He knows Rovena is too disappointed to discover that the Dren she knew changes a lot. He wants to be called by my name Ajdin rather than Dren but she just allows her to call him Dren because that is what she prefers to call him. Anyway his real name really is Ajdin Dren Wolf. But Ivano and his parents prefer to call him Dren rather than Ajdin. Only his grandfather used to call him Ajdin before.

When Dren saw Rovena finish eating her food he asked her to go.

"Let's get out of her"

"Okay",

They walked on a path full of snow. After an hour of walking, it was almost a few meters away before they could reach the roadside. Because the snow was too cold, Rovena's feet felt hurt. She can hardly walk on the way out of the thicket.

"Dren, can we stop for a while? I can't walk anymore."

"Yes, but it would be better if we could get out of here immediately. Let me carry you."

"No! Just a minute of rest and I can walk again."

"Don't be stubborn. It seems that your feet hurt badly."

Without waiting for her permission, Dren lifted her and carried her in his arms. Then he continued walking to get out of that place. Rovena keeps on asking him to put her down, but he never listens to her.

"Dren, put me down."

"I won't."

"Dren, I can walk now."

"I will put you down if we reach the roadside."

"But it's still a few meters away from here."

"So what?"

"Are you not tired?"

"Of course not."

"But I'm too heavy."

"Stop those nonsense reasons, Rovena."

Rovena didn't talk again when she saw that he frowned. He frowned because he felt so annoyed because she kept on asking him to put her down while he could see that her feet hurt badly. So he wants to carry her as long as he can.

When they reached the roadside, he put her down. Then they continued walking down the road to look for a possible transportation that they could find to go home.

While they were walking down the road they saw a passenger bus coming so they rode. They will go to Sarajevo to take a flight back to Vienna.

While they are riding on the bus the situation that happened last night still lingers in Dren's mind. Rovena and him slept together but he was able to control himself last night so nothing happened to them unlike when she slept over at the mansion that he really forced her to. And in the resthouse, he really hurt her badly because of the lust and anger that he felt for her. He's been acting like a beast towards her the last few days but not last night.

But he knew Rovena was afraid of him last night. She was worried that something would happen between them but he is glad that he proved to her that she can still trust him.

Dren didn't notice that the bus already reached the terminal. He heard Rovena's voice asking him;

"Dren, we are already here at the bus stop. Are we not going down?"

"We will. I just didn't notice that we were here. "

"As if you were lost in deep thoughts."

"Yes, I am."

"What are you thinking of?"

"It's just the bad weather last night."

"What about the bad weather?"

"Stop asking me. Let's just get down so that we can go to the airport right now."

" Why? "Don't you want to tell me?
"It's personal. Hope you understand."
"Okay."
Few hours later.

The plane that they boarded reached Vienna. Dren called to the mansion and asked their family driver to fetch them from the airport. Now they are heading back to the mansion. After another 25 minutes, they reached the mansion. Dren woke up Rovena who fell asleep while they were on a trip.

"Rovena, wake up. We are here at the mansion. "

Rovena opened her eyes when she heard his voice. When Rovena is awake, he steps out of the car and helps Rovena step out of the car. When she is outside the car, she talks to him.

"I will go home now..."
"Take a rest first before going back there.
"I really want to go."
"No. Get inside the mansion first. "

Dren said in an irritated voice. He got irritated at her when she refused to take a rest first before going back to her apartment. He is just showing concern to her but she rejected it. He hates rejection and embarrassment. But he felt Rovena kept on rejecting and embarrassing him.

He knows Rovena feels annoyed too but she chooses to keep silent. She just follows behind him when he enters the mansion.

He doesn't know why he can't forgive Rovena easily. And he doesn't know how long it will take before he can forgive her.

When they are inside the mansion, Rovena takes a deep breath and sits on the long sofa. Dren sat down beside her.

"You don't have to go back to the apartment where you are renting."
"What do you mean?"
"You know that we will become husband and wife soon."
"Yes I know that."
"So instead of living in your apartment just live here."
"But still I'm not your wife so why do you want me to stay here that early?"
"I just want."
"But..."

"No buts. Do what I said. Let's go to my room. I want to take a nap. I feel too exhausted."

"I will stay here. You can go to your room."

"Fine. If you want to go with me I'll ask a maidservant and the driver to accompany you to get your things to your apartment. "

"No need.I can do that alone. Don't worry I will obey you."

"I don't trust you that you will do that as soon as possible. "

After talking to her he called the maidservant and the driver. He gave them instructions and went to his room after their conversation.

"Ma'am Rovena let's go. Don't be stubborn. There is no way you can change Sir Dren's mind. You need to move here as soon as possible."

"Alright."

Rovena and the maidservant left to go to Rovena's apartment. While Dren is now inside his room. He threw himself on the bed. He feels too stressed about Rovena.

He can't determine his true feelings about her right now. He hates her but he doesn't want to let her go. What he knows is that the attraction that he feels for her right now is not love but lust. He feels obsessed with her amidst the hate that he feels for her.

The intercourse that had happened between them always lingers in his mind. And everytime he sees her he wants to do it over and over again. But he still knows that it's wrong to abuse his rights over her. He has all the right to ask Rovena again and again about that thing because their marriage was arranged. But he needs to stop himself. He doesn't want Rovena to always think that he is insane.

Now that Rovena wants to leave him he doesn't know how he can stop her from leaving. He doesn't want his Uncle Ivano to get disappointed with him. But what can he do if Rovena wants to leave and doesn't want to marry him.

He feels sleepy but he just can't sleep because of those thoughts in his head.

The moment Rovena arrived at her apartment, she rushed to her room and packed all her things. The maidservant helps her. While she packs her things he can't stop thinking about Dren. His attitude towards her is too much. She is slowly getting angry at Dren. She is not supposed to love him anymore. There's no sense of loving him. He loves him but he hates her. She asked for his forgiveness but he can't forgive her. She thinks there's nothing left but to say goodbye to him.

It's nearly evening when she and the maidservant finish packing her things. The maidservant and the driver loaded all her language into the car. Then they go back to the mansion.

It is dinner time when they arrive at the mansion. Ivano and Mila also arrived from their vacation. They are in the dining room waiting for her but Dren is not there. They started eating but Dren is still not around. She can't stop herself from asking.

"Where is he? Is he gone on a date or what?

"He is in his room. Why are you looking for him, Rovena?"

"Is he not going to eat dinner Sir?"

"He has no appetite to eat dinner..."

"Why, Ma'am?"

"He didn't tell me the reason when I called him to eat dinner."

"Okay."

"Why not just bring Dren a dinner to his room?"

"Alright, Sir."

The maid servant prepares the food that she will bring to Dren's room. After the maid servant prepared it, she brought it to Dren's room. Since she thinks the door of his room is open she just pushed it. When it opens, she enters his room. She sees Dren standing near the door going to the balcony of his room. He is holding a bottle of brandy. He is drinking.

He looked at her when he noticed that she was inside his room.

"What are you doing here?"

" I'll bring your dinner...."

"I don't want to eat..."

"Why?"

"I'm not in the mood to eat..."

She took a deep breath when she heard his excuses.

"What is your problem?"

"Does it matter to you?"

"Yes. You skip dinner. I just don't want you to get sick."

"You better bring back that food to the kitchen. As I was saying, I'm not in the mood to eat dinner."

"But Dren..."

"Don't insist because I won't obey you..."

"Eat your dinner,please?"

Dren took a deep breath and walked to the table where she put his dinner. He started eating his dinner while she sat on the single sofa opposite him.

Dren looks at her from time to time while he is eating his food. She is feeling nervous. She wants to regret that she came to his room and brought him dinner. She knows what that looks means. When he is finish eating half of the food he talks to her;

"It seems you regret your decision to come to my room and bring me dinner."

"No..."

"Really?"

Dren held her hand all of the sudden. Then he smiled at her like a devil. Because of that she is drowning in fear because she doesn't know what he is thinking of. And what he is planning to do...

Chapter 31

The night is over. Dren gets up from his bed to prepare to go to his office while Rovena is still sleeping. Dren asked her to sleep in his room last night.

Rovena regretted it a lot. Last night was probably one of her worst nightmares because of what Dren did to her. She was hurt because he just can't stop himself from hurting her. Because of mixed feelings of lust and hate that he felt for her.

Dren felt pity for her afterwards but he didn't regret what he did to her. He didn't deny that what had happened between them last night satisfied his obsession towards her.

He knows Rovena has classes today so I woke her up because he thinks she is still in a deep sleep while she has already finished taking a bath and putting on his clothes. He prepared to go to work while she was still sleeping.

"Rovena, wake up. You will be late in your class this morning..." He said Rovena while he touched her on her shoulder to wake her up but when she felt his touch she flinched. Then he heard her talking;

"Will you please stop! Are you not finished doing all the things you want from me..."

When he heard what she said he felt too annoyed so he couldn't stop himself from raising his voice at her.

"Here we go again. It's too early in the morning but you start sending me into a bad mood. As I was saying you need to wake up! It's already morning, and you have classes, right?"

"I will not attend my class today..." Rovena said and covered her face with a pillow. She is still sleepy.

"And why?"

"What do you think?"

"I will not ask you if I know the answer..."

"I'm sick..."

"Sick? What do you feel?"

"Body pain..."

"Oh, If you don't want to attend classes today it's fine. But you need to come to my office today. No more excuses. I have an important meeting today in the afternoon. You need to go with me..."

"I don't understand why I need to go with you to that meeting. You have a secretary to assist you. I told you I'm sick."

"Rovena, Stop making excuses like that before I send you to the hospital...."

"Hospital?"

"You heard it right. I will send you there if you don't show up in my office after lunch. Do I make myself clear?"

"Okay. Fine. I will go to your office. Don't send me to the hospital..."

"Good."

He decides to leave his room but before he can step outside the door he hears Rovena says something that really irritates him;

"Devil! You have an angel-like face but have a devil-like attitude!!!"

He felt so annoyed at her and wanted to answer her but he chose to leave her alone in his room before he totally lost his patience with her.

He goes to the garage and rides in his car. He starts to drive to his company. When he arrives at his company he goes to his private office immediately.

When he reached his office his secretary informed him that someone was waiting for him. He saw Mister Sajin Feratovic sitting in the waiting area of his office. He felt glad when he saw him. I know it's about the property that he wants to buy from him.

He received a message from him last week that if he really decided to sell the property to him he would just come to his office. He greets Mister Sajin Feratovic while he is walking towards him;

"Good morning, Sir! What can I do for you?"

"Good morning. I came here to inform you that I decided to sell my property to you. I brought the documents..."

"Glad to hear that, Sir. Lets get inside my office to talk about it. "

"Alright. Thank you."

"No worries, Sir."

They get inside his office and talk about the price of the property. When Mister Sajin Feratovic was satisfied with the price that Dren offered him, Dren issued him a dated cheque. After that he thanked him and left.

When Mr. Sajin Feratovic left him; he was lost in deep thoughts. Reminiscing about how he met Mr. Sajin Feratovic...

Sajin is Dana's father. Dana is one of his ex-girlfriends from high school days. Dana thinks that one of Dren's friends is better than Dren so when his friend tells her that he likes her Dana breaks up with him and goes for his friends.

Dren can't blame her. That time he was a penniless highschool student. He can't blame Dana for thinking that his friend Niko is a better man than him. And her future is secure if she chooses Niko over him because Niko is the son of a millionaire.

That time Sajin was not in favor of the relationship between Dana and Dren. His reason was he sees Dren as an opportunist gold digger and a social climber. He regards him like that because their family is wealthy while Dren is just a poor orphan and still not a citizen of their country before. Sajin is in favor of Niko to become Dana's fiance.

Years had passed so quickly. Dren was able to finish his studies. He got a job and was able to save money from his salary that he used to start a small business. Because he is good at handling businesses like his parents, his small business began to gain more clients. That startup business of his became his stepping stone. And the rest is history.

At present, he is a billionaire while those people who belittle him like Sajin come to him one by one, asking for his help when their companies fall into bankruptcy.

When the family of his ex girlfriends fell into a financial crisis he helped them to show them that he is a better man than the man whom they chose over him.

He was awake in deep thoughts when the door of his office suddenly opened. Rovena entered his office. He didn't notice that it's already 9 o'clock in the morning. He expected her to come to his office after lunch but it's good that she came earlier than what he expected.

Rovena walks towards her desk without greeting Dren. She starts doing some paperwork while she frowns a lot. So he can't stop himself from asking her;

"What is your problem, Rovena?"

"Stop asking me."

"I just want to know. What will you do if I won't stop asking you?"

"If you don't stop asking me I will leave you today..."

Dren really feels annoyed when Rovena answers him that way. So he stood up and brought a swivel chair beside her chair. He sat down and wrapped his arms around her waist. And whisper something in her ears.

"Do you want me to lock you somewhere? I will do that If you say that again."

Dren noticed Rovena's face suddenly looked pale when she heard what he said. She didn't answer him. He knows she feels afraid that's why she keeps silent. He feels that she wants to remove his arms on her waist but she doesn't dare to do it. Dren speaks to her again.

"Now tell me, why are you frowning?"

"Because I feel like I can't finish my studies anymore."

"And why?"

"I want to resign from my job and I don't want to marry you anymore because I don't want to become a battered wife."

"So you are afraid that you will become a battered wife if we get married?"

"Honestly yes. I'm afraid of marrying you..."

"Okay. Fine. Let's don't get married! I have nothing to lose. I can replace you whenever I want to."

He said to Rovena then he laughed softly. To end their conversation he asked her to get him a cup of coffee.

Rovena makes him a cup of coffee while thinking of her plans. She really decided to leave him; she decided not to continue her studies and go back to her own country. She really feels afraid of Dren. She will leave after office hours. She will just accompany him in a business meeting today for the last time. She goes back to Dren's private office and brings his coffee.

"Here is your coffee."

" Thanks. We need to go to the venue of the meeting after lunch."

"Alright."

Before 1:00 pm they arrived at the venue of the business meeting. Some of the clients arrived already at the venue but they are just standing on the hallway instead of staying inside the conference room. When they see Dren,

they greet him. Dren mingles with the clients while Rovena remains standing at the corner of the hallway away from Dren and his clients.

Chapter 32

After office hours Dren goes for a date with Selene, a beautiful CEO of one of the companies that supplies raw materials at his manufacturing company and a sister of one of his friends.

He wants to show Rovena that their relationship is over because his pride and ego was touched when she said that she doesn't want to marry him anymore. He wants to show to her that he is not hurt about their decision to end their relationship. And most of all he wants to show Rovena that he can replace her easily anytime he wants. But deep inside of him he still wants Rovena badly. He still can't overcome his obsession towards her.

While Dren is having a good time with Selene, Rovena picks up her belongings from Dren's mansion and decides to leave. Mila and Ivano tried to stop her but she really made up her mind.

"Rovena,Please don't leave Dren just like that. I know Dren doesn't mean what he said."

"I made up my mind Madam. I can't take his treatment towards me these past days."

"But Rovena you know Dren's condition, right? Maybe he doesn't want to behave like that towards you but his personality disorder keeps on pushing him. Give him time to go back to his real self."

"Sir Ivano, maybe it is better for me to leave him so that he will realize what he really wants, what he really feels towards me. I give him space."

"Alright if that is your decision we will allow you to leave but don't lose contact with us, Rovena. Me and Ivano are working on the documents so that you can get your inheritance from your father that his step sister doesn't want to give you. We will not stop until you get it."

"Thank you, Sir and Madam. I will leave my contact number and address where I am going but please don't tell Dren."

"Alright, Rovena."

"Mila and I promise."

"I will go back to my own country and work for one of my friends from the orphanage who was adopted by one of the rich families there in Albania. They own a seafood restaurant. I will work as a helper in their kitchen."

"Alright. Please write your address here in my book."

"Okay. Madam."

Rovena takes the favorite book that Mila is reading and writes her address. Then she saved her contact number on Mila's phone.

"I'll go ahead, Madam Mila, Sir Ivano."

"Alright. Take care."

"Thank you Sir"

"Don't forget to call me when you get there."

"Yes, Madam."

After their conversation, Rovena left the mansion and went back to Albania. After 17 hours of traveling by bus she reached Albania. When she gets there she immediately makes a phone call to her friend Sara who is expecting her to call ones she gets in Albania.

"Hello!"

"Hello, Sara."

"Yes, Rovena. I'm here at my parents' restaurant. Please proceed here. I will introduce you to my adoptive brother who is managing this restaurant so that you can start working here."

"Alright. I'm on my way. Thank you."

"No worries. I'll wait for you."

After half an hour Rovena reached Sara's family's restaurant. Sara meets her and introduce to her stepbrother.

"Chester, This is my friend Rovena."

"How are you, Rovena?"

"I'm fine, Sir."

"Alright. Sara, you haven't told me that Rovena is beautiful."

"Is that necessary?"

"Nope. But If I don't have a fiance for sure I will date her."

"Oh, don't even think about saying that in front of your fiance Chester."

"Yes. Of course. I know she will get jealous. Huh! I don't understand why our parents arranged my marriage to that woman."

"Stop saying that. Mother might hear you. You know she will get disappointed in you if she knows that you don't like Sabrina."

"I know. I only agree with them to that arranged marriage so that I wont lose my inheritance."

"We both know that. So when will Rovena start working here?"

"Maybe by tomorrow. Let her take a rest first."

"Alright, brother."

"Thank you, Sir."

"No worries, Rovena."

"You can go home now, Rovena. Don't be late for tomorrow."

"Alright, Sara. Thank you. I'll go ahead."

"Take care. I will."

Rovena left the restaurant and looked for a room for rent near the restaurant to save fare. Fortunately she got a small room in one of the apartments walking distance from the restaurant.

Since it was already evening when she was able to find a new home she decided to take a rest after eating an early dinner. She lay down on her bed to go to sleep.

On the other hand, It's 8:00 o'clock in the evening. Dren is laughing with his friends, they are at the private resort owned by Adam Smith, one of his friends. They are enjoying the scenery but still Rovena lingers in his mind.

Her beautiful face flashbacks to him while he is looking at the clear water in the huge swimming pool. He remembers the last time when he and Rovena were in his resort in Bosnia. It's all coming back to him.

Dren is back in reality when his phone rings. He received a call from Selene, the woman he dated last night. She is a sister of his friend Faris.

"Hello, Selene. What can I do for you?"

"Is Faris with you? I need to talk to him. He is not answering his phone."

"Yeah. Wait, I'll give the phone to him."

"Thank you, Dren."

"No worries. Faris, your sister wants to talk to you."

Dren said while handling his phone to Faris. Faris gets the phone from Dren. He stands up and walks a little distance from his friends before he talks to Selene.

Faris reaction is like that because he knows her sister is only making way to talk to Dren but Dren didn't notice it. He feels ashamed of what his sister is doing. In fact Selene is the one who insisted on the date last night. Dren only agreed to her to cover up the pain Rovena gave him.

Dren's other friends Sanin and Niko know that also so they are smiling while looking at Dren.

"Oh, why are you looking at me like that?"

"Are you numb?"

"Why, Sanin?"

"You haven't noticed that Selene is only making a way to get noticed by you?"

"I know but our friend Adam is interested in her so I would rather not come between them now when I learned that a while ago from him."

"Seriously?! Or is there something stopping you aside from that?"

"For sure Niko, it's Rovena."

"Is Sanin right, Dren?"

"I don't want to talk about it, guys. Let's just enjoy tonight, okay?"

"Alright! You said it. "

"Let's just drink!"

"Alright! Cheers!

"Cheers!

Dren drinks the glass of brandy straight. The glass is empty when he puts it down on the table. Niko and Sanin look at each other. They both shrugged their shoulders. Then drink the brandy on the glass that they are holding while Dren looks far away.

Chapter 33

Two years later.

It's a cold rainy evening. In one of the pubs in Vienna, Dren is sitting on the bar counter. He goes to the pub just to drink again.

On a bar counter glasses of brandy are served. He is still drinking even though he is too drunk. He takes a deep breath and drinks another glass of brandy. After he emptied the glasses of brandy on the counter he ordered another several glasses of it.

Dren is in disguise this time. He is wearing a dark black jacket. The collar of her jacket almost covers half of his face. He doesn't want anybody who knows him to recognize him. He is worried that if someone recognizes him drinking again in that kind of place they will tell his uncle about it. And for sure he will send him to his doctor again.

Dren is feeling shattered because until now he still can't accept that Rovena left him just like that. And it has been two years since she left him but he can never really move on. He is longing to see her again.

Because of those thoughts, when the bartender gave him his order he drank three glasses of brandy continuously. He dropped by a pub again, just to drink so that he could forget Rovena. That was 2 years ago, but the memories are still there in his heart and mind.

He drank the last glass of beer that he ordered. He decided to go home. He has an important business trip outside the country for tomorrow so he needs to go home.

It's raining in torrents outside the pub but Dren still went outside the pub. He is feeling dizzy. He needs to lean on the car before he can get inside. He feels too dizzy. He can't stand up properly. He slowly sat down on the roadside. He is talking even though he is alone because he is drunk. His whispers turn into shouting. He just needs to get it off his chest that Rovena will always have his heart.

"I'm holding on forever...wanting to see you once again, Rovena!"

Dren shouted while he was under the falling rain. But when he was back to reality he immediately composed himself.

"Shit! I can't handle myself. Is this the effect of the brandy that I drank?"

He needs to force himself to stand up and get inside his car to drive home. He stands up but he still feels dizzy so he falls down on the street and he can't manage to stand up. He can't get inside his car.He falls asleep beside his car under the falling rain.

Fortunately their family driver who was asked by Ivano to look for him saw him. Their family driver carried him back home to the mansion.

Dren woke up to the strong smell of coffee aroma.He realized that he is in his own room now because the place smelled fragrant.Unlike in the pub, which smells of alcohol and cigarettes is in the air. He got up from bed. He saw Ivano sitting on a single sofa, drinking coffee. He looks worried.

When Ivano saw that he got up from bed and sat down he walked towards him. He brings him a cup of coffee and puts it on the bedside table. Then he talked to him while holding a cup of coffee;

" How are you? Our family driver saw you last night beside your car parked outside the pub. You were unable to drive home due to intoxication."

" Yeah. I remember."

Dren picks up the cup of coffee that Ivano brought for him.

"Are you out of your mind? You're doing nonsense again. You drank too much last night."

Dren laughed out softly before he answered Ivano;

"I'm sorry. I only remember Rovena last night."

"How many times I told you to forget her. She will not come back to your life. You can't change her mind."

Dren shook his head then spoke to his Ivano;

"That is true. But I can't forget her. I'm still longing to see her."

Ivano takes a deep breath. He is worried about what Dren is doing because of Rovena.

"You better empty your coffee cup before the coffee gets cold. "

"Alright.

"Fix yourself. Remember, you have a business trip today to Albania. Take your chance to look for her there. Here is the address of the restaurant where is working at present."

Ivano gave him a small sheet of paper with an address written on it. Dren's face lit up when he read the address.

"Why haven't you told me that you know where Rovena is?"

"Because I thought you will forget her also like your previous girlfriends. Women just come and go in your life. And you move on easily."

"But Rovena is different from them. "

"Yes. I can see that. She is the only woman that drives you crazy. So after what you did last night I decided to let you know where she is. "

"Thank you, Uncle. I know this place. This restaurant is under the Collins group of companies where me and my friends are going to invest. "

"No worries. Go ahead. Talk to her."

"Alright. "

When Ivano left the room, Dren emptied his cup of coffee. Then, after a few minutes, he decided to take a bath and prepared for his flight outside the country.

Thirty minutes later. He asks the head of the maidservant to inform their family driver that he is about to leave to go to the airport.

Dren went to the airport to meet his friends who were on their way to their meeting place. Before Dren's car reached the airport, he saw a salesman on the street. He asked his driver to stop the car. He buys all the items that the salesman is selling. Dren does that because he remembers himself before. He works as a salesman before helping Ivano to support his studies in college because Ivano's small business before is not doing well so they suffer from financial problems. That is unknown to the society that he belongs to at present.

After several minutes he is at the airport. He stepped outside his car. His driver carries his suitcase. When he got near his friends, they asked him;

"What took you so long, Dren?!?"

"Sorry, Niko. I stopped for a while on the street."

"We see you talking to a salesman...!"

"Yeah. Sanin is right. What comes into your mind and you entertain those kinds of individuals?"

"Faris, Instead of interrogating me, why don't we just board the plane now so that we can't be late to our flight! I'm excited to visit Albania again after a long time. "

Dren said to his friends , laughing to hide his feelings, that he got offended by their behavior towards the salesman. He thinks for sure they will not talk to him if he meets them when he is still a salesman.

" Yeah. That's right! Let's go!" Niko agreed to him in an excited voice.

Chapter 34

1:00 pm, Tirana Albania

Collins Group of Companies Boardroom.

Dren is sitting now in the boardroom together with the board members of Collins Group of Companies. He is listening to Alexander Collins who is conducting a meeting with the board members of the group companies owned by his family and relatives. His grandfather Elmo, the company's CEO is on a business trip to the next city that's why Alexander is the one who conducts the meeting as a representative of his grandfather.

Alexander starts his discussion about the investment proposal. Then he recognized the presence of Dren and Dren's friends . He introduced them to the board members as the new investors in their group of companies.

"This is Dren, Sanin, Faris and Niko. They are our new investors. The billionaires from Austria. To be specific they are from Vienna."

Alexander noticed that Dren cannot concentrate on the meeting, that's why he decided to talk to him in private after the meeting while Dren's friends are busy talking to other members of the board.

"I noticed that you are not paying attention well while I'm discussing in front. Do you have any problem, Dren?"

"It is just about one of your employees."

"Employee? From which company?"

" Yes. Working in the seafood restaurant under the management of your brother, Chester."

"Who among them?"

"Rovena."

"Rovena? Are you interested in her? She is an assistant cook and sometimes a delivery driver in the restaurant."

"Alright."

"Alright. Since it's nearly evening I will prepare dinner for you and your friends. And after eating dinner, let's go to a party."

"A party? Sorry but I don't have any interest in going to a party tonight..."

" Oh come on Dren. Go with us. To feel relaxed."

"Maybe you are right. Okay."

"Glad to hear that."

At 7:00 pm in the evening they go to the restaurant where Rovena is working. Dren is very excited to see Rovena but unfortunately it's Rovena's day off so she is not around in the restaurant. Dren feels so disappointed because of that. He lost appetite eating his food.

At 8:00 pm their dinner was over. Alexander, Dren and their friends go to the party. That is Lily's birthday party. Lily is one of Alexander's friends who owns a luxurious nightclub so the party is held at her own nightclub.

They started to drink. Lily has many female friends who attend her birthday party. Including Sara and Rovena. Rovena is not Lily's friend. She only attends such parties because she is also doing a part time job as Sara's personal assistant. Sara asks Rovena to go with her at that party.

Alexander notices that as soon as they arrive at the party Lily and her female friends all look at Dren but Dren has no interest in them. His eyes are fixed on Rovena as soon as he sees her at the party venue. Rovena doesn't recognize Dren. Because Dren's appearance is too different from the last time she saw him.

Because Dren is busy looking at Rovena's angelic face and whose vital statistics are too perfect than the last time they saw each other he didn't notice that he drinks more and more brandy. And when the effect of alcohol consumed him he stood up and made an excuse to his business partners because he decided to talk to Rovena.

Rovena is standing away from their table and away from Lily's friends. It is obvious that she is working as Sara's personal assistant because she is running some errands from time to time if Sara asks her.

" Excuse me guys. I need to talk to someone for a while."

"Alright."

" Go ahead."

"Be careful, I think you are already drunk."

"No Niko. I can manage."

"Alright."

He saw Rovena leaving the establishment so he wants to follow her. After making excuses, he goes outside the nightclub to follow Rovena who is now walking down the street.

He clears his throat when he is behind Rovena. She turned around when she heard there was a man following behind her. She wants to know if the man is really following her to avoid the man immediately if he has bad intentions towards her.

Dren was mesmerized when Rovena turned around. He can't imagine that she is more beautiful now, especially from a closer look. He greets Rovena who is staring at him.

"Hi"

Rovena didn't recognize Dren. Since Dren has a splitting personality disorder. Rovena is seeing his another alter ego aside from what she already saw as Ajdin.

She can't imagine that the man who makes her heartthrob the moment he stepped inside the nightclub is now in front of her. Talking to her. Rovena warns herself not to talk to him because he is a stranger. But the feeling of attraction that she feels towards him is stronger than her fears. So she entertains him despite her doubts and fears.

"Hi. What can I do for you?"

"I want to talk to you a little. "

"Alright. So what is your name?"

"Dean."

Dren intentionally didn't tell her that he is Dren so that Rovena will not avoid him. He knows Rovena will avoid him if she knows.

"Nice to meet you. Are you a tourist?"

"Yeah. Are you working in that nightclub? Are you off from work?"

"No I'm not working there but I'm off to work. My friend who is also one of my employers allows me to go home."

"Really? Please go with me. "

"Where?"

"Somewhere ...In a private place... where we can be alone to talk. "

"Alright."

The moment Rovena agreed to go with him he held her hand and led her to his newly bought car. Rovena didn't think twice when she agreed with him. Even though she knew what the possible things may happen to her. She likes him a lot. Never in her life has she felt that way again towards a man aside from Dren. Unknowingly that the one in front of her is Dren.

They get inside the car. Dren started to drive. Rovena just kept silent while looking at him. She feels like she was hypnotized by his appearance because he looks like a drop dead gorgeous dignified looking man. His business style haircut fits him. His green eyes shine like a star in the night. The color of his business suit matches his white skin complexion and fits his muscular body.

Rovena was back in reality when he heard him was talking to her;

"Why are you staring at me like that?"

He smiles at her. His pure white beautiful teeth show up.

"Nothing."

Rovena felt embarrassed when he asked her so she looked away from him and focused her eyes on the road.

After more than several minutes of driving, Dren stopped his car in front of an old huge house. That is Dren's parents' house. He and his parents lived there when he was a child, not until his parents died. He stepped outside the car and said to Rovena;

"Let's get inside."

Rovena stepped outside his car. She has no plan to go with him. She started to walk away because her fears consumed her this time. But Dren held her hands immediately and did not let her go.

"You agreed to go with me, remember? Are you afraid now? Do I look a monster or a beast in your eyes all of the sudden."

"No. But I changed my mind."

"You can't change your mind just like that. As I was saying, let's get inside. Please?"

When Dren looks straight in her eyes and seems like he is begging at her she finds herself in the next moment walking with him going inside the house.

When they got inside the house Dren led her to one of the rooms. He started to lose the necktie of his business suit. Rovena feels afraid. Her nervousness added up when he started to remove his suits. And now he is half naked. She feels like she was frozen in the chair where she sat down.

The next moment, they are both in bed. This time even though he feels a lustful desire towards her, she takes her with respect and gentleness unlike before.

He never forced her. He acts with care, respect and gentleness. Because of that she willingly gave herself to him even though she knew that it is quite not right to just be with a man in bed who is a complete stranger unknowingly that he is Dren.

Afterwards, Dren was satisfied. He gets all the cash that he has in his wallet and gives it to Rovena. The amount of money that he is giving to Rovena is equivalent to her whole year's salary as an employee of the restaurant where she is working at present.

"Here... please take all these and stop working at the restaurant. "

Rovena can't say anything. Her tears fall down from her eyes while she looks at the money that Dren put in her hands. She felt insulted because she thinks that he is mistaken for a prostitute like those women working in that nightclub.

She saw that Dren had already put on his clothes and lighted a cigarette so she talked to him.

"I can't take this money."

"And why? Do you still want to work there?

"Yes. I'd rather keep my job than to accept your money."

"Why not just come back to me, Rovena?"

"What are you talking about? We only met this evening."

"No."

"What do you mean?"

He picks up her clothes that are scattered on the floor and gives it back to her.

"Put on your clothes. I'm Dren."

"You are Dren? I didn't recognize you. How did you find me?"

"It's not important how I was able to find you again. You will go with me back to Austria when I go home."

"No! I won't go with you."

"Rovena, Please?"

"What between us is over?"

"It's not over."

"I said it is!"

"Rovena, I know I hurt and scared you before that's why you go. Please give me another chance. I promise I won't do that to you again. "

"No. I don't want to go back to you. Leave me alone."

Dren takes a deep breath while looking at Rovena who is putting back all her clothes. He doesn't know what to say to her.

When Rovena decided to go home he was not able to stop her. But he won't give up until she convinces her to come back to his life again. He made up his mind that he will stay in Albania for a while to convince Rovena.

When Rovena gets home the dawn is breaking. Penny, her roommate asks her when she saw her enter their apartment.

"Where have you been, Rovena? The dawn is breaking. "

"I go with Dren Wolf."

"Dren Wolf? Wait? I think I know him. He is the new investor at Collins Group of Companies."

"How did you know?"

"You forgot. I'm working as a cleaner in the main office of CGC. I saw him. And he is too handsome. My God! Rovena, how did you know him?

"He was my fiance."

"Fiance? Stop kidding me. Do you accept another part time job? Do you work as his maid? "

"No!"

"As his personal assistant?"

"No!"

"No? Or maybe as a part time driver?"

"No. I don't work for him. And I will never go back to the restaurant . I will look for another job. "

"What?!"

"I want to avoid him. I know he will insist on seeing me again and again if he knows where to find me."

"Seriously? Are you not kidding me?"

"Do I look like I'm kidding?"

"Alright. I think you are not. You look pale and worried."

"I'm afraid of him. He wants me to go with him when he goes back to Austria."

"Why don't you want to go with him? My goodness. He looks so handsome and a billionaire. You don't need to live a poor life like this if you go with him. Use your head Rovena."

"You don't understand."

"Oh Rovena what did he do to you that makes you afraid like that?"

"I don't want to become a battered wife if I agree to marry him. I managed to get away from him before so I will never go with him."

"Marry? You mean he wants to marry you? So it means you do not belong to the woman whom he only needs to satisfy his lust. It means he loves you. You're so lucky Rovena."

"How I wish I am but I think I'm not."

"Rovena, take a rest first and think. If I were you I would go with him and accept his marriage proposal."

"I made up my mind. I will hide from him again."

"Rovena don't be a fool!"

"I'm not a fool. I just don't want to marry him."

"Alright. As you have said."

Rovena lay down in bed when Penny left her alone. She fell asleep immediately because she felt too tired.

Chapter 35

The dawn is breaking but Dren just keeps tossing on his bed and still doesn't get some sleep after Rovena left. He can't go to sleep. In his thoughts Rovena still lingers.

Hours passed by. It is already morning. He can't go to sleep anymore. It's time for breakfast so he decided to just get up and take a bath. After taking a bath he decided to join his friends to eat breakfast. He proceeded to a nearby restaurant where his friends were. It is one of the finest restaurants in the city known for its delicious foods.

While they are eating breakfast, his friends keep on teasing him.

"Dren, where did you go last night?" Niko asked, smiling at him.

"Yeah, you never came back when you left us in the nightclub. " Sanin second the motion.

"I felt I was drunk so I decided not to go back." Dren shrugged his shoulders in response to their teasing.

"What a pity! Those women who join us in the nightclub are looking for you. You know they are the best in bed." Sanin snapping his fingers.

"Yeah, they are. But we know Dren is not interested in those women." Faris looks at Dren who is now in deep thoughts.

"Because I think he is really in love with Rovena." Niko tapping Dren's shoulders. He notices Dren lost in deep thoughts.

"How many times have we told you to move on Dren? Accept that she will not come back to you." Faris is frowning because it's been so long they are telling Dren that but he is not listening.

"Alright. You know I'm trying. " Dren taking a deep breath.

"We hope you will really move on Dren," Sanin tapped his shoulder.

"Yeah I hope so, I can do that."

Dren keeps silent and continues eating his food. While his friends continue talking about their experience in the nightclub last night.

On the other hand,

Rovena still goes to work when Sara calls her over the phone. But she is really planning to resign from the restaurant where she is working.

When Rovena looks outside the seafood restaurant something catches her attention. Her eyes are fixed on the store opposite the restaurant.

Rovena sees a job vacancy posted on the store. After a few minutes of looking at the store she mumbles;

"I will apply for that job."

When she finished washing the seafood that their chef cook asked her to prepare she went to the store to inquire.

She has really decided this time to look for a new job and leaves her present job. She will hide from Dren again.

Rovena proceeded to the store. She notices all the employees there are male, except for the middle-aged woman at the cashier.

Rovena saw a middle-aged man sitting beside the cashier. She thinks maybe he is the owner. She walked to the store counter to inquire about the job vacancy. She asked one of the sales boys.

"Excuse me. Where can I apply for the job vacancy posted outside the door? "

"You can talk to the owner. Wait for me, I will just inform him that there is an applicant. "

"Alright, thank you."

The sales boy talked to the shop owner. While speaking with the shop owner, Rovena noticed him pointing to the counter. She sees the shop owner looking at the counter where she is still standing. Then he talked to the sales boy. After their conversation, the store owner goes to the counter to talk to Rovena.

Rovena greet him politely;

"Good morning, Sir. I'm Rovena."

"Good morning, I'm Mr. Martin.So what can I do for you? "

"I want to apply for the job. I saw on that post that you are looking for a waiter. "

"Alright, You can go to the next city to apply for that job..."

"Next city? "

" Yes. My sister who is living in the next city needs another waiter at her restaurant ..."

"Alright, I know how to get there."

"Good. So here is the name of my sister and the address of her restaurant in the next city."

"Thank you, Sir. I will try to find it.I'll go ahead."

" Goodluck."

After their conversation, Rovena immediately goes home and starts to pack all the things that she needs to bring on the trip.

After she prepared all the things she needed she set on her trip going to the next city. She rode on the bus. It was nearly evening when she arrived there. She can see the different neon lights from a distance that signifies the modern city life.

On the street ahead from the bus station, Rovena sees the restaurant where she is going to apply for a job. It's near a luxurious salon. It looks like one of the first class restaurants in the city. She feels hungry all of the sudden. She thinks that kind of restaurant serves yummy dishes.

When she was near the restaurant, she stopped in front of it to see where she would inquire about applying for the job vacancy there.

While she is standing in front of the restaurant a gorgeous women who will about to enter the restaurant talk to her;

"Do you think a poor person can afford to buy food in such a restaurant?"

"Maybe yes. And why not?"

"Hah! Can't you see that almost all the people inside look rich unlike you?"

"Yeah. I noticed."

"So get out on my way. A poor person like you has no business here."

"Alright. I'm sorry..."

Because of that she started to stepped backward to gave way to the woman who is about to enter the entrance of the restaurant but before she could walk away, she heard a loud horn blowing coming from the latest model of Honda Civic, which parked in front of the restaurant and wanted to pass by immediately going to the parking area of the restaurant.

"BEEEEP! Beep, beep!Beeeep!"

The driver blew the horn so that Rovena would get out of the way faster. Then the beautiful woman who drives the car shouted at her;

"Get out of my way! You poor people have no room in this kind of place. What are you doing here, Huh? "

Rovena heard some of the woman's friends who are with her in the car laugh out loud while pointing at her. She slowly burns in anger but she chose to keep silent and got out of their way immediately.

She wanted to shout back at them, but she stopped herself from doing so because she only arrived in the city and didn't want to get into trouble.

But before she could start walking away the woman stepped out of her car and grabbed her jacket. Then shouted at her;

"Haven't I told you to get out of my way? Are you deaf?!"

Rovena removed the hands of the woman on her jacket before she talked to her;

"I heard you. That's why I'm leaving."

Rovena humbly said to the woman . The woman continued talking to her even though she saw that Rovena was leaving.

"Oh, it seems that you are angry with me."

"Who do you think will not get angry with your bad manners?"

"Hahaha. Do you have the courage to talk to me like that? Don't you know me?"

"Nope. And who are you?"

"I am the daughter of one of the millionaires in this capital city. We own many establishments here. And my father has the power to ban you in the city if I tell him to do so."

"I'm sorry..."

"So a poor person like you should fear an influential person like me? "

After the woman says that to Rovena she calls her bodyguards who are riding in another car following behind her car.

"Teach her a lesson!"

Her 3 female bodyguards drag Rovena away from the restaurant and throw her on the street. She fell down on the street side but she stood up immediately.

One of the bodyguards kicked her on the stomach. She fell down on the ground with bent knees. Two of them grab her arms to make her stand up. They hold both her arms so that she can't get away from them.

One of them was about to kick her again, but she stepped on the feet of the two women holding her arms. They lost grip on her arms and she was able to move away before the kick of one of them landed on her again.

One of them grabbed her again but a man from an approaching sports car happens to saw the commotion, he shouted at them;

"Heyyy! What's happening there?!"

When the woman's friends heard the man they stopped the bodyguard from assaulting Rovena

"Stop!"

"That's enough."

"Let her go!"

When they stopped, Rovena was thankful to the man. But the body-guards are still blocking her way even when they stop assaulting her. The man stepped out of his car. He talks to the woman;

"You better stop this before you suffer punishment from our parents."

"Why? What can a poor woman like her do against me? We belong to a rich and influential family. Why should I be afraid of her?

"But what if our parents know this because there are some witnesses like the guards and people inside the restaurant? Let her go, Tracy. "

"Fine! But I swear you will regret that you intervened, Calvin."

Tracy said and walked back to the restaurant like a fashion model together with her friends and bodyguards.

"Alright. See you at home!"

Calvin shouted at her while she was leaving. Then he talks to Rovena;

"Hey, beautiful are you okay, now?"

"I'm fine. Thank you for saving me..."

"Oh, no worries. By the way, I'm Calvin and that woman is Tracy, my stepsister."

"Nice meeting you, Calvin."

"Your name please?"

"Rovena. "

"A beautiful name just like you."

Rovena touches her chin after saying those words. Rovena started to feel afraid of him. So she started to make excuses to get away from him.

" Ah, I have to go. I have some important matters to look for..."

" Oh! Wait! After what I did to you, will you just leave me like that?"

"I'm sorry but I really need to go..."

" Oh, why don't go with me first. Let's eat dinner."

"Thank you for inviting me but I'm not hungry...I have to go..."

"Seriously? Alright. May I know where you are going?"

"I need to look for an inn to stay in tonight. I just arrived in this city..."

"An inn? Why not just go with me to my hotel? I own a luxurious hotel here..."

"I'm sorry I can't go with you there...I can't afford to pay for a room there..."

"You don't need to pay for it, sweetheart, Just lay on my bed and it's quits!"

"I can't do that...I'm sorry..."

Rovena starts to walk away but Calvin catches her arms before she can get away. He drags her to his sports car and pushes her on the passenger seat. After that the man slammed the door and got inside the car. He starts to drive away while Rovena is begging from him to let her go but Calvin just laughs softly and never listens to her.

"Where are we going?...Please let me go. I'm begging you!"

"I like hearing you beg.I feel excited! Don't worry when we arrive there you will know."

Calvin is planning to bring Rovena to his resthouse in the outskirts of the city where some of his male friends are staying for a vacation.

Calvin slowly loses patience with Rovena because she keeps on asking him to let her go while they are on the trip so he sprays some sleeping liquid spray on Rovena to make her fall asleep.

While driving to his resthouse Calvin notices that there is a car following his car. But he felt relieved when the car passed his car. So he continued driving to his resthouse.

The owner of the car who follows Calvin's car is Dren. He has been following Rovena ever since Alekxander informed him that Rovena decided to leave her job at the restaurant. He won't let her get away from him again.

Dren knows that Calvin has bad intentions at Rovena so he is thinking how he can save her from him. He intentionally passed Calvin's car because he knew that Calvin noticed that he was following his car. But he doesn't totally drive far away from Calvin's car to see where he is going.

After a half an hour of driving, Calvin reached his resthouse. He parked his car. Because Rovena fell asleep he carried her in her arms and brought her inside the resthouse. When his friends see him arriving carrying Rovena they feel the excitement especially when they see how beautiful she is.

They bring Rovena in a huge room of the resthouse. Put her in bed. Then they want to start their bad intentions towards her. Since Rovena is unconscious she doesn't know what they are planning to do to her. She doesn't know that she is in danger and is about to suffer at their hands.

All of them have lustful desires towards Rovena. Calvin started to undress Rovena and enjoy seeing her body but all of the sudden Dren jumped from the open window of the room and punched his face.

That made Rovena wake up. She immediately covers her nakedness when it syncs into her mind what is happening to her at the hands of Calvin. While Calvin falls on the bed beside her unconscious because of Dren's punch. Calvin's friends were shocked and were not able to move for a moment.

But After a minute, Marko, one of Calvin's friends, points a gun towards Dren while the two of them check what happened to Calvin. They help Calvin get up.

Rovena felt so nervous when Marko pointed a gun at Dren but Dren didn't feel afraid. He just puts his hands up while Marko is walking towards him, still pointing a gun to his head and questioning him.

"Who are you? How did you manage to get here?"

"It's none of your business how I manage to get here. I just want to fetch this woman."

"Seriously? Man, I think there are lots of women out there. With your looks you can easily grab one for yourself. Why are you trying to snatch this woman from Calvin?"

"She is my fiance. Do you think I will allow any of you to touch her?"

"Oh, Really? If you are lucky to save yourself from the bullet of this gun you can save her from us but if not you will see how me, Calvin and my two other friends tear her apart in front of you while you are slowly losing your breath."

Marko laughed out loud at Dren after saying those words to him. Rovena can't move from her place. The two friends of Calvin holding her tightly. While Calvin is sitting on bed composing himself.

"That will never happen!"

Rovena shouts at Marko upon hearing his words. All of Calvin's friends' attention is focused on Rovena. They are laughing at her. Teasing her. While Dren is still in the same position but thinking how they can get out of that trouble.

"Oh what are you thinking of? Your fiance can save you?"

"Sad to say he is not a superhero to do that."

"Watch how he will die while we are enjoying your beautiful body."

Since their attention is focused on Rovena, Dren takes advantage of the situation. He kicks the gun that Marko is pointing at him. Marko lost grip on it. The gun falls from Marko's hand. Marko and Dren exchange punches and kicks. When Calvin and the two of his friends saw that Dren nearly defeated Marko, Calvin started dragging Rovena out of the room while the two of his friends helped Marko, assaulting.

Rovena shouted at Dren asking for help because of nervousness when Calvin started kissing her. Planning to continue what he started before Dren came out of the blue.

"Dren! Help me!"

Dren is now lying on the floor. He fainted when Marko hit him on his head with a base. He is half conscious. Blood is dripping from his rosy pink lips. He was beaten by Calvin's friends. They are laughing at him now. But when Dren hears Rovena asking for help he forces himself to stand up.

Since Dren has a psychological disorder and he hears his two alter egos talking to him saying that they came to help him Dren's behavior and strength suddenly change. His alter ego, who he named Ajdin is manifesting. He is the bravest among his two alter egos.

Calvin's friends were shocked when Dren's movements suddenly became quick. He started assaulting them again and this time he won over them.

Dren gave them a hard kick and punch. They fall down on the floor one by one. And was not able to fight back to Dren because they felt all their bones broken.

One the other hand Rovena is struggling to escape from Calvin. And continues to shout Dren's name.

"Dren! Help me!"

"Do you think he can still hear you? He is now dead in the hands of my friends."

"It's not true! Let me go!"

"Not until I get what I want from you."

"Drennn!"

Dren makes sure Calvin's friends will not be able to get up and assault him again.When Dren hears Rovena's voice again calling his name he runs outside the room to save Rovena from Calvin.

When Dren gets near Calvin he punches him which makes Calvin let go of Rovena and fall on the floor. That time Calvin fainted. He is not able to follow Dren and Rovena when they walk away immediately out of the rest-house and get inside Dren's car. Dren's drives away from the place.

Rovena is still catching her breath while she and Dren are traveling back to the heart of the city because of nervousness and trauma she got from that incident. In addition to that Dren keeps silent. She sees that Dren is annoyed. She knows one wrong move of hers, Dren will erupt like a volcano and will scold her.

Chapter 36

It's past 12 midnight when Dren reaches the old house of his parents where he is staying. He drove Rovena home from the city downtown because she really doesn't want to go with him even after he saved her from danger that is about to happen to her in the hands of Calvin if he doesn't come on time. His heart felt heavy because of that. It is clear that Rovena really doesn't want to come back to him to be his fiance again.

Dren immediately parked his car in the garage. Step outside the car. and walk towards the front door of the huge house.

He wants to go immediately to his room. He

wants to change his soiled clothes because it gives me an uncomfortable feeling. His clothes got dirty because of fighting back with Calvin's friends.

He feels his mouth is still bleeding. He still tastes the blood on his rosy pink lips. His whole body is aching. He entered the house quickly. Walk across the large living room to reach the staircase going up to his room.

He is in a hurry because he's feeling so bad now. But before he could reach the staircase Jacob, his phone vibrated in his pocket. Niko is calling him.

"Where are you all day Dren?" Niko asked him. His voice seems worried.

Dren cleared his throat then he answered. "I've followed Rovena all day..."

"What?! You know you missed the conference meeting, right. And the signing of a contract for investment."

Dren takes a deep breath before he speaks.

"Okay... okay. It's not a problem. I will talk to Alexander tomorrow and I will sign the documents."

"Alright. So what happened? Have you talked to Rovena again to convince her to go with you back to Austria. "

"Yeah. But she still didn't agree. Maybe she is just a little stressed because of the problems she faced the whole day. I will talk to her later."

"Problem?"

"She was forced by a man named Calvin to go with him. He wants Rovena. And that is the reason why I got into trouble to save Rovena from him. " Dren explained while frowning because the incident still lingers in his mind.

"Here we go again. You got into trouble because of Rovena. How many times have I told you to forget her?" Niko said and at the same time scratched his head.

"I can't hear you, Niko. I will call you back. I will just change my clothes." Dren said to Niko instead of answering his question.

"I'm still talking to you. Don't make excuses..." Niko said in an irritated voice.

"Alright. I just help her..."

"Dren, Why do you still cry for her? As I always tell you, learn to forget her. There are a lot of women out there. I'm only concerned for you because you are my friend. That's why I'm telling you this."

"Look. I'm trying but I just can't. I admit that I'm dying to get close to her again but she fears facing me. Can you please just help me to make her go with me to Austria instead of telling me that?"

"Alright. What's the plan?"

"I will tell you later."

"Okay."

"I will call you back."

"Alright."

After their conversation Dren went upstairs as fast as he could. He left the living room. He reached his room. He immediately removed his clothes. Take a bath.Then he gets an ice bag and ice from his personal fridge inside his room. Put the ice bag on his body parts that swell. Then he drank a pain reliever. After drinking medicine he goes to bed.

But before he can take a nap he hears his cell phone message notification. He got a message from an unknown number. He read the message;

"Hi. I just text to know if you're okay?"

Dren typed his reply;

"Who are you? And where did you get my number?"

Dren gotta reply from the sender;

"From a calling card that dropped from your pocket here in my boarding house." The sender replied.

"Oh, Okay. I didn't know that my calling card dropped somewhere so who are you?" Dren replied while wondering who the sender was.

He got another reply from the message sender;

"Rovena."

When Dren read the name of the message sender he was surprised. He felt glad. A smile crossed his face while typing his reply to Rovena;

"Oh okay. Don't worry about me. I'm okay. How about you?"

Rovena replied;

"I'm fine. Goodnight."

Dren replied;

"Goodnight. See you around."

When Dren didn't receive any reply from Rovena he decided to go to sleep.

On the other hand...

Rovena decided to go to sleep. She is too tired because of what happened to her earlier. She was thankful that Dren helped and saved her. She didn't expect that Dren would come and save him. She is so sure that Dren got more body pain. She saw that Dren fought back with all his might against Calvin's friends. She saw that his mouth was bleeding. And she saw that the kick and punch of Calvin's friends landed repeatedly on his body.

She got too worried about Dren even though she doesn't like to go with him again so when she saw Dren's calling card on the floor she picked it up and decided to text Dren when.

Rovena wants to go to sleep but she can't. The image of Dren's handsome face still lingers in her mind. She felt that she would find it hard again to resist her feelings for Dren. But she doesn't want him to be his fiance again, not anymore, maybe only friends.

She wonders if Dren already forgives her from the humiliation that she caused to him when she is still working at his company. And that incident sent their relationship into chaos.

Rovena thinks maybe he is because he never thinks twice to save her from the devilish plan of Calvin to her.

Rovena fell asleep with those thoughts in her head about Dren...

Chapter 37

The next few days Rovena got a job outside of her country. She was hired as office staff at one of the distributing companies in Bosnia and Herzegovina. She accepted the job because she wants to get away from Dren again. She learns from Penny, her roommates who is working in the office of Alexander Collins that she heard that Dren Wolf is planning to stay in Albania for a while. Rovena knows that Dren will come to her apartment again and again as long as he knows that she is there. So she decided to accept the work outside Albania.

When Dren learns that Rovena already left Albania he goes back to Austria to inform his staff that he will stay in Bosnia and Herzegovina for a while to observe his newly bought distributing company there. And his work will be temporarily given to the assistant chief executive of his company.

Rovena doesn't know that the company where she is going to work was bought by Dren to save the company from shutting down. It belongs to Niko's cousin.

Niko helped Dren's plan to carry out. Dren asks Niko to tell his cousin to hire Rovena in their company which now belongs to Dren. Because Dren is really dying to get close to Rovena he plans to send Rovena to that company for work so that he can see her around while he is at that company. He will stay there for a while to know what he can do to increase its sales.

Rovena traveled to Mostar. One of the cities in Bosnia and Herzegovina to report at the HRD office of REN Distributing Company. It is a distributing company of raw materials for making bread and cakes.

Rovena met Miss Venice, the head of the HRdepartment. Miss Venice is a very sophisticated and pretty woman.

"I'm Ms. Venice from the HR Department of REN Distributing Company. Are you Rovena?" she asks in a soft voice. Her voice sounds too beautiful in Rovena's ears.

"Yes ma'am. I'm Rovena." Answers her in a very polite manner as she admires Miss Venice's beauty and sweet voice.

"Okay. You are hired not because your qualification is suitable for the requirements set by the HR. We hired you because the new owner of this company wants you to be here. Come on time everyday and obey your superiors while working here because if you don't I will give the position to those who are more qualified than you. And I will assign you to a janitorial position.Do you understand?"

Hearing Miss Venice's words makes Rovena so embarrassed that she can't even speak to answer her question quickly. It feels like the word "not qualified "keeps on ringing in her ears. Even though Miss Venice was finished in her talking still Rovena can hear the words she said. Because Rovena didn't speak and answer Miss Venice's question she heard Miss Venice talking again in an irritating voice.

"Hello, are you still listening?" Miss Venice asks in an irritable manner.

"Yes... ma'am...Thank you."

Rovena said, stammering in a voice. She cannot speak properly because she is in panic mode. She is afraid that she will lose the job because she didn't answer her immediately.

"The new owner wants you to be assigned in a higher position but I will only assign you as an all around clerk but I will just give you a lower position because your qualification didn't meet the company requirements for the job positions that you are recommended for."

Miss Venice said while looking at Rovena from head to foot.

"Thank you Ma'am..." Jessica forced herself to smile.

"Alright. I will show you your workplace. Let's go." Miss Venice said to Rovena while walking like a ramp model going to the place where she is going to assign Rovena

Rovena followed behind her. Rovena wonders where Miss Venice is going to assign her as they ride on the elevator going down. Rovena can't determine what floor Miss Venice had pressed because there are also other employees who ride the elevator and press the floor where they are going.

Rovena realized that Miss Venice and her were going to the basement when the two of them were left at the elevator.

Miss Venice gave Rovena the job assignment. Rovena was assigned to sort all the old files coming from different departments of the company and put it in the filing cabinets. In that area there are only a few people around. It is the room where all the old files of the company are stored.

Miss Venice is too afraid that if she assigns Rovena to a higher position she will just mess up.

After their conversation Rovena got mixed feelings. She feels both happy and sad. She is happy because she got a new job with a high salary rate but she feels sad at the same time because she is hurt and was too embarrassed about what Miss Venice said about her qualification. Yes she knows that she is not qualified most of the time for a job position in the office because she is an undergraduate but it still hurts when she hears it from the mouths of others. And to think that even in this clerical position her qualification isn't fit. It made her so much hurt and sad. But she needs to ignore such feelings to get a job that will give her a good salary and from this job she will be able to survive her daily expenses.

ONE WEEK LATER...

In Rovena's working area, it is hot like hell, with no air conditioning. Only a ceiling fan

It has been almost one week since Rovena started working there. She still wonders who is the owner that recommended her to that company. She still didn't see him in those past days. She thought that maybe one of Sara's cousins is the owner of the company or the agency where she applied in Albania recommended her to the owner of the company.

But the head of the HR department in that company looks down on her and tells her that her qualification doesn't even fit their requirements and she was hired just because of the recommendation. But Rovena is thankful that she still got a job in spite that her qualification doesn't fit the requirements of the company. So all she needs is to do her job well without complaining whatever her superior told her.

Chapter 38

It's 7:00 a.m. in Bosnia and Herzegovina...

REN Distributing Company.

Rovena arrived late at work. She is mumbling while walking too fast going to her workplace.

"Oh, what bad luck is this! It's Monday and I'm late!I'm sure it will cause my supervisor to get more irritated at me."

In her workplace, there are three clerks including her and a strict supervisor.

"Hey Rovena, are you late today?" asked Dina. Another employee at the company.

Rovena answers, "Yes because my alarm clock didn't make a sound, so I woke up late."

Dina and her are in the same position. She is also a clerk, but she is in the other company department .

Rovena arrived at her workplace. She arranged the things in her workplace and started sorting some documents on the table.

"Hey Rovena, did you hear? "The owner of this company will visit here today, right?" said Ezma, approaching her. They work in the same place. She is also an all around clerk.

"Yes, I heard that."

"And .. Sir Ajdin will visit all departments today. I heard he looks so handsome! And no woman can resist his charm!" Ezma said, smiling wide.

Rovena laughed at what Ezma was saying. Ezma is really crazy most of the time.

"What? You're really crazy! He's probably married. How old is he? Wait, if he's already the owner of the company, he's probably old! "

"Nope! I heard he's still young. He's only in late twenties. "

"Weh?Really? "

"Yes, Rovena! Let's just see later if you do not feel attracted to him. Hahahahaha."

"You're crazy! Go back to your work before our strict supervisor shouts at us." Rovena said, frowning at her.

She returned to her work still laughing at Rovena while Rovena continued sorting all the files on the table.

"Girls, the owner of this company is about to come here . Arrange your things before he arrives. Everything needs to be in order."

"Yes Ma'am," the three clerks said in chorus.

"And you, Rovena. Why are you late? Come on time if you want to continue working here."

Rovena's strict supervisor said to her while raising her eyebrows and looking sharp at Rovena.

Rovena mumbles,"Seriously! scary! Her eyes blazed over. I thought she was going to kill me !! She looks like a monster!"

"I can't hear your answer, Rovena!"

"Yes Ma'am. It will not happen again." Rovena answered quickly in a soft voice while looking at her supervisor.

"Just make sure!" The supervisor said, raising voice at Rovena before returning to her desk.

"As if she wasn't late even once. So annoying!" Rovena mumbles again.

Two hours had passed before the owner arrived. He first went to the other department. Their working place is in the basement.

"Girls, Sir Ajdin is here. Behave."

"Yes ma'am." The three clerks answer in an uninterested manner.

"How did you answer me? When Sir Ajdin talked to you, that's how you answered? "

They did not answer because their supervisor is overreacting. Instead they whisper to one another.

"Why? Will all of us be fired if he doesn't like it the way we answer??"

"Immediately??!"

"Seriously?!"

Several minutes later...

"Good morning." greetings of the owner who just arrive

"Good morning." The four employees said in chorus.

Rovena sees that Ezma was stunned. Her table is in front so she can see immediately whoever was coming

While Rovena's table is behind Ezma's table. So she will not immediately see who will come.

Even their supervisor Miss Jenny was stunned and unable to speak. Her eyes winkle in a little while as if there are stars hanging on her eyes. She looks so funny.

Rovena slowly turns to Ezma's table. She is stunned. She can not breathe.

"Oh my God! This can't happen!" Rovena whispered. She can't move. She doesn't know what to do.

She mumbles, "No! I am just dreaming. Oh my God! It's just a dream! Then soon I will wake up. Promise!"

"Hi, who's the Supervisor here?" Dren suddenly said

"Wahhh it doesn't look like a dream !! My God! How come? This can't be happening ! What will I do?!" Rovena is whispering again.

"Ah, I'm the supervisor here, Sir. I'm Ms. Jenny." Rovena's supervisor said she emphasizes the word "Ms" when she offers her hands to the owner for a handshake.

Rovena whispered again. "No shame! as if he would like her. She looks like a monster! She wants to be noticed. He's even older than Dren!"

"Nice meeting you, Ms. Jenny. I can see that you only have three subordinates here," said Dren while reaching out the hand of Ms. Jenny, who seemed to be flirting.

"Just call me Jenny, Sir.Yes Sir, I only have three clerks here since there's not too much work here unlike in other departments."

"Ok. If that's the case, I'll go ahead. I just want to see my staff since I just bought the company." said Dren.

"By the way, welcome to the company Sir." said Ms. Jenny, smiling as sweetly as possible.

"Thank you." Dren said. Then he looked at Rovena before turning away completely.

Rovena wishes that it's just her imagination even though she knows that it's not. She didn't expect that Dren is the owner of that company where she is working at present because Dren uses the name of his alter ego which is Ajdin. And Rovena almost forgot that name.

"He's so handsome!" Nea screamed when Dren left. She is the clerk on the third table.

"Yes, Sis! Heyy Rovena, why are you so quiet ?? You feel attracted to Sir Ajdin, right?" Ezma said, teasing her.

"What? Is he that handsome? He only has a white skin complexion and is tall." Rovena said softly.

"Oh my gosh! Do you have poor eyesight, Rovena?! You need eyeglasses. You're the only one who said that!" said Nea in disbelief.

"Hey, be quiet! Go to work. But he's really handsome, isn't he?"said Ms. Jenny, whose eyes are twinkling again when she talks about Dren.

Rovena can't deny the truth and lie to herself but it is true that Dren is handsome even before she ran away from him and looks more handsome today.

Well. If she is to describe his appearance earlier, this is probably how she will describe him; he is a good-looking dark-haired man who is almost 6 feet and 2 inches in height; has green eyes; a white skin complexion and a muscular body. His black business suit gives him a dignified look.

"Huh!" Rovena sighed.

"Rovena, please send these reports to Ma'am Ena." Miss Jenny said that made Rovena back in reality.

"Ok Ms. Flirt." Rovena whispered. She doesn't know why she felt irritated when she saw her supervisor openly show that she likes Dren.

She just whispers " Ms. Flirt". She'll be fired if I say it out loud. She took the reports and brought them to the other room to be signed.

"Excuse me Ma'am Ena." Rovena said with a smile on her face as she approached the Department Head.

"Ah ok. Please just put it there."

Rovena is about to leave when Ena calls her name.

"Ah Rovena, just a minute. Please take this to Sir Ajdin as well. He said he needs it. Everyone here is busy. Then I can't find the messengers. You don't have much to do at this time, do you?"

She emphasizes even though Rovena will obey her !!

"Alright. Ma'am."

"Ah, please hurry up. Sir seems to need that now." Ena said in a demanding voice.

"All right, I'll bring it now, Ma'am."

Rovena is mumbling while going to Dren's office.

"What bad luck do I have today ?? Now I have to face that man again."

Rovena took the elevator to the 5th floor where his office is based. When she arrived there, she informed his secretary that she would give the files to Dren.

"Oh okay. Please wait." The secretary said while she called Dren at the intercom;

"Sir, the files you requested are already here."

Then she nodded as if the Dren could see. "Yes Sir."

When she put the intercom down, she turned to Rovena.

"Take that inside." She said to her, smiling.

"Okay thanks."

Rovena proceeds at the door. She takes a deep breath and whispers. "Okay. This is it. Oh my gosh! I feel so nervous."

She knocked first before she opened the door. When she opened the door, she entered Dren's cozy office. All the walls in his office are white and still a few things are there. The things he only needs.

Dren is busy looking at the files on his table and doesn't seem to notice her presence. Rovena called him.

"Ahh excuse me, sir. Here are the reports you are asking for from Ma'am Ena." She said and handed the documents in front of him.

He looked up. She could see that he was not surprised . As if she is expecting her to take those documents to his office.

"Ahh Okay. Kindly put it there." he said while pointing to a part of the table.

Rovena puts the papers there and immediately wants to leave. She doesn't know but she feels like Dren will do something that she can't figure out. He felt that she wanted to leave immediately so he held her hand to stop her from leaving.

"Do you need anything else Mr. Wolf?" She emphasizes the word "Mr. Wolf."

Dren couldn't speak right away because he felt like he was frozen. Especially because she called him Mr. Wolf.

"Hey, do you need anything?" she asked again, afraid of him.

"Yes. Please stay." he said when he noticed that she wanted to turn away.

Dren stands up from where he is sitting and holds her face with his both hands. Rovena feels afraid of him. She wants to run away but she knows she can't just do that easily. She knows Dren. He will not let her escape from him if he wants to do something to her. She knows that very well. She knows she is cornered by him again.

Chapter 39

Rovena doesn't know how she is able to come back to her workplace after what Dren did to her. She sits down on the swivel chair behind her table immediately because she feels her knees are shaking. She feels too nervous. She didn't expect that Dren would throw away all the things on his table when she rejected his feelings for her.

But she felt relieved when he stopped throwing things and let her leave his office after he was able to express his displeasure with what she did...

The lunch break came but Rovena had no plan to eat lunch because she is aiming to save money because her budget is limited. She will count several more days before she gets her first salary. Because she will not eat lunch she will just continue her work.

Rovena doesn't know that Dren is watching her through the CCTV camera that is connected to the large monitor in his office.

Dren can't stop himself from watching Rovena's every move on the monitor. When lunch time comes Dren notices that it was almost lunch break but Rovena doesn't stop working as if she had no plan to eat lunch. He wonders if Rovena is on a diet and wants to skip a meal. He notices that Rovena touches her stomach as if she is hungry but instead of taking a break she continues her work.

Dren's eyes got fix on the monitor and watches Rovena's every move. He sees that Rovena touches her stomach again, takes a deep breath and gets her wallet in her pocket. She counts her money in her wallet and takes a deep breath again. Then she slips back her wallet in her pocket and continues her work.

Dren knew the meaning of her action. She wants to eat lunch but maybe she has no enough money to buy lunch so she just decides to skip the meal.

Dren loses appetite to eat lunch earlier because of the pain Rovena caused him when he said to her that he still has feelings for her but Rovena ignores him.

But now he decided to go down to the basement where Rovena is just to ask her to eat lunch with him. He took pity on Rovena. That's why he decided to take a lunch break even though he doesn't want to eat.

Dren rides on the elevator heading to the ground floor. The elevator reaches the basement where Rovena's workplace is.When the elevator opens Dren stepped outside. He decides to approach Rovena.

Dren sees Rovena glancing at him so he smiles at her but Rovena pretends that she doesn't notice him . Rovena looks quickly in the opposite direction of where she is sitting. Rovena stands up quickly to put some files on the filing cabinet. Dren fails to approach her.

Dren has no choice but to call Rovena's name. He wants her to notice him and stop walking away.

"Rovena!"

Dren calls Rovena but she pretends that she doesn't hear him calling her name.

"Rovena! Do you hear me?!"

Dren called her again but still she ignored him and continued pretending not to know that he was calling her.

Because of that Dren decided to just get near Rovena and hold her shoulder for her to notice him.

"Hey! I called you twice but you didn't hear me."

Rovena looked at him.

"What can I do for you, Sir?"

"Sir? Just call me Dren, okay? It is lunch break but you didn't eat your lunch."

Rovena smiles and says, "I'm not in the mood to eat lunch."

"Alright but I want to invite you to eat lunch. Go with me. Let us eat at a nearby restaurant. Let's go."

Dren touches her hand and pulls her going in the direction of where his car was parked.

"Sir! Wait. I'm not finished doing my work. My supervisor will get angry if I leave my work like this."

Rovena tried to pull her hand from Dren's grip but he held her hand tight so she was not able to lose from his grip.

"She is only your supervisor. My position in this company is much higher than her. So you need to obey me instead of her. "

Dren led her to the car while still holding her hand.

"But... Sir..."

Rovena is full of hesitation.

"As I have said, just call me Dren. No buts, Okay!"

Dren opened the door of his car in front and pushed her inside. Rovena could do nothing about that. Then Dren immediately gets inside the car to drive.

They arrived at the nearby restaurant after a fifteen-minute drive. Dren led her inside the restaurant. He chose a table good for two located at the corner of the restaurant. The waiter gave them the menu. He started to choose food from the menu and told it to the waiter.

But he noticed Rovena didn't touch or read the menu given to her so he asked her.

"Come on. Look at the menu and choose. What do you want?"

"Nothing. I have no money to buy..."

"Don't you worry I'll pay for it."

Because Rovena still had not touched the menu Dren decided to order for her.

Then the waiter takes his order. After several minutes the waiter served their food. Dren started eating his food but he noticed Rovena still didn't eat her food so he talked to her.

"What's wrong? Eat your food before it gets cold."

Rovena looked at Dren. In her eyes Dren can see that she is wondering why he insisted on inviting her to eat lunch. So even though she is not asking anything he found himself explaining to her.

"I just know that you are short of budget. That is why I treat you to lunch. Can we still be friends?"

Dren smiles at her.

"Yes, Sir."

She smiled a little bit while looking at Dren. She feels afraid of him deep inside.

"You're calling me Sir again?!Why don't you just call me by my name instead of calling me Sir?"

"No I can't because you are ..."

"No? Because I am the owner of the company where you are working?"

Dren cut what Rovena was about to say.

"Yes."

Rovena speaks shyly.

"Never mind my position in the company. I insisted you call me by my name. Okay?"

Dren said to her while putting more food on her plate because he noticed that she didn't eat well. He thinks that maybe Rovena felt shy around him or maybe uncomfortable because she feels afraid of him. He notices Rovena's face looks pale whenever he smiles and looks at her.

Rovena took a deep breath before she answered him.

"Okay I will just call you by your name if that is what you want."

"That is good."

Dren looked straight into Rovena's eyes.

Rovena cannot look at him the same way. She immediately turned her eyes away from him, lowered her head and focused on eating her food.

They were about to finish eating lunch but Dren noticed that Rovena remained silent. She never asked or said anything to him. So to break the silence between them Dren talked to her again.

"So where do you live now?"

"Just nearby the company's location."

Rovena answers without looking at Dren.

"Good so I can drive you home after office hours because you're residing just near the company."

"Thank you but no need to drive me home I can go home alone..."

" I insist..."

Dren said, smiling at Rovena. Rovena felt nervous. She knows she can't stop Dren from doing so.

After they finish eating lunch, they go back to REN Distributing Company. Rovena continues her work while Dren goes back to his office.

When Rovena goes to do her work, she notices that her two co-workers Ezma and Nea are whispering to each other while looking at her. Rovena hears some of their talkings about her.

"She goes with Sir Ajdin during lunch break?"

"Yes. Some of our co-workers saw her."

"Well, as far as I can see, she is beautiful..."

"Yeah. That's why she was easily noticed by Sir Ajdin just like that ..."

" Oh she is so lucky..."

"Yes."

"Imagine Sir Ajdin is the owner of this company and he is interested in knowing her..."

"But I think she and Sir Ajdin had a past relationship."

"What makes you think of that?"

"Can't you see how she reacts when Sir Ajdin arrived here earlier."

"I also noticed her weird reaction."

"As if she is running away from him and feels so shocked when she knows that he is the owner of the company."

"Yes. Her reaction is like that. "

They stop talking when Rovena walks towards their working table.

Chapter 40

Rovena's working shift ends. When she goes up to the ground floor to swipe her ID for time out, she notices that other employees are whispering to each other while looking at her. She heard some of them talking about her loudly. And she felt so small when she heard what they said.

"Her name is Rovena..."

"She is a flirt..."

"We saw her together with the company's owner during lunch break."

"She is not a citizen here..."

"She is an overseas contract worker..."

"Well, as far as I can see, she is beautiful."

"Yeah, That's why she was easily noticed by Sir Ajdin. "

"Oh she is so lucky..."

"Why...?"

"Imagine Sir Ajdin is the CEO and owner of this company, and he is interested in knowing her..."

Because of what Rovena heard from other employees, she felt that she didn't want to continue making friends with Dren again because of what other employees thought about her. Other employees think that she does a flirtatious act to get Dren's attention while she never does that. She felt annoyed about it because they easily judged her without even knowing that Dren and she knew each other before she even came to work at REN Distributing Company.

Rovena was awake in deep thoughts when Dren approached her.

"Rovena , it's the end of your working shift. I can drive you home. "

"No. Thanks. " Rovena said ,looking at Dren.

Dren didn't speak for a minute. He feels annoyed by the way she answers him. But before she could walk away, he spoke to her.

"Are you not really interested in me? This is your chance to get a good position in this company. Just flirt with me... " But he was not able to finish what he was going to say when he received a slap from Rovena.

"Sir, I'm not flirting..." Rovena said. She can no longer hold her anger because she doesn't like what Dren said to her.

"Alright. But as far as I can see there's nothing wrong with that if you will do that. Believe me, you will not remain in the lowest position in this company... Never mind what other employees are talking about you. They are just envious. "

Dren smiled at her. Then he held her wrist and pulled her out of the lobby.

"Let me go!" "Leave me alone."

"Oh, why are you angry at me?"

"You are too much. "How dare you say that to me? "

"Huh! What do you want to hear from me? "

"Nothing. "Just let me go." "Leave me alone."

"Not until you go with me tonight to my house and cook dinner ."

"What do you mean? You will stop bothering me if I do that. "

"Yeah, so what do you think?"

"Fine!"

"Really? So you agree? "

"Yes."

"Good."

"Just be sure that you are not fooling me, Dren."

"Do I look like I'm fooling you?"

Rovena didn't answer him. She was too irritated by what people around her were looking at and discussing the moment they saw Dren and her talking to each other.

Rovena decided to get inside Dren's car immediately when Dren opened the car door for her.

While driving on the street near his company, Dren sees a supermarket. He decided to ask Rovena to go with him to the grocery store to buy some food ingredients for cooking dinner.

Then, after half an hour, they finished buying what she needed to cook dinner. They walked out of the store. Dren put all the stuff that they both had inside his car. Then he opened the door of his car in front of her and said to her,

"Let's go. It's getting cold here. The snow is starting to fall. "

When Rovena rides in Dren's car, Dren can't stop himself from smiling. He immediately closed the door of the car behind Rovena and got inside the car. He started the engine of his car and drove home.

After a twenty-minute drive, they arrive at the house where Dren is staying. When the car stops, Rovena opens the car door immediately and steps outside while Dren gets the groceries they bought at the grocery store, which are in the backseat of his car.

Rovena offers to help him carry those bags up to his house. Because Rovena was already holding some stuff, Dren let her carry it. They get inside the house. Dren put down the grocery bags.

Since Rovena was his visitor, Dren decided to offer him a cup of coffee.

Three months later,

It's a winter afternoon.

The wedding chapel was decorated with pure white flowers, as white as the snowflakes falling because it's winter.

Dren is on the altar waiting for Rovena to walk down the aisle. He is so handsome in his wedding suit. He is wearing a black suit.

Rovena is wearing a white wedding gown with a purple color motif. The motif of her wedding gown is like the color of the purple flowers that she is carrying in her hands.

She walks slowly to the altar, where Dren is standing. Dren waits patiently for her

As she begins to walk towards the altar, the wedding theme song is sung by the famous singer in town. The music with the title " Never Thought ('That I Could Love")" was written by Dan Hill.

Rovena reached the altar. The wedding ceremony begins. A few hours later, the wedding ceremony was over. They are now husband and wife.

Dren feels so happy because, in spite of the doubts and fears that Rovena feels for him, he gave him a second chance.

Winter ended and springtime came.

Rovena gave birth to a son. Dren can now say that his life is so complete now that he has his own family, which he has been longing for.

He just realized ,in a relationship that Rovena and he have, that when love is truly right, it lives from year to year. It changes as it goes, but it never disappears.

After all the stops and starts that they have been through, she and he keep coming back to each other. He guesses it's meant to be forever for her and him.

—The End—

Author's note